THE WARNING

There were a few cars in the lot as I approached the car service driveway, and suddenly the lights on one of the cars went on. I thought nothing of it, figuring it was just someone heading home. Suddenly, the car accelerated and jumped the curb. It shot straight across the street, then veered left and headed right for me.

I only had a second to decide which way to jump and when I did my boxer's legs added the extra distance I needed to avoid the car . . . .

My friend Billy Palmer came running. "What happened?" he asked, helping me to my feet.

"I think somebody just tried to kill me."

THE STEINWAY COLLECTION

Robert J. Randisi

PaperJacks LTD.

TORONTO   NEW YORK

AN ORIGINAL

PaperJacks

THE STEINWAY COLLECTION

PaperJacks LTD

330 STEELCASE RD. E., MARKHAM, ONT. L3R 2M1
210 FIFTH AVE., NEW YORK, N.Y. 10010

PaperJacks edition published January, 1988

ISBN 0-7701-0659-5

Prologue

It was almost 9:00 P.M. when I arrived at my client's apartment house. There was no doorman on duty, which was odd, so I stepped through the lobby and into the elevator and pressed the button for the penthouse, where Aaron Steinway had his apartment.

When the doors opened again and I stepped out, something struck me a blow on the back of my head. I went down, but not out. I struggled to my hands and knees, trying to beat the count and wondering why the ref wasn't counting out loud. Turning my head to the left, I saw the door to the stairway swinging shut. Trying to shake the fuzziness from my head, I lurched towards the door. I could hear someone taking the steps fast and breathing raggedly. I started down, taking the steps two and three at a time, despite the protestations of my aching knees and head. I finally spotted him four or five levels down. The lighting on the stairway was very bad and I saw only his back, but at least I was gaining on him. From the sound of his breathing, he was just about run out.

I finally reached the top of one flight of steps just as he was reaching the bottom. I took a chance and launched myself in a flat-out dive. I hit him high and

1

we both went down, and I had the added misfortune of banging my head on the wall. I tried to get back to my feet, but he hit me, and the chase was over.

When I woke up I had to try a couple of times before I was able to get to my feet and support myself against the wall. I looked around for my handlers, but when no one came to help me back to my corner, I staggered through the door of whatever floor I was on and made my way to the elevator. When it arrived I entered, leaned against the wall, and pressed the button for the penthouse again.

When the elevator stopped I stepped gingerly from it to the entry foyer of Steinway's apartment, but there was no longer any need for such care.

I went through the apartment, snapping on lights as I went along. When I reached the door to what apparently was his study I leaned against the doorjamb and felt for the wall switch. When I flicked on the light, I found Aaron Steinway, my client.

He was seated behind his desk, considerably more bloody than I was, and dead.

The phone on his desk was off the hook, explaining the busy signal I had received earlier. I picked up the receiver and called the police.

After that, I called time out and dreamed about what had gone before....

Chapter One

I was in the ring again for the first time in months, but it wasn't the way it used to be. We were only in the second round of sparring, but my breath was coming raggedly and my opponent was landing punches virtually at will. I could see the punches coming, but when I tried to move to block or counter, it was as if I were moving in slow motion.

"Time!" Willy Wells shouted from the ring apron.

I stopped, letting my gloved mitts drop to my sides like lead weights. Willy jumped into the ring, threw me a sour look, and started tending to his boy.

"You're a little slow with the left, Vito," he was telling him, rubbing the back of his neck at the same time.

"He seemed okay to me," I said, while trying to loosen the laces on my gloves with my teeth.

Willy turned and gave me a nasty look this time, then said, "There's a call for you over on the pay phone."

"For me?" I said, ignoring his cloudy looks. I slipped my right glove beneath my left arm and tugged until it came off. "Thanks."

I climbed out of the ring, dropped to the floor on legs that felt like noodles, and walked to the phone. The receiver was hanging down towards the floor and I took a couple of good, long breaths before picking it up and trying to speak.

"Yeah, Jacoby."

"Uh, excuse me, but is this Miles Jacoby, the private detective?" a man's voice asked.

"Yes, it is," I said, even though he mispronounced my name. It's *Jack*-u-bee, not Ju-*co*-by.

"Uh, yes, Mr. Jacoby, I called your office and was given this number by your answering machine. My name is Aaron Steinway."

I tried not to sound too breathless as I asked, "What can I do for you, Mr. Steinway?"

"I'd like to hire you to find my pulp magazine collection."

"Your, uh, pulp magazine collection?" I asked. "What happened to it?"

He went on to explain that he owned one of the most extensive collections of old pulps—including Black Mask, Doc Savage, The Shadow, Dime Detective, etc.— in the world. He had gone away on business and when he returned, he found the entire collection missing from his home.

He offered to pay me a generous fee to try and find it and suggested that I come out to his home in New Hyde Park to "look for clues." I stifled a trite remark about my Sherlock Holmes magnifying glass being in the shop for repairs and told him I'd be there as soon as possible. I know the sound of money when I hear it, even over the phone, and business wasn't so good that I'd let myself be put off by the prospect of a trip out to New Hyde Park.

I hung up and began to unlace my other glove. I still felt winded, but pretty good about possibly having a client. Of course, that didn't mean that I didn't want the money I'd get paid for sparring with Willy's new boy.

For the first few weeks after hanging up my own gloves for good, I had tried to stay away from boxing, and the gym; but pretty soon I realized that was foolish. I still enjoyed the sport, even though I was no longer competing. Recently, however, when money became very tight, I had entertained the thought of possibly putting the gloves back on and sparring for some extra cash—

4

with which to pay for some food and my rent.

This had been my first session as a sparring partner, and it showed me how out of shape I'd become in the three months since my retirement from the ring.

I pulled off the other glove and walked over to where Willy Wells was helping Vito DeLuca off with his headgear.

"Willy—" I started, but the grizzled old bantamweight turned on me and silenced me with a look.

"I know, you want your money," he rasped. He reached into his pocket and took out a few bills. "You're stealing this money from me, Kid. When you called and said you needed some bread and wanted to spar, I expected you to give my boy three good rounds."

"We didn't go three—"

"You went two, and you didn't even go a decent two," he said. He shoved the money into my hand and said, "Call me when you're in better shape and can do my boy some good."

He turned away and started talking to DeLuca again. The kid was looking over Wells's shoulder at me, smirking, and I wished I had the strength to throw a decent punch.

I remembered a time when Willy Wells wanted to manage me and help me become middleweight champ. Now I was an annoyance to him. I looked down at the bills in my hand and saw two twenties and a ten. Fifty bucks just wasn't worth the fatigue—not to mention the ear-burning shame I was feeling.

I went to the locker room and showered in cold water, trying to wash away the burning, but it didn't help. When I left I did so without looking at or speaking to Willy Wells again.

Chapter Two

The man who answered the door was a painfully thin six foot four. He had great, gaunt hollows under his cheekbones, hooded gray eyes, and a thin slit of a mouth. His gray hair came to a widow's peak and, in defiance of his years, was full. I knew he couldn't be the butler, because he was dressed in an old sweatshirt, faded blue jeans, and sandals, so I had to assume that he was Aaron Steinway, my prospective client.

"Mr. Jacoby?" he asked, mispronouncing the name again, as he had on the phone. Even while I was fighting, the referees and ring announcers could never get the name right.

"Jacoby," I said, correcting him. "Miles Jacoby."

"Come in, please," he said, taking no notice. I stepped past him and he closed the door behind us. "I am Aaron Steinway," he introduced himself. "I spoke to you on the phone."

His voice was very deep and his mouth barely moved when he spoke, as if he knew he had bad breath and was trying to protect the world from it.

"This way, please," he said, without offering to shake hands. He led me down a long hallway to a room packed with comic books, magazines, and old hardcover and paperback books. You couldn't miss the spot where the pulp magazines had been. Directly across from the door was a full wall of shelves, and they were empty.

"That's where they were when I left," he said, indicating the empty shelves.

He looked at me hopefully and asked, "Do you think you can find any clues?"

I looked at him then, to see if he was serious, and saw that he was. I decided to humor him and walked up to the empty shelves.

"Have the police been here?" I asked as I pretended to inspect the shelves for, uh, clues.

Behind me I heard him snort harshly and I turned to look at him. He looked as if he had just bitten into a lemon.

"The police! They were here yesterday and didn't even bother to take fingerprints. They just looked around and told me that they would be in touch. If there isn't a clue that they can trip over, the police simply close the case."

I nodded and decided not to try to defend the actions of the police, who got so many cases each day that they couldn't devote their time to the ones where there wasn't a clue you could trip over. That would just have alienated me from my new client, and I didn't relish being alienated from all that money he wanted to pay me.

"Are you married, Mr. Steinway?"

He bit into another lemon and said simply, "No," indicating that his opinion of marriage—and women—was on a par with his opinion of the police.

His answer didn't surprise me. He probably had very little time after his work and his collection to devote to a marriage.

Looking down at my hands, now black because I'd made the mistake of touching the empty shelves, I asked, "Could we go somewhere and talk about this? I'd like to ask some questions and perhaps...wash up?"

He glanced at me for a moment as if he weren't quite seeing me, then shook his head abruptly and said, "Oh, yes, of course. This way, please."

We went back down the hall and into a smaller, cleaner room that was apparently his den. There were books there as well, but they were newer, cleaner. He showed me a small bathroom, where I washed the dirt off my hands. When I came back out he was seated behind his desk, staring off into space. Behind him, on the shelves, I could make out some titles: *The Hardboiled Dicks* and a book called *Cheap Thrills,* both by Ron Goulart, and a book entitled *Gun in Cheek,* by Bill Pronzini. I hadn't heard of any of the books or authors, but then I wasn't much of a reader.

There were other books, but I turned my attention to Steinway.

"Mr. Steinway, how many people knew of your trip?"

For a moment I thought I was going to have to repeat the question, but then he looked at me and said, "Several people. My partner, a few clients—"

"I'll need names, sir, and addresses," I said. "A list of people who knew you would be out of town, and another list of anyone who has shown a recent interest in, or has made an offer for your collection."

He nodded, took a pen and pad, and began preparing the lists. While he did that I walked to an expensive-looking bookcase and peered through the windows on the door, which I assumed were locked. This had to be where his rare, valuable items were kept. I saw books by Raymond Chandler and Dashiell Hammett, presumably first editions. The only titles I recognized were *The Maltese Falcon, The Thin Man,* and *The Big Sleep,* and those only from the old movies.

"No one broke into this room or this cabinet?" I asked.

He looked up from his desk and said, "Thank God, no."

He finished up the lists, which were relatively short. When he handed them to me, I produced a pen and began to put check marks next to the names that appeared on both lists. One name in particular caught my eye, and I asked him about it, even though it appeared only on the list of people who had made offers for his collection.

"This James Denton, did he offer you any cash up front?"

"Denton," he said, thinking. "Yes, he did, but I simply was not interested."

"How long ago was this?"

"Last week."

"When did you leave town, and when did you return?"

"Today is Friday," he said. "I left Monday morning and returned Thursday evening. I immediately phoned the police, and they came and took a report that evening."

"How was the house entered?"

"Apparently through a window in the back."

"Was it broken?"

"No, forced. I called the police yesterday to ask if they had accomplished anything, but that was when they told me they would be in touch. That was also when I decided to hire a private investigator."

"Where did you get my name?"

"From my attorney, Hector Delgado."

I knew Heck very well, and this was not the first time he had steered some business my way. However, he had never sent me a client as affluent as Aaron Steinway.

I decided that Heck would be one of the first persons I spoke to when I left Steinway's house. I checked the two lists again, but did not see his name.

"Did Heck—did Mr. Delgado know that you were leaving town?"

"No, he did not."

"Um, Mr. Steinway, excuse my ignorance, but how much money are we talking about here?" I asked. "I mean, I don't know anything at all about these magazines, so I don't have any idea of their value."

"Are you asking me to put a value on my collection?"

"I guess that's what I'm asking, yes."

He thought a moment, then said, "It's impossible. It's difficult to put a monetary value on something you have never had any intentions of selling."

"Well, then, what about individually? What do they go for? A buck, two bucks—"

He looked at me as if I had just pissed on his rug.

"It is true," he said, rather stiffly, "that some of them did come rather inexpensively, but there are magazines in my collection that cost me as much as a thousand dollars...each!"

I was stunned.

"Really? I, uh, had no idea," I said lamely.

"Obviously not."

A thousand bucks for a book that was forty years old? What must the entire collection have been worth?

"How many magazines were there?" I asked, trying to establish my professional tone again.

"Oh, almost ten thousand now."

That meant it would have taken a truck, or a van, to move them, and time to load. There were no windows in that book room of his, and I made a mental note to check the carpet in the hallway again for some kind of tracks. They had to have used something, maybe a wheelbarrow, to move the books to a window or a door, where they could load them up.

"Tell me something about some of these names that appear on both lists," I said. "Who's Walter Brackett?"

"Walter is my partner—"

"Excuse me," I said, stopping him, "but what kind of business are you and your partner in?"

"We are stockbrokers and investment counselors."

"Okay, go on."

"Walter and his wife, Laura, have been after my collection for a few years now. He is a foolish old man who married a woman much younger than he. Laura collects also, and he seems to feel that if he could present her with my collection, he would have a better chance of keeping her."

I checked the lists again and found Laura Brackett's name on both.

"How much of a collection does she have?"

"Modest," he said. "No more than three or four thousand. Nothing at all like mine. She has been pushing Walter to buy the collection from me ever since she first saw it."

I picked another name from the list and asked, "What about Michael Walsh?"

"Walsh is a client of mine. He has been a client for a few years and a collector for many years, but his collection does not compare to mine any more than Laura Brackett's does," he finished proudly.

We discussed some of the other clients on the two lists, and then discussed my fee—which I shamelessly hiked—and agreed on a retainer. When he gave me the check, the fact that it wouldn't have bought me even one of those thousand-dollar pulps did not depress me in the least. I tucked it away in my wallet with great satisfaction, because it was more money than I had seen in months.

Before leaving, I took down Steinway's office phone number, his home number, and the address and phone number of his New York apartment. Getting out of my chair, I said, "I'll call you the moment I find out anything, Mr. Steinway."

"Even if it's only about a single copy," he insisted anxiously.

"Even if it's only about a single copy," I assured him.

We shook hands and he got mine dirty again. He also mispronounced my name again, but I refrained from correcting him this time. He had paid for the privilege.

Chapter Three

The sign on my office door said WATERS & JACOBY, PRI-
VATE INVESTIGATORS. It was a fairly new sign, but then
I was fairly new to the business.

Eddie Waters had been my employer for three years,
allowing me to accumulate the time and experience I
needed in order to apply for my own license. While
working for him I also pursued my career as a middleweight boxer. Aside from all of that, he was also my
friend. When my brother was arrested for killing Eddie,
it had been up to me to prove that my brother Benny
was innocent, and also to find out who really killed
Eddie. I did that, and then I had one more fight during
which the referee saved *me* from getting killed. After
that I hung up my gloves and decided to keep Eddie's
office open, and keep his name on the door. Unfortunately, keeping his name on the door did little to satisfy
his regular clients, and they went elsewhere. So did his
secretary, Missy, who felt she simply could not work in
the same office any longer. She and Eddie had had much
more than a professional relationship. So, with Missy
gone and most of Eddie's steady clients gone, I had a
hard time keeping things together; but the job from
Steinway would help a lot.

Entering the office, I scooped up my mail from the floor and put it down on the desk, next to the second-hand answering machine that was supposed to replace Missy. I also put Aaron Steinway's two lists down on the desk, sat next to them, turned the phone around, and dialed Heck Delgado's number.

I had met Heck while working for Eddie. After my brother was arrested and charged with Eddie's murder, I imposed on Heck to defend Benny, which he would have done had I not eventually turned up Eddie's real killer.

Hector Domingo Gonzales Delgado was a young and damned good lawyer, and he had become a good friend as well. On occasion he pushed some work my way, as he had done with Steinway.

Heck answered his own phone and I said, "What did you do to lose this one?" He had a habit of running through secretaries like babies run through diapers.

"This one," he replied, "is out to lunch." In that Ricardo Montalban accent of his he added, "Secretaries do eat lunch, you know. Not like some lawyers and private eyes I know."

"Right. Listen, I just came from talking to Aaron Steinway. What can you tell me about the man?"

"Not much. I've handled some work for him from time to time."

"He said that you were *his* attorney."

"Anybody who works for Aaron Steinway once is *his*," Heck said, "which tells you more about the man than I can. Ah, well, he's hard, but fair. He hasn't got much of a heart, but then that's not what his clients pay him for. They pay him for results, and that's what they get. What did he want?"

"Didn't he tell you?"

"He did not. He simply asked me to recommend a reliable private investigator."

"What's the matter," I asked, "was Walker Blue busy?" Walker Blue was a first class P.I. that Heck used regularly.

"You should know, Miles, that I did give him Walker's name as well as yours."

"Really?" I asked, feeling good about having been picked over Blue, who was one of the best in the busi-

13

ness. Then I had a thought and asked, "Did he call Blue?"

"You mean, did he call you after Walker turned him down?"

"That's what I mean."

"I don't know the answer to that, Miles, and were I you I would not worry about it."

"Take the money and run, huh?"

"Take the money and work for it, my friend."

"Right."

"Is it none of my business?"

"What's that?"

"The reason he needed a private investigator."

"Oh, no, it's no secret. Somebody copped his collection of pulp magazines and he wants me to get it back for him. Piece of cake."

"I am sure. What do you know about pulp magazines?"

"*Nada*, but I know somebody who does, so if we can get off the phone I'll call him. Is there anything else I should know about Mr. Steinway?"

"Yes. He'll probably pay you very well indeed if you find his precious collection."

"That's good to know, Heck. Thanks for the referral."

"My pleasure, Miles. Uh, how have you been these days?"

"Fine, Heck, just fine," I said. "I'll let you know what happens."

"Good luck."

"Thanks. Be good, *amigo*," I said, and hung up.

I did know somebody who could fill me in on the world of pulp magazine collecting, but before I made that call I wanted to see if I could get a copy of the Steinway police report.

I called the Seventeenth Precinct and asked for Detective Hocus, in the "squad."

When he came on I said, "Hocus, it's Jacoby."

"Good afternoon, Mr. Jacoby," he greeted, "and what can the New York City police department do for you today?"

"Well, seeing as how you asked—"

"Why shouldn't I ask?" he cut in. "You only call me when you want something."

14

"Just trying to keep up with the TV image of the private eye, Hocus."

"And doing a fine job of it," he added. "You're all get and no give."

"Hey, if you ever have need of my facilities—" I started to offer.

"What do you need?"

"I'm working—"

"That's a switch."

"There was a burglary in New Hyde Park that was reported Wednesday night. I'd like to get a look at the police report. Think you can help me?"

"I could if I was inclined to."

I had met Hocus while working on Eddie Waters's murder. He was the cop who arrested my brother, but after a rough start we got along. I called him for help or information from time to time—as he pointed out— because he was the only cop I knew well enough to call. He always made himself sound unwilling to help, but he was okay, and in the end he usually gave in, if he could, without putting his neck in a noose—which he did for no man.

"All right," he sighed, when I wouldn't bite. "I'll make a call and see what I can do. If they've got the same computer setup that we've got, I might be able to get you a hard copy."

"I'd appreciate it."

"Yeah. I'll call you. Why don't *you* call *me* sometimes when you don't want something?"

"Aw, come on, Hocus," I said. "What would we have to talk about then?"

"Forget it," he replied. "I've got work to do, Jacoby. I'll be in touch."

Hocus had never struck me as the kind of man I would call to have a beer or go to a fight. It had nothing to do with the fact that he was about fifteen years or so older than me, it was just the way the man felt to me. He didn't seem like the type of person who would socialize easily—with anyone.

Once while I was working for Eddie, he sent me to San Francisco to find a guy who had jumped bail. The bail bondsman had hired Eddie to bring him back, but

15

Eddie had to stay in New York to testify before a grand jury, so he sent me instead.

Since I didn't know San Francisco I'd had to get some help from a local P.I. The man I got was a big, bearish private eye of about fifty or so who, amazingly enough, collected pulp magazines. If anyone would know about a large collection of pulps suddenly showing up on the market, it would be him, so I called him after Hocus.

When I dialed his number I got one of those phone company messages telling me that his number had been changed and giving me the new one. When I dialed that one, he picked it up.

"Detective Agency."

"Don't you send out change-of-phone-number notices, Lone Wolf?"

"Jack? Is that you, Kid?"

After we'd found my bail jumper, he had invited me to his place in Pacific Heights, where he showed me his better than six thousand pulp magazines. We killed a couple of pizzas and more than a couple of six-packs of Schlitz. He started calling me "Kid," and I started calling him "Wolf" or "Lone Wolf," because a newspaper out there had once described him as the "last of the Lone Wolf detectives."

"It's me, Wolf. What's with the new phone and the high-class greeting?"

"I'm trying to attract a higher class of clientele."

"That means you're going to have to buy another suit."

"You should see my new office," he went on, ignoring my remark.

"The P.I. biz must be booming in the City by the Bay," I said.

"You couldn't tell by me. What's up, Kid? Are you in town? Nope, I can tell from the echo you're not."

"I'm calling from New York," I verified. "I've got a case I think might be right up your alley," I added, and went on to tell him what it was all about.

He whistled soundlessly into the phone and said, "The guy must be climbing the walls. I know I would be if it was my collection that got snatched."

"Hey, was he bullshitting me about having paid as much as a thousand bucks for one book?"

"No bull, Kid. A first of Black Mask just recently went for almost three times that much."

"Well, I guess there's no telling what people will spend their money on," I said, taking a playful dig at him.

"Up yours, Kid," he replied, good-naturedly.

"Seriously, you buy a lot of these things. Do you know any of the people I've mentioned?"

"Sorry, Jack, but I do most of my buying through the mail. The only name I recognized was your client's, and that's only because I've read about his collection. Other than that, I can't help you."

"You could keep your ears open, just in case there's a glut of magazines on the market."

"I can do that, sure. I'll let you know as soon as I hear something," he promised.

"Okay, I appreciate it. There's just one other thing."

"What's that?"

"Do you know anyone in the New York area who could be called an authority on the pulps?"

"Let me think a minute," he said, and got off the phone for just about that length of time. "I thought I had one here," he said, coming back on the line. "I don't know the guy personally, Jack, but I've bought some stuff from him through the mail. He's got a catalogue, but the guy is only known as Mr. Pulps. I can give you his name and address."

"That's great," I said, picking up a pen and turning one of my client's lists over so I could write on the other side. He read the info off to me, giving me the guy's name and a New Jersey address.

"I hope this is just what I need," I told him when he finished reading.

"I hope so, too—and I hope you find your client's collection. Hell, I hope I find it," he added, laughing.

I laughed, too, and said, "You'd give the damned thing back."

"Yeah, I wonder."

"I don't. Your honesty is part of your fatal charm, and it's probably also your fatal flaw."

"Thanks...I think."

"Listen, behave yourself and come to the Big Apple real soon, huh? I owe you a pizza and a hangover."

17

"I'll collect, don't worry. Take care, Kid."

"So long, Lone Wolf."

As I hung up, I couldn't help but think that if ever a man personified the "Lone Wolf" private eye of the thirties and forties, whether it be on film or in print, it would have to be the man I had just been talking to, a man I liked very much and had a tremendous amount of respect for.

I moved around to sit behind my desk and turned the phone to face me again. I placed the two lists side by side in front of me and knew that I had to transpose the names that appeared on both over to a third list, according to where they lived. It was times like these that I especially missed Missy. She used to do things like that for Eddie without his even having to tell her. The last time I had heard from Missy, she was working for one of those temporary secretary services. I was tempted to call her while I had the phone at hand, but pushed the thought away. I picked up the receiver and dialed Knock Wood Lee's number. As usual, the phone was answered by his main lady, Tiger Lee.

The number I dialed was Wood's private number, which I was privileged to know. When Tiger Lee answered, she was not using her "John" voice, which was the singsong Oriental tone that most men expected from a Chinese woman.

"Hello?"

"Hello, Lee."

"Jack, hi," she said, making me feel like she was really glad to hear my voice. Tiger Lee, whose real name was Anna Lee, had the most fantastic phone voice I had ever heard, and when she was using the "John" voice, its effect was doubled. "How are you?"

"I'm working. Is Wood around?"

"Where else would he be? I'll put him on."

I waited a moment, and then Wood came on the line. His real name was Nok Woo Lee, and he was a Chinese-American bookie who ran some girls on the side, got his fingers sticky from time to time, and did it all from a loft in Chinatown that he rarely left.

"Jack, you're working," Wood said, sounding as if he could barely believe it.

"Don't sound so surprised. I need your help."

18

"Now I'm not surprised," he said. "What can I do for you?"

"Keep your ears open," I answered, and went on to tell him what I wanted him to keep his ears open for.

"Old books?" he asked.

"Old and valuable are two words that usually mean the same thing," I informed him.

"Yes, tell that to an old whore," he replied. "Well, if it's a collection, chances are it will be split up fairly soon."

"I don't think it would be as valuable that way."

"Perhaps not, but it would certainly be easier to dispose of," he reminded me. "That is usually the most important consideration."

"I guess you're right."

"As usual," he said immodestly. "I will call you if I hear of anything."

"I'd appreciate it," I said, picking up the bundle of mail and leafing though it. I stopped short when I came to a particular envelope, and then became aware that Wood was speaking to me again.

"Jack, hey, Jack? Are you there?"

"Uh, yeah, Wood, I'm here. Thanks for your help, okay?"

"Sure, anytime," he said, sounding puzzled. "Are you all right?"

"I'm fine. I was just going through my mail."

"Bills, huh?" he asked, as if he suddenly understood.

"Yeah," I said, "bills. See you, huh?"

I hung up before he could reply, put down the rest of the mail and examined the envelope in my hand. It was a normal 4⅛-by-9½-inch white envelope, with my name and office address typed on it. Nothing unusual about that, until I looked at the return address.

The name was Jacoby, and the return address was a post-office box in Chicago.

There were only three Jacobys that I knew of. Me, my brother, Benny, and my brother's wife, Julie. Julie had left town three months ago, after I'd cleared Benny of the murder rap. While he was in jail, we discovered that we felt the same way about each other, but I'd also found out that she was involved in the murder of Eddie Waters. So I forced the woman I loved, my brother's

19

wife, to leave town—which, believe me, hadn't been easy.

It was also not easy to get a letter from her and not open it, but that's what I did.

I dropped the letter into the top drawer of the desk, picked up the two lists I'd gotten from Steinway, and left the office.

Chapter Four

I needed someplace else to sit and recopy the names onto my third list, and with that letter from Julie in my desk, the office wasn't the place. I didn't want to go home, because my brother, Benny, was there. That always seemed like a good reason not to go home.

I decided to go over to Bogie's, claim a small spot at the bar, and do it there. At the bar I wouldn't interfere with their lunch business.

Bogie's is a restaurant on Twenty-sixth Street, between Seventh and Eighth Avenues, that named itself after Bogart and dedicated itself to supporting the mystery. On Sunday nights they played old radio mystery shows, and on the last Sunday of every month they had mystery writers there, speaking and autographing their latest books. I wasn't a mystery fan, but I liked the place because it was small and comfortable, and the owners, Billy and Karen Palmer, were nice people.

Billy was in when I got there and greeted me at the door. Karen usually got in a little later in the day.

"Jack," he called from the far end of the bar. He waved me over with one hand while holding the phone to his ear with the other. "Be off in a minute," he said when I reached him.

I sat on the last stool and took the lists out of my pocket.

When Billy hung up I said, "I need a piece of paper and a beer."

"You need to work out," he said, patting my stomach, "and no beer. Why don't you come down to the dojo and get back in shape, Jack?"

"Sure, Billy, maybe next week," I said. "Right now I need a beer."

He frowned at me, but said, "Sure, but light beer, okay?"

I grinned at him and said, "Yeah, okay."

I was upset over the letter from Julie, and I'd taken it out on him. He understood something was bothering me, though, because he was good with people.

"Thanks," I said when he set it down. Next to the beer he put a sheet of paper, and again I said, "Thanks."

"You working?" he asked, and I knew it had nothing to do with my tab.

"Yeah."

"Good. I'll let you concentrate. I've got to go in the back, anyway. Don't leave without calling me, huh?"

"Sure."

I started copying names and addresses—Brackett, Walsh, Brackett again—but my mind wasn't on it. My head was back at the office, in that top drawer with the letter from Julie. What did she want after three months? Did she think I'd feel less anger, less hurt after that time?

I drank down half the beer, then tried to turn my full attention back to the list. When I got to the name James Denton, I saw a way to keep my mind off of that letter.

"Ed," I said to the bartender.

"Yeah?"

"Tell Billy I had to leave, huh? I'll see him later, maybe."

"Okay, Jack."

I pocketed my lists, left my beer, waved to Ed, and left Bogie's. I was heading downtown to find James Denton, otherwise known as "Jimmy the Dime."

22

Chapter Five

"Jimmy the Dime" Denton got his name because, for the right price, he was always ready to "drop a dime" on someone, which was another way of saying he was a snitch. I knew Eddie had used him, and Hocus had also thrown some cash his way. Now it looked like someone was using him as a front man in an attempt to buy Steinway's collection.

For the right price, Jimmy would tell me who.

On my way downtown to find him, I stopped at my bank, deposited most of Steinway's check, and pocketed the rest.

Jimmy Denton hung out downtown, in Chinatown, or Little Italy, or wherever, as long as it was below Houston Street. Normally, that is, he hung around down there, but on that particular day I couldn't locate him. As well as acting as somebody's front man, he was either lying low or they'd stashed him somewhere. I spent the better part of the afternoon trying to locate him, but no one had seen him in at least a week.

I ended up at Packy's, a bar in the Village not far from my apartment that was run by an ex-heavyweight. Packy himself was behind the bar, as he almost always is.

"Hiya, Kid," he greeted me. "How's the boy?"

"Fine, Packy, just great."

"What'll it be, beer?"

I almost said yes, but thought better of it and said, "Let me have a ginger ale, Packy."

"Ginger ale?" he asked, frowning. "You ain't going back into training, are you, Kid?"

"I don't *look* stupid, do I?"

He frowned mightily and said, "Geez, I never said you looked stupid, Jack."

"Just bring me the ginger ale, Packy," I said, and he grinned and went to get it. Packy was not always as punchy as he liked to make people think.

He brought back the ginger ale and said, "I guess you *could* stand to lose a little weight, huh?"

"So I've been told. Packy, have you seen Jimmy Denton lately, or heard of anyone who has?"

"Jimmy the Dime?" he said. "He doesn't drink here."

"I know that, but maybe you heard from someone..."

He shook his head and said, "Sorry, Jack. I can't help you."

"Yes, you can. Just keep your ears open."

"What do you want with Jimmy the Dime?"

"I'm working, Packy."

His eyes lit up and he said, "Does that mean you're paying, too?"

"Is my tab that high?" I asked, kidding, but he was only half kidding.

"Not yours, Jack," he said seriously.

"Shit," I said viciously. "Packy—"

"I'm sorry, Jack, but if I don't give it to him, someone else will. At least here I can watch him."

"You don't have to watch him!" I snapped. "He's *my* brother." I dug into my pocket and came up with the money from Steinway's check.

"What does he owe you?"

"It can wait, Jack," he said, apologetically. "I shouldn't have even mentioned—"

"How much?"

"Fifty-five bucks."

I counted it out and gave it to him, then told him, "No more, Packy. If he wants to drink someplace else, let him. If he gets rolled staggering home some night, they won't find anything on him."

"He could catch a beating, Jack."

"It won't be the first time," I said of my brother, who was also an ex-boxer. It had been Benny who pushed me into fighting, wanting me to win the title he hadn't even been able to get close to. As it turned out, neither one of us got a sniff of it, and that was fine by me.

"Has he been in today?" I asked Packy.

"Not today, no."

"He's probably passed out at home," I said, half to myself. I still didn't want to go home, but I couldn't really think of a good alternative, so I got off my stool and said, "I'll see you, Packy."

"Be good, Jack."

I knew that if I didn't find Benny out cold on my sofa bed, I'd find him out on his feet. He had been a lush before Julie left town, but during the past three months he had gotten even worse. I took him in to live with me because if I didn't he would've ended up dead in the street somewhere, but sometimes I found myself wishing I had the guts to kick him out. I used to think that old TV series "The Odd Couple" was funny, but lately it had lost its appeal.

I stopped on the way home to pick up some hamburgers and French fries from a greasy spoon. Knowing my brother, he hadn't eaten a thing all day, and I was pretty hungry myself. When I reached my apartment I paused outside the door and tried to think of a good reason to go in. Actually, the only reason I was ever able to come up with was the same one that kept me from kicking him out.

He was my brother.

Chapter Six

My apartment was what they called two rooms, but I called it a room and a half with a kitchenette. Whatever you wanted to call it, when I didn't see Benny as soon as I walked in, it meant he was either in the john, or gone. I heard the john flush.

The sofa bed was still unmade, and my sleeping bag was still on the floor. I walked to the table in the kitchenette and dropped the greasy bag on it.

"Miles, you're home," Benny said when he came out of the john.

"Yeah," I said, "I brought dinner."

My brother shuffled across the room, sat at the table, and opened the bag.

"Burgers and fries, huh?" he asked. He rooted about a little more in the bag, then withdrew one burger and one order of fries.

"No bottle, Benny," I said.

He looked at me with his mouth full and said, "That's not fair, Miles. I ain't had a drink all day."

"You didn't clean up, either, did you?" I said.

"What?" he asked, looking around. "Oh, the bed? Well, I took a little nap, you know? I was gonna clean up before you—"

"And my sleeping bag."

"Oh, that. I just forgot—"

"Have you been home all day?"

"Why?" he asked, with a crafty look in his eyes. "Did you call?"

"No, I didn't call, Benny," I said. I sat down opposite him and tore the bag open so I could get to my food.

He looked relieved that I hadn't called, and turned his attention to his food.

Benny was about five years older than I was, but he looked fifteen years older. Since Julie left, he'd really gone to seed. He'd gotten fat and sloppy, and I hoped to God I wasn't looking at a future version of myself. I looked down at my belly, which had gotten bigger since I left the ring, and I pushed the remains of my burger and fries over to him and said, "Here, you can have it."

"Not hungry, huh?" he said, grabbing it.

"No, I'm not hungry," I said. "I been thinking that maybe I've put on a little too much weight over the past few months."

"You look fine," he said. "What's the difference, if you ain't gonna fight anymore?"

"The difference is I don't want to end up looking like you," I snapped, standing up.

"That ain't nice, Miles," he said, giving me a hurt look.

"I'm going out, Benny, I've got work to do."

"You got a client?"

"Yeah, I've got a client."

He put down the burger and, wiggling his greasy fingers said, "Do you have any money?"

"Yes, I do, and I'm going to keep it, too."

"That ain't fair, Miles. I've got to have some money..."

"I gave your money to Packy, Benny," I said, "to pay your tab."

"Oh, that."

"Yeah, that." I started for the door and kicked the sleeping bag on the way. "When I get back I expect to find this place cleaned up, Benny."

"What for?" he called after me. "You're just gonna have to open the bag again to go to sleep—"

I slammed the door behind me to drown out his voice and banged my feet loudly on the steps going down.

Christopher Street was getting dark now, and I looked around for a direction to go in. I needed someplace where I could go and relax and decide how I was going to proceed on this Steinway thing.

I decided to walk just a few blocks and go to the only place I could think of that fit the bill.

Chapter Seven

"You know, you come around more often now," Tracy Dean said.

"What?" I asked. I was seated at a table in her apartment, putting my new list in order of who I was going to see first.

"Since Julie left, you've been coming around more often," Tracy said.

I looked up at her and said, "What do you mean?"

"I mean I don't feel like such a substitute anymore."

Tracy and I had met when she came to one of my fights, and we got on pretty well for a while. Later, I used to go to her apartment when I started thinking about my brother's wife too much, and she would help me forget for a while. She knew that she was sort of a substitute and she accepted it. Tracy was twenty-four, brunette, and incredibly energetic. She was an actress and model, although most of her acting was done in movies of the blue variety, but she enjoyed the independence her chosen profession gave her, and she enjoyed sex for its own sake.

"And you don't come around just to fuck anymore," she added, smiling. She touched my arm and said, "Jack,

I know you miss Julie, but I feel like since she left we've become more like...friends."

I touched her hand and said, "We were always friends, Tracy. At least, you were always a friend to me."

She kissed me on the cheek and then walked to her sofa and picked up her jacket.

"Where are you going?"

"I have a scene to shoot tonight. I should be back in a couple of hours...if you want to wait?" she asked, wiggling her eyebrows suggestively.

"I, uh, I may have to go out and do some work myself," I said. "Why don't we play it by ear, okay?"

"Sure," she said, looking disappointed. "See you."

"Be careful."

She waved and was gone.

If Tracy was right about our having become closer "friends" lately, then that had to have something to do with my not particularly liking the way she made her living. I wasn't wild about the prospect of waiting for her to come back from doing her "scene" and our then going to bed together. I'd be wondering just what kind of scene she had done, and that wouldn't be fair to either of us.

Then again, our relationship had never been a particularly fair one.

I finished up my list, deciding that it was time for me to put everything else aside and start acting like a detective.

Jimmy the Dime was still tops on my list, but finding him was going to be hard. I'd have to call Wood again in the morning and enlist his aid to that end as well.

The Bracketts, Walter and Laura, both lived in Manhattan, and seeing them tomorrow would be fairly easy. Michael Walsh lived in Staten Island, so I'd need a car to go and see him. The same went for the man who put out the catalogue. He lived in New Jersey. I wrote his name down last, then folded up all of my lists and put them in my pocket. The easiest course of action was to see the Bracketts tomorrow, and then work on borrowing a car.

With tomorrow planned, I readdressed the problem of where to spend the night. I sure as hell didn't want to go back to my apartment, and now I had reservations about spending the night with Tracy—at least until I had time to think things out.

One alternative was to register in a hotel for the night, but that seemed like an awful waste of Steinway's money. I was just going to have to go home and go right to sleep...in my sleeping bag...without talking to Benny....

There had to be a better way.

Chapter Eight

Bogie's wasn't mobbed, but they had a nice midweek dinner crowd on their hands. I hated to bother Billy and Karen, but I remembered Billy offering me the use of his back office once if I ever needed it. According to him, it was equipped with a desk, a cot, and a working john with a shower.

"Hi, Jack," Karen said, greeting me with a lovely smile and a kiss on the cheek. "Twice in one day; to what do we owe this pleasure?"

"I'd like to talk to Billy, Karen," I said.

"Sure, he's in the back," she said, frowning. "Is anything wrong?"

"No, I just need a favor, that's all."

"Why don't you sit at the bar and I'll call him."

"Thanks."

Karen went around to the far end of the bar and picked up the phone. A few moments later, while I was working on a ginger ale, Billy came out from the kitchen.

"Jack, what's up?" he asked, approaching me on my side of the bar while Karen came over on the other side.

"I, uh, need a place to spend the night, Billy, and I was thinking about your back room. I wondered if—"

"It's yours," he said, cutting me off.

32

"I just need it for tonight."

He put his hand on my shoulder and said, "Jack, it's yours for as long as you need it. Use the shower, use the phone, use whatever you need."

"Thanks, Billy."

I felt Karen's hand touch my other shoulder and she said, "Is everything all right, Jack? You look so down."

I smiled at her as best I could and said, "I've just got a bad case of the moroses tonight."

"Do you need a change of clothes for tomorrow?" Billy asked. "I keep some stuff around."

"No, that won't be necessary," I told him, "you've done enough by letting me stay—"

"Don't be silly," he interrupted me. "We're about the same size. I'll lend you something. Come on, I'll take you in the back."

I got off the stool to follow him, looked at Karen, and said, "Thanks, beertender."

"Anytime," she said, grinning back.

Billy took me through the kitchen, out a back door, and up a small flight of stairs next door. Using a key he opened the door and admitted us to his back office, which at one time had been an apartment.

"There's a door to the outside there," he said, pointing towards the front. "We keep it locked, but you can either use that or go back through the kitchen if you prefer. There's also a small alleyway that leads to Eighth Avenue, if you have to get out in a hurry."

"I'll only be here one night, Billy," I reminded him.

"Jack," he said, "obviously there's a reason you don't want to go home tonight. In fact, I've noticed quite a few nights when you haven't wanted to go home. This place is yours for as long as you want it. It must be pretty cramped in your apartment with Benny there."

"More than you think."

"Business obviously isn't good enough for you to get either a larger place or a place of your own, so why not stay here?"

I looked around and liked what I saw. The desk was large, the bathroom was clean, the cot against the wall was certainly big enough and probably comfortable enough—more comfortable than my sleeping bag.

"There's an intercom between here and the bar," he

added. "You could even see clients here, if you wanted to."

"I don't know what to say," I said, staring at him.

"Don't say anything," he suggested. "We're friends, aren't we? That intercom works both ways, you know. If I need somebody thrown out, you're the first one I'll call. Deal?" he said, putting his hand out.

"Deal," I said, taking his hand, "but you've got to let me pay you."

"When business is better for you, we'll talk about that. Okay?"

"Okay."

"Good. Have you eaten anything?"

I thought about the greasy burger and fries I'd barely tasted and said, "No."

"I'll have the cook make you something and send one of the waitresses back with it."

"Something nonfattening."

He smiled and said, "All right. What about working out with me at the dojo?"

"I'll get to that," I promised.

"I'll see that you do," he replied. "See you later, Jack. The place is yours."

"Thanks, Billy."

When he went out I sat myself down at his desk and took out my lists. I transposed every name onto one single sheet of paper and tore up the rest.

Since I was going to have to interview the Bracketts and the other names on my list, that meant I wouldn't have time myself to go looking for Jimmy the Dime, who obviously didn't want to be found. I had to get someone else to find him for me, and since Steinway was footing the bill, it might as well be another P.I. Tomorrow, at my office, I'd go through my phone book and see who I could commission to help me out.

Billy stocked his booze on a floor-to-ceiling set of shelves against the right wall, and I was admiring the variety in brands when the intercom buzzer went off.

I picked up the phone and said, "Yes?"

"I told you this thing worked both ways," Billy's voice said.

"You got a rowdy customer already?"

"Nope, but I need a fill-in bartender for about an hour. You interested?"

"Why not?" I said. "At least I can work for my keep."

"You can eat behind the bar—and bartenders eat on the house."

"Lucky me. Be right there."

I hung up, shut the lights, and went out the back door the way he had brought me in, through the kitchen, and into the bar.

Billy met me at the base of the steps that led from the kitchen into the dining room and said, "Ed had to leave for a while, but he should be back soon."

"No problem," I told him, "as long as nobody orders anything too fancy."

"If you get into a jam we can work it out together," he said. "Get behind the bar and I'll get your dinner."

"Right, boss."

I was so busy behind the bar for the next half hour that I barely had time to eat my dinner—chopped steak and vegetables, all with very little seasoning—let alone worry about Benny, Tracy, Steinway's pulp collection, or even that letter in the top drawer of my desk.

In short, I had a ball.

After an hour and a half Billy came over to the end of the bar and said, "I've got a problem. Ed can't come back and I can't locate Laura. Do you mind..."

"I don't mind at all," I said. "I'm having the time of my life. This may be what I was born to do."

He laughed and said, "Thanks."

About eleven o'clock it slowed down enough for me to start worrying about my problems again. At that point, a man I recognized walked through the front door and approached the bar. He was in his forties, not overly tall, and had only one arm.

His name was Dan Fortune, and he was a P.I.

I walked over to him and asked, "What'll it be, Danny?"

He looked up at me in some surprise and said, "Miles Jacoby!"

"Irish or beer?" I asked him.

He thought a moment, then said, "Beer, I think."

I brought him a draft and he asked, "Change of professions in the works?"

"Just helping out," I answered, "but I'm having a good time doing it. A change might not be so bad."

"I've often thought that myself," he admitted, and I thought he looked a bit sad for a moment. It must have been going around.

I'd met Danny while working for Eddie, and I had learned a few things from him then, and since. Chelsea was his bailiwick and, although we never socialized, we crossed paths once or twice a month.

"As a matter of fact," I said, leaning my elbows on the bar, "I've got a client right now, and maybe you can help me out with something."

He drank some of his beer and said, "I'm working myself, but if it's something I can do, consider it done."

"I'm looking for Jimmy the Dime."

He thought a moment, then said, "Well, I haven't come across him in a while, but I'll keep my eyes open. You want me to sit on him if I find him?"

"Not unless you have to. I'd rather you just gave me a call and let me know where he was." I grabbed a matchbook and wrote down my office number—which he may or may not have had—my home number, and then as an afterthought added Bogie's number.

"You'll either find me or be able to leave a message at one of these numbers," I said, handing him the matchbook.

"Okay," he said, putting it away in a pocket. "I hope I can help you out."

"Thanks, Danny."

He put away his beer and slid off the barstool.

"I've got to get going, Miles. It was good to see you. I'll keep my eyes open for you."

"I appreciate it, Dan. If I can give you a hand with anything, let me know."

I winced as I realized what a pun that was to a one-armed man, but he just grinned, waved, and left. I'd always wondered how Dan had lost his arm, but he had a different story for every day of the week, and I had long ago given up asking him.

When closing time rolled around I sat at the bar with Billy, had a last one with him, and accepted the key for the office front door.

"You did a good job, Jack," he told me.

"Thanks, I enjoyed it. Now I don't feel so guilty about going to sleep in your office."

"You never should have, but if you have to feel like you earned it, I can tell you that you did. You bailed me out."

I slid off my stool sleepily, patted him on the shoulder, and said, "I guess that makes us even, Billy."

Karen came out of the kitchen to collect her man and I said good night to both of them and got out of there so they could shut the lights and go home.

Tomorrow, I told myself, you start making like a detective and earn that big fat fee you're going to charge Mr. Aaron Steinway.

Chapter Nine

To tell the truth, I didn't really expect to find any trace
of the missing books. As Knock Wood Lee had pointed
out, collections of almost any kind are usually broken
up and sold separately. However, as long as Steinway
was willing to pay me, I was willing to look.

I woke in the morning with a new game plan. I left
Bogie's and took a train uptown to my office. Once there
and armed with a phone book, I called as many used-
book stores as I could find, plus Manhattan's three mystery bookshops—The Mysterious Book Shop, Foul Play,
and Murder Ink—none of which I had ever heard of
before. The mystery bookstores did not deal in old pulps,
although they all agreed to call me if they heard of any
for sale, but a few of the used stores admitted having
gotten in new shipments.

I spent the morning and a good part of the afternoon
checking out those stores. They showed me what had
come in, and I bought a magazine from each place and
took them to Steinway's office on Wall Street. He examined them briefly and announced that they were not
from his collection. I didn't know how he was able to
tell—they all looked the same to me, dirty—but he
was.

When I finished with the bookshops I was fairly certain that the collection had not yet been broken up and sold—at least, not in the New York area. I put some feelers out with other P.I.'s in New Jersey, Pennsylvania, and Upstate New York, even though I was planning a trip to New Jersey myself, and I also put the word out on the street that I was interested in finding out if anyone had been hired to do a number on Steinway's house while he was away.

With all of that done, I started checking out the names on my list, starting with Walter Brackett, my client's partner. He had not been in the office when I went to see Steinway, so I tried him at home, a plush apartment house on Fifth Avenue and Sixty-first Street, opposite Central Park. Steinway had called ahead, so I was admitted with no problem by the doorman, who looked like an ex-marine.

Brackett answered the door to his apartment himself and led me to the living room. He was nudging sixty, but he was in pretty good shape, and had dyed his hair and eyebrows to help the look. As far as I was concerned, "the look" was that of a sixty-year-old man who had dyed his hair and eyebrows, but I kept my opinions to myself, since I was not being paid for them.

"I assume Mr. Steinway has told you why I've been hired?" I asked him.

"Yes, yes, Aaron mentioned that you were looking for that infernal collection of his."

"You don't like your partner's collection?"

"I have no feelings about it one way or the other," he said. "Aaron's collection is the reason Laura started one of her own, but she hasn't been able to build it up to anywhere near his."

"I imagine she hasn't been at it as long as he has," I commented.

"No, she hasn't," he said. "I suppose the fact that I've repeatedly tried to buy the damned thing makes me some sort of suspect?"

"I'm not the police, Mr. Brackett, I don't have suspects. I'm just asking questions."

"Well, then, before you ask, I did not steal Aaron's collection. I am a businessman. I deal in buying and selling, certainly not in stealing."

"I'm sure," I said. "How about your wife?" I asked, before I realized how it would sound, coming on the heels of the previous remark.

"I beg your pardon?" he asked, stiffening.

"What I mean is, is she home? I'd like to speak to her as well," I said.

"I'm afraid Laura is not at home at the moment, Mr. Jacoby, but I can assure you, she had no more to do with Aaron's books being stolen than I did."

"I'd like to take your word for it, Mr. Brackett, but unfortunately that's not the way this business works. Can you tell me when she'll be home?"

"No, I can't," he said, starting to look annoyed. "I have some work to do, Mr. Jacoby, so if you would come back again—"

"When?"

"Some other time," he said tightly. "I don't mind helping my partner, but I won't stand for my wife being accused—"

"I'm not accusing anyone, Mr. Brackett," I said, puzzled by his sudden change of heart. He'd been very cooperative until I started asking about his wife. "I *will* come back another time to speak to Mrs. Brackett. I'm sorry if I've upset you."

"I'll talk to Araon about this," he assured me. "I'm sure he won't want you bothering Laura with this."

"I'm sure he'd want me to do whatever I have to do to find his property, Mr. Brackett," I said. *"We'll* talk again as well, when you have more time. I'll show myself out."

"Good day," he said, standing rigidly in the center of his expensively furnished living room.

When I got downstairs I found a pay phone on the corner of Fifty-ninth and Fifth and called my client.

"Have you found anything yet?" he asked anxiously.

"Yes," I said, "a very uncooperative partner."

"Walter? I told that idiot—"

"He was fine until I mentioned his wife," I cut in. "What's the story there, anyway?"

"Damn, don't tell me she's moved out on him again."

"Moved out?"

"Well, actually, she does keep an apartment of her

40

own, but you never know which one she'll be staying in. The woman is as unpredictable as—as—"

"—as a woman," I finished. "Where does she live, Mr. Steinway?"

He kept me waiting while he found the address, and then read it off to me. It was an apartment house on East Eighty-second and First Avenue.

"I'll get back to you," I said. "Call ahead, would you?"

I walked to Lexington Avenue and caught the Number 6 local up to the East Eighties and found Laura Brackett's second address. The doorman had been given the word, and I was allowed up.

Laura Brackett was not quite what I had expected. I'd envisioned her as a flashy young blonde out for a rich old husband's loot. What I got was something quite different.

I had to ring her bell three times before she answered, which I thought odd, since she was expecting me. When she answered, she apologized.

"I'm sorry," she said, "I was reading." She held up a worn copy of *Black Mask* with a half-dressed blonde and the name Carroll John Daly on the cover.

"My name is Jacoby, Mrs. Brackett. I'm working for Aaron Steinway."

She was not nearly as young as I had expected—early thirties, I figured—and she was a brunette. "Classy" was the first word that popped into my mind. She was tall with subtle curves, high cheekbones, and long legs. Her dark hair hung down past her shoulders.

"Do you have I.D.?" she asked.

I reached into my pocket for my wallet and showed her the photostat of my license. She examined it intently, the tip of her tongue resting on her full bottom lip, and then she said, "I've never seen a real one before."

"It's real," I said, putting it away. "I can vouch for that."

She smiled, backed away, and said, "Come in, then." She shut the door and said, "I was just curled up with Race Williams. He's a private eye, too." She held up the book to show me where he did his private eyeing, and then led me to the living room. The apartment was smaller than the one she shared—sometimes—with her husband, but it was no less lavishly furnished. Against one wall was a set of shelves smaller than Steinway's set, but these were filled.

"Mrs. Brackett—"

"Laura," she said. "I insist."

"Laura, then—"

"Your first name is . . . what?"

"Miles."

Her eyes widened and she said, "Oh, just like Spade's partner. He was Miles Archer, you know."

"If you say so, ma'am."

"Laura."

"Laura, would you mind if we got down to business?"

"Oh, of course. I'm sorry to be prattling on like this, but I'm really quite excited, you know. I've never met a real-life private eye before."

"I understand."

"I'm glad. Please sit down. Can I get you a drink?"

"Thank you, no," I said, sitting in a large armchair. She sat down on the couch and spread her arms along the back, pushing her chest out.

"Mrs.—Laura, how did you feel about Aaron Steinway's refusal to sell your husband his collection?"

"Ooh, angry," she said. "I can't blame him, but he still made me angry."

"Angry enough to steal it?"

"Of course," she said, laughing. "I rented a truck, drove to his house, loaded the collection up, and brought it . . . where? Here?"

I stared at her and she said, "I'm sorry, really I am. No, I did not steal his collection. God, I wish I had."

"How badly did you want it?"

"Bad enough to make it part of my settlement with Walter."

"Settlement?"

"Didn't Walter tell you?" she asked, then she added, "No, he wouldn't. That would be 'airing his dirty laundry in public.'" She sounded as if she were quoting him exactly. "I'm divorcing him, and I told him that he either gets me that collection, or I'll take him for everything he has."

"Could you do that?"

42

She said, "Yes," with great satisfaction and confidence.

"What do you have on your husband that would make that possible?" I asked.

"Ask him."

"I suppose I'll have to."

"Am I making him your number-one suspect?" she asked with avid interest.

"Are you trying to?"

"Not really," she said. "I'm simply telling you the truth." She put her hands down flat on the cushions next to her and continued to pose for me.

"Were you a model before you married Mr. Brackett?" I asked.

"Why, yes, I was. Why do you ask?"

"You looked familiar," I lied.

The lie pleased her and she said, "How nice of you to remember. I haven't done any modeling now for a few years."

"I'm sure you could, though," I remarked.

"Possibly," she said, eyeing me suspiciously now. "Mr. Jacoby—Miles—are you trying to butter me up?"

I tried to look surprised and said, "Why would I do that?"

"I don't know."

"Is that what Race Williams does?" I asked. "Butter up his female suspects?"

She opened her mouth as if to laugh, and said, "Ha, is that what I am, a suspect?"

"Would you like to be?"

She looked positively gleeful as she cupped her face in her hands and said, "You know, I believe I'd like that very much!"

Chapter Ten

There were probably other questions I should have asked both of the Bracketts, and if I'd expected to find the pulp collection I might have asked them.

After Laura Brackett, I packed it in for the day and went back to my office. Tomorrow I'd see about borrowing or, better yet, renting a car and going out to Jersey and Staten Island.

I sat behind my desk and checked my machine for messages. There were two, neither of which had to do with business. One was from Benny, wanting to know where I was, and the other was from Tracy, wanting to know where I was. I shut off the machine and reset it, then opened the top drawer of the desk and stared at the letter from Julie.

I hadn't thought about it much during the day, but it had always been there at the back of my mind. I hefted it, and figured that whatever she had to say, she'd said on one or two pages. My problem was, did I want to know what she said?

The phone rang and I dropped the letter back in the drawer, closed it, and answered the phone.

"Private detective," I said, having yet to come up with a better way of answering.

"Miles, it's Benny," my brother's voice said, fuzzily. It was plain as day, even over the phone, that he'd been drinking. "What happened to you last night?"

"I spent the night somewhere, Benny," I said. "I didn't feel like coming back."

"You could have called," he said, sounding like a petulant wife.

"You're not my wife, Benny, and you're not my mother."

"We live together—"

"Not anymore."

"What's that mean?"

"It means I'll be staying at Bogie's for a while, Benny. That apartment is too small for the both of us."

"What? How am I supposed to live and pay the rent?"

"Get a job, Benny. That's what I should have made you do months ago."

"Miles, I'm your brother..."

"Don't rub it in," I said, and hung up. Sooner or later I'd have to go back to the apartment to pack my things and deal with my drunken brother, but I decided not to do it on an empty stomach.

I picked up the receiver and dialed the phone number of the temporary service Missy was working for. When someone answered I asked where I could get in touch with her and was given another number. It was almost 4:30, so I should have still been able to catch her wherever she was working.

I had to ask for her twice, but I finally got her on the line.

"Missy, it's Miles."

"Hello, Miles. How are you?"

"I'm fine. I was wondering if you'd like to have dinner with me tonight."

"When?"

"When you get off, unless that's too early for you."

"Well, to tell you the truth, I'd rather not have to take the train home to Queens and change, so if it's not someplace too fancy I'd like that just fine. We haven't talked for a while."

"No," I agreed, "we haven't. Where are you?"

"I'm at an insurance company on Park Avenue and Fifty-first," she said.

"Hey, ritzy."

"Yeah, sure. I get off at five-thirty. Meet me here?"

"Sure. Thanks, Missy."

"Thank *you*, Miles. I assume you're paying," she said, and hung up.

That might have been unfair of her, had it not been for the fact that last month, when we had dinner, she had to pick up the tab.

At five-twenty-five I was on the corner of Park and Fifty-first waiting for my date, and at five-thirty there she was.

She gave me a kiss on the cheek and a hug and said, "Hi, Jack."

"You look great," I told her, and I wasn't lying. She was still on the right side of thirty, had red hair, green eyes, and was smart as the proverbial whip.

"Where shall we go?" she asked.

"Someplace not fancy, you said?"

"Right."

"I know just the place. Let me get a cab."

I grabbed a cab—which, in New York, is not always just a figure of speech—and told him to take us to Eighth Avenue and Thirty-third Street, across the street from Madison Square Garden.

"Where are we going?"

"A place I've been meaning to try."

It was a restaurant called The Way Things Were, with a bar, a small dining room, and some outside tables in the back. It's usually pretty crowded at lunch, but we were a little early for dinner and had no trouble getting a table. The menu was basically real meat-and-potatoes fare, which was just fine with both of us.

Once we had a couple of plates of burgers and fries in front of us—good burgers and fries, this time—she got right down to it.

"Are you working, Jack?"

"Yeah, I've got a client wants me to find a collection of old pulp magazines that were taken from his house while he was out of town."

"A paying client?"

"That's the best kind, isn't it?" I replied. "And he can pay, too."

46

"Ah, a rich client," she said, widening her eyes. "Dinner is on him, huh?"

"Right."

"What else is on your mind?"

I hesitated a moment, then said, "You're too smart, Missy."

She put her right hand over mine and said, "I know you too well. I know when something is bothering you, and I know when you need to talk."

Shaking my head, I said, "I've got a client, Missy, and one who can pay. Things should be going great guns, but they're not."

"Tell me."

I told her how Benny was getting on my nerves and that I was staying at Bogie's; I told her about the new feelings that were popping up regarding Tracy; and I even told her about the problem I had trying to make some extra money sparring.

"Jack, those are not insurmountable problems," she said, staring me right in the eye. I popped a French fry into my mouth and listened to her. "As far as Benny is concerned, you're doing the right thing by putting some distance between you. I knew it was a mistake when you took him in to live with you. That's one," she finished, ticking it off on her index finger. "Number two is Tracy, and all you've got to do is talk to her. As far as wanting to spar—or needing to—just get back in shape, Jack. You can do that without going back into the ring for real."

"Boy, you sure have got a way with words, lady," I said.

"Now tell me what's really bothering you."

I had to smile at that and shake my head.

"You're amazing."

"I care," she said. "People who care can always tell when something is bothering the person they care about. Come on, Kid Jacoby, let me have it."

I toyed with my French fries and said, "I got a letter yesterday."

"Who from?"

I looked at her and she said, "Wait a minute. Not from...Julie?"

I nodded.

"What does she want?" she demanded, nostrils flaring.

"I don't know," I answered. "I haven't opened it yet."

"You haven't opened it?" she asked, staring at me in disbelief.

Suddenly she got a determined look on her face and she told me, "Don't open it, Jack. Throw it away."

"That's what I wanted you to say," I said, pointing at her over my burger.

"And now that I've said it?"

I shrugged and bit into my burger.

"I don't know, Missy."

I ordered two beers and when they came she picked hers up and said, "Well, I've told you what I think. The rest is up to you."

"I know that," I assured her. "I've known that all along, but I guess I needed to hear you say that, too."

She held her beer mug up over the glass, clinked it with mine, and said, "Good luck, Jack. I hope you do the right thing."

Yep, I knew she was going to say that, too.

Chapter Eleven

For once I was glad to see Benny passed out drunk on the sofa bed. I packed my things, left him a note telling him essentially the same thing I had said on the phone, and left. Lugging my single suitcase, I made for Bogie's, entered the office through the private entrance, and then went into the bar through the kitchen and had a few light beers.

After that I went back to the office and checked in with my client on the phone, calling him at home.

"I'm going to have to put another man on the job, Mr. Steinway," I told him, "and I'll have to rent a car to drive to Jersey and Staten Island."

"Very well," he said, "I will mail you another check. Just try and find my collection, please."

Ecstatic that I wasn't going to have to attempt to squeeze some more money out of him, I said, "I am trying, Mr. Steinway, I assure you."

"Very well. Keep me informed."

"I will," I promised, and hung up. At that point the back door opened and Billy came in carrying a couple of cups of coffee.

"You look like the cat," he said.

"Well, maybe I feel that way a little," I admitted,

taking one of the cups. "I've got a place to stay, and a client who doesn't mind parting with his money, plus I had dinner with Missy, which always puts me in a better mood."

"Then you should do it more often," he suggested.

"Don't think I haven't thought about it," I told him, "but I get the feeling Eddie would always be there between us."

"And Julie?" he asked. Immediately he added, "I'm sorry, Jack. I shouldn't have said that."

I waved his apology away and said, "Forget it. You may be right."

"And we both may be wrong," he said, moving towards the door. "You should ask her one of these days."

"Maybe I will," I said. He waved and went back to work and I sat back and thought about calling Tracy. Thought about it, and rejected it. I didn't feel up to discussing new feelings with her, not over the phone. Maybe later...

In the morning I called a P.I. friend of mine named Hank Po who lived in Chelsea and promised him a few bucks if he came up with Jimmy the Dime for me. He said he'd give it his best shot, which was all right with me.

I went out and rented a car from the "try harder" people, and was on my way to Parlin, New Jersey. The Jersey Turnpike, Garden State Parkway, and Route 9 got me in the general neighborhood, and then I had to ask directions to get to the house I wanted.

The house was one of those big old ones you get cheap and then fix up, only this one hadn't been fixed up— on the outside, anyway. I parked my rental in front, mounted the rickety steps, and rang the doorbell.

The man who answered was about five foot two and weighed in at about one hundred and ten pounds, if he was lucky. He wore thick glasses with heavy black rims, and reminded me a lot of the actor Wally Cox.

"Can I help you?" he asked.

"I hope so," I said. "My name is Miles Jacoby, and I'm working for a man named Aaron Steinway."

"Steinway?" he asked, cocking his head to one side. "I know that name. What do you mean you're working for him? In what capacity?"

I took out my photostat and said, "I'm a private investigator. I've been hired by Mr. Steinway to recover something that's been stolen from his home."

"How can I help you with that?" he asked, looking puzzled.

"What was stolen was his collection of pulp magazines."

"That's where I know the name from!" he exploded. "My God, that collection has been stolen?"

"Yes, it has. May I come in and discuss it, please?"

"Sure, of course," he said, backing up to let me in. "God, I can't believe it. Let's go into the sitting room."

The inside of the house had been fixed up only marginally better than the outside had. The floors were bare, the walls hadn't seen any new paint in years. There was very little furniture beyond the barest necessities, and even that looked like your bargain variety, garage-sale specials.

"Can I get you something to drink? I have no liquor, only soft drinks or juices."

"Some ginger ale would be nice," I said.

"I'll get it. Please sit down."

The only thing in the room that there was to sit down on was an old wooden church pew. There was a small plastic table with some kind of a plant on it, and a card table with two chairs that were folded up and leaning against the wall.

"Here you go," he said, coming back into the room with a tall glass of ginger ale and ice. "Now, how can I help you, Mr. Jacoby?"

"Well, first of all, you could tell me your name." I took out my list of names, and for him I had "Mr. Pulps" and his address, which my friend from San Francisco had given me. "All I know you as is 'Mr. Pulps.'"

"Ah, you got my name and address from my catalogue?"

"A friend of mine in San Francisco gave it to me, yes."

"Who was that?"

I told him and he nodded and said, "He's a pretty regular customer of mine. I don't put my name on the catalogue for privacy's sake, but it's Leon Battle."

"Mr. Battle, I'm told that you—or Mr. Pulps—are

51

the foremost authority on pulp magazines in this area."

"That's very flattering, as well as true," he said, leaning his shoulder against the wall. He had not gotten himself a drink, and he folded his arms across his chest. "Do you want to know if I've heard anything about the collection surfacing, or if I stole it?" he asked, bluntly.

Glad that I wasn't going to have to fence with him, I said, "Either one, actually."

He showed me his right index finger and said, "Let me show you something," wiggling the finger to indicate that I was to follow him. I got up, left my glass on the table, and did so.

We walked through the kitchen to a door that obviously led to the basement. I trailed him down the rather steep steps and when he turned on the lights I was totally unprepared for what I saw.

Aisles and aisles of wooden shelves, all of which were packed with books of one kind or another. There was barely enough room between the shelves to walk, but he said, "I've got a place in the back. Follow me," and led me through.

I was impressed, even though the air did have a terminal case of the mustys.

He took me to a small space where he had a desk and a couple of file cabinets and positioned himself behind the desk.

"This is my stock, Mr. Jacoby," he said, spreading his arms wide to indicate the scores of floor-to-ceiling bookshelves. "I have almost every pulp magazine that it is humanly possible to obtain. Do you really think that I would have to steal someone else's collection?"

"I guess not," I said. "I'm impressed...although I think you could use a few air fresheners down here."

He frowned, sniffed the air, and said, "Why would I?"

"Forget it. All right, let's say you didn't steal the collection. If it showed up on the market, would you hear about it?"

"I guess I would," he said. "Mr. Pulps usually hears about everything that comes up for sale."

"Have you heard anything?"

He shook his head and said, "Nothing about a collection that size."

"What about some rare books appearing on the market alone?"

"You mean, maybe whoever stole it is going to split it up?" he asked, looking horrified.

"That's generally the rule when it comes to fencing hot merchandise," I said.

"But breaking up that collection, that'd be a sin!"

"I guess you would look at it that way," I said. "Look, Mr. Battle, I'd leave you a card, but I don't have any. Would you take my number and call me if you hear anything?"

"Of course I will," he said, picking up a pencil and pulling over a pad. I gave him my office number, and the number at Bogie's, and then he guided me back up the stairs.

"That's amazing," I said, standing at the top of the basement steps and looking back down.

"That's my own little world down there, Mr. Jacoby," he confided. "You can see that I don't spend very much money on other things." He looked down at his sweatshirt and jeans and said, "Not clothes, not furniture, not anything. I can't afford to."

I remembered how Steinway was similarly dressed when I first saw him, but for different reasons.

"I'll tell you something, Mr. Pulps," I said. "It probably wouldn't make any difference even if you could."

Chapter Twelve

Instead of getting off the turnpike for Manhattan, I kept going until I got to the Goethals Bridge. When I crossed the bridge, I was in Staten Island. Next to me on the car seat was the newest Mr. Pulps catalogue.

Michael Walsh lived in the rather exclusive Todt Hill section of Staten Island, on the top of a hill. Steinway must have done all right by Walsh as far as investing his money, and Walsh's home was almost as impressive as his investment counselor's.

I parked right in front and rang the doorbell. I told the dowdy maid who answered the door who I was and what I wanted and, after checking with her employer, she led me to his study.

"Mr. Jacoby?" Walsh asked as I entered the room.

"Yes."

"I'm Michael Walsh," he announced, approaching me with his hand held out.

Walsh was a tall, handsome man approaching forty, with an open, friendly face and a quick, infectious smile.

"Aaron called me about his loss," he said, making it sound as if someone had died. "I'll be glad to help you in any way I can."

"Thank you."

Walking back to his desk, he asked, "Can I offer you a drink?"

"Not right now, thanks. I'd just like to ask you a few questions, if I may?"

"Fire away," he said, seating himself.

"You've made offers on several occasions to buy Mr. Steinway's collection, haven't you?"

"Uh, well, yes, I have, but I imagine I haven't been the only one," he said.

"Do you have a collection?"

"Why, yes, I do. Uh, it's in the next room."

"Could I see it?"

"I don't see why not," he said, standing up. "Follow me, please."

We went to a connecting door, which he opened with a key. Once inside I saw that he did indeed have a modest collection, not nearly as large as Steinway's.

"I've limited myself to pulps, whereas Aaron's collection is much broader."

"I realize that," I said, "but all that was stolen was his pulp collection."

"I see. Uh, am I a suspect or something?" he asked nervously. "I mean, just because I offered to buy his collection?"

"I'm just asking questions, Mr. Walsh. I don't suspect anyone."

"I mean, my entire collection is indexed right here," he said, indicating a mini-file with three index-card-sized drawers that was atop a table by the door. "You could check it out."

"I wouldn't know one copy from another, Mr. Walsh. As I said, right now I'm just asking questions and collecting data." I sounded like some kind of a computer expert.

We backed out of the room and he locked the door again, then turned to me, nervously shifting the keys from hand to hand.

"Why are you so nervous?" I asked.

"Look, I read about cops and robbers, and private eyes, but I've never been involved with anyone like that," he explained. "I've never been suspected of anything before."

"What business are you in, Mr. Walsh?" I asked.

55

"Insurance."

I raised my eyebrows and said, "And you've never been suspected of anything?"

While he was trying to think of an answer I told him that I would be in touch if I had any more questions for him, and that I could find my own way out.

Chapter Thirteen

"What kind of a day did you have?" Packy asked. I had turned the rental car back in and gone to Packy's for a few beers and a sandwich. Cold cuts was all the food Packy offered, but since I was staying in Billy Palmer's back room, I didn't want him giving me dinners on the arm as well.

"I don't know, Packy," I said, my right hand hovering over my beer mug, "I just can't seem to get into this missing book thing."

"Why not?" he asked, leaning a pair of formidable forearms on the bar.

"Well, for one thing, I don't really expect to find the damned things," I admitted.

"Don't put yourself down, Jack," he said, "you're a pretty good detective."

"Thanks, Packy, but it's something I'm still learning. I don't feel I've been asking enough questions, or the right ones, for that matter. I also feel a little guilty."

"About what?"

"About taking Steinway's money."

"He can afford it," Packy assured me.

"I guess."

"Hey, Jack, you need the money and he needs to feel

that someone is looking for his stuff. It's fair and square."

I looked at Packy's beat-up face and said, "You're pretty smart, Pack."

"I didn't get all my brains punched out," he responded, tapping his temple with a forefinger the size of a sausage.

"I never thought you had," I said. "I guess we were two of the smart ones, huh, Packy?"

"You're smarter than me," he said.

"How's that?"

He stroked my cheek and said, "You got out while you were still pretty."

"My friend," I said, "you were a good fighter, and you're a good friend, but you were never pretty."

Chapter Fourteen

I went to my office after leaving Packy's and listened to my answering machine. There were two messages, from the same two people as last time. Benny cursed me out drunkenly, and Tracy wondered why I hadn't returned her other call. I rewound the tape and set it up to accept calls again.

I opened the top drawer, stared at Julie's letter for a few...long...seconds, then closed it again with a slam. Damn the woman, but she did have some hell of a nerve writing after all these months. My life didn't need the extra complications, or grief.

I thought about some of the things Benny had said on the tape—about how I was abandoning him and leaving him penniless, to die—and decided that if he wasn't going to try and get himself a job, I might as well. Once he was working, it would keep me from feeling any guilt where he was concerned.

I walked across town to the gym on Forty-second Street. It was after five, but I was hoping to find Willy Wells still there.

As I walked in I saw him working on a heavy bag, making some repairs on a split.

"What happened?" I asked from behind.

"A kid," he said over his shoulder, "a super heavy-weight with a heavy punch and a glass jaw. Every time somebody knocks him on his ass he takes it out on my bag."

He turned around at that point to see who he was talking to and when he saw me, a pained look crossed his face.

"Hello, Kid," he said. "You couldn't have gotten back into shape that fast."

"I haven't," I said, "but I took your comments to heart and I'm working on it."

He looked at me again, then released the bag and turned around to face me. Willy was in his sixties, and had been a trainer for over forty years, a good one. He worried about his fighters, played mommy and daddy to them when he had to, and it all showed in the lines on his face.

"Look, Kid, what I said...I didn't mean—"

"Forget it, Willy," I said. "You had a right, and if I hadn't needed the money so bad, I wouldn't have taken it."

"Look, Kid, if you need a loan..."

I waved him off and said, "I'm not one of your boys, Willy, you don't have to bankroll me. As a matter of fact, I'm working on something right now."

"As a private eye?" he asked, looking interested. "You're really working?"

I stared at him and then said, "What's so hard to believe about that? I'm at least as good a P.I. as I was a fighter."

I thought he was going to make me sorry I said that, but instead he said, "If that's the case, all you need is a little desire and you'll be a damned good P.I."

"Well, thanks, Willy."

"What brings you here? Business?"

"No, not exactly," I said. "I've come about Benny."

"Your brother?" he asked, and now there was a look of definite distaste on his face. "What about him?"

"He needs a job."

"Why? I thought he was living with you."

"Not anymore he isn't," I said. "I gave him the apartment and moved out."

"Best thing you could have done, Kid. Get away from him. You should have done it a long time ago."

"Willy—"

"I'm sorry, Kid, but you know how I feel about Benny," he stated and then added, "and you know how I feel about you. You saved my life a few months ago, but even before that...Look, if I didn't care about you I wouldn't have tore into you like that the other day—"

"Okay, Willy, okay," I said, holding my hands out to him with my palms showing. "Look, just give Benny something to do around here and pay him minimum—"

"A job?" he asked, incredulously. "You want me to give that lush a job?"

"Just for a while, Willy," I said. "Give it a try and if it doesn't work, fire him."

"Look, Kid, I'll save time by just not hiring him—"

"Look, Willy, if he gets a job, has something to do, he might straighten up. The fact that he'll be around boxing might even help as well."

"I doubt it."

"Willy," I began, but then I stopped and took a step back. "All right, let's just forget it."

I started for the door and he called out, "Wait, damnit!"

"Yeah?"

He was standing there with his arms folded across his chest, staring at the point of one of his shoes.

"Have him come in tomorrow, early...as early as you can get him up, that is. I'll see what happens."

"Thanks, Willy," I said, and continued to the door.

"And you get back in shape if you wanna spar for me!" he shouted after me.

Chapter Fifteen

I've gotten into the habit of walking distances that are not too extreme, rather than springing for a cab or risking the subway. This may be the reason why I hadn't fallen completely out of shape, and the fact that I hadn't was probably the reason I didn't die that night.

I decided to walk from the gym on Forty-second to Bogie's on Twenty-sixth. During the walk I went over the questions I had asked the Bracketts, Leon "Mr. Pulps"—who looked more like "Mr. Peepers"—Battle, and Michael Walsh.

What would Eddie have asked, I wondered, or Danny Fortune, or even Walker Blue? What would they, experienced detectives, have asked that I hadn't?

Passing F.I.T.—the Fashion Institute of Technology—I wished it were earlier so that I could get a glimpse at some of the women and girls who went there. Some of the best New York girl watching is done at F.I.T. in the spring. It wasn't spring now, though. It was October, and at that moment it was getting dark, and a little chilly.

As I turned the corner of Twenty-sixth Street from Seventh Avenue, darkness had just about totally fallen. The streetlamps were on, and cars were using their headlights.

Bogie's is farther down the block, closer to Eighth Avenue than Seventh. Next door to the restaurant is a car-service office and garage. Across the street is an open-air parking lot that has no attendant at night and no gate to keep it from being used when it is technically closed.

There were a few cars in the lot as I approached the car-service office and garage. Across the street is an the cars went on. I thought nothing of it, figuring it was just someone who had used the lot and was now heading home. Suddenly, the car accelerated and jumped the curb instead of using the entrance driveway. It shot straight across the street, then veered left and headed right for me.

I had only a second to decide which way to jump and when I did my boxer's legs added the extra distance I needed to avoid the car. In that split second I thanked God my legs hadn't gone.

My jump brought me into contact with a garbage pail and a few plastic bags of trash. The metal pail struck me painfully across the knees, but the plastic bags cushioned my fall and prevented any real damage. The car, having missed me, straightened out on Twenty-sixth Street and sped away. I didn't recover in time to get a look at the license, or even a good look at the car itself. The only time I had really been looking at it, the headlights had been shining directly in my eyes.

The door to Bogie's opened as I rolled around, trying to get away from the garbage and to my feet, and Billy Palmer came running out. Karen was right behind him, and I snapped, "Get her back inside," just in case the car came around the block for another try.

He turned and told her to go back inside, which she did, reluctantly.

"What happened?" he asked, helping me to my feet.

"Well," I began, "there are a few possible explanations, any one of which could be very innocent, but I guess I'm just basically the suspicious type."

"Which means?"

I checked the corner, then looked at him and said, "Which means that I think somebody just tried to kill me. Let's go inside."

Chapter Sixteen

"And you didn't see the driver?" Hocus asked later.

"All I saw were the twin headlights coming at me," I said, rubbing my knees.

He saw that I was hurting and said, "You want to go to the hospital and get checked?"

"No, I want another beer."

A half hour had gone by and we were seated at Bogie's bar, discussing why someone would want to kill me.

"For a collection of old books?" he asked, looking dubious. "Jacoby, are you sure this was deliberate?"

"Valuable old books, Hocus," I reminded him, accepting another light beer from Ed, the bartender. He looked at Hocus with raised eyebrows, but the detective shook him off. "Very valuable."

Hocus shook his head and looked into the dining room, where his partner, Detective Wright, was consuming some of Bogie's fine Italian cuisine.

"As if I didn't have enough problems," Hocus said, half to himself. "Old books and a new ulcer."

"You've got an ulcer?" I asked.

"No, he does," he said, inclining his head towards his partner, "but he refuses to admit it. I'm gonna have to hear him whine when that spicy food starts eating away at him."

"He's got an ulcer?" I asked, disbelievingly. "That man's got two speeds, Hocus, slow and slower. If he was any slower he'd be moving backwards."

"Yeah, tell me about it."

He closed his notebook, picked it up off the bar, and slid it into his jacket pocket.

"Well, if you don't want a ride to the hospital and you can't tell me anything about the car or the driver—"

"I wish I could," I said fervently. "I'd like someone to pay for these bruised knees."

"Luckily, you're used to bumps and bruises," he said.

"Hey, I used to dole out a few as well," I reminded him.

"Yeah," he said, sliding his wide buttocks off the bar stool. "Let me go and see if the galloping ulcer is ready to roll."

He started away, then stopped and turned to me again.

"Listen, just in case this was deliberate, why don't you try being a little careful."

"Like how?"

"Try taking the subway next time."

"You call that being careful?" I asked him. He shrugged and went over to pull his partner's ulcer away from sure destruction.

Billy went over to talk to the two detectives, and then approached me as they left.

"Did they pay?" I asked.

"I'll never tell," he said, grinning. "How do you feel?"

"Sore, but alive."

"You're sure it was deliberate?" he asked, sitting next to me.

"Now you sound like Hocus," I answered. "How can I be sure? But I'm relatively positive. That car swerved and headed straight for me, and there's no denying that it took off after it missed me." I grimaced and rubbed my knees, adding, "In my book that spells deliberate."

"Well, you'd know better than me," he said. "Why don't you go in the back and take it easy?"

"Yeah, maybe I will. Hey, Ed, let me have one to go, will you?"

Ed brought me a bottle of beer, and I slid off the stool and limped to the kitchen. There were still diners in the place who had been there when it all happened, and they watched me curiously as I climbed the stairs.

Walking through the kitchen, I saw Karen and said, "I'm sorry if I disrupted your dinner crowd, Karen."

"As long as you're all right, that's all that matters," she told me. She was holding an appetizing-looking sandwich, which I plucked from her on the move, saying, "Thanks, love."

She slapped me on the shoulder as I went by.

In the office I sat at the desk, ate the sandwich, drank the beer, and went back over the incident in my mind. No matter how many ways I went at it, I was still sure that the whole thing had been planned. It had to have something to do with Steinway's collection, because I wasn't working on anything else, and hadn't worked on anything else for weeks.

Somebody obviously did not want me looking for, or finding, that collection; but who?

I called my buddy Hank Po for a progress report on finding Jimmy the Dime, but progress was nil.

"Jimmy's done a disappearing act, and somebody just tried to pound me into the pavement with a Plymouth."

"Sounds like you're onto something more than just old books," Hank commented.

"Wait a minute," I said. "Did I just say 'Plymouth'?"

"You did."

"I don't recall that it was a Plymouth, but maybe I picked that up subconsciously," I said, half to myself.

"Maybe you did," he agreed. "And maybe we should end this conversation in favor of the one you're having with yourself."

"Huh? Oh, I'm sorry, Hank. Listen, keep after the little weasel, will you?"

"I'll do my best to scare him up, Jack," he promised.

"I'll check in with you, Hank. I don't know where I'll be."

"Fine. Good luck, Jack."

I hung up and thought again about the scene in front of Bogie's. Yeah, I guess it had been a Plymouth. Color was impossible to tell under the streetlights, but I figured it was safe to say that it was a Plymouth.

A plate number would have been a lot more helpful.

I showered and changed into fresh clothing. My knees were still sore—and visibly bruised now—but I tried not to think about them. I dialed Steinway's home number and received no answer. It was too late to try his office, so I tried his New York apartment and found the line busy. I decided to go over there and see him and find out if there wasn't something he hadn't told me.

Which is when I got hit on the head, found him dead, called the cops, and conked out...

...until someone started to shake me.

I woke up and stared fuzzily at the person who was doing the shaking.

"Hocus," I said.

"Well, glad you're back with us," he said.

I frowned, trying to remember the time, place, and circumstances. After I phoned the police I must have passed out in a chair. I looked over at the desk and saw Steinway, still slumped over his desk. There was a man examining him, and a man dusting the desk and everything on it.

"I touched the phone," I said.

"No fooling," Hocus said. "I thought maybe you went next door and used a neighbor's to call nine-one-one."

I made a move to get up, but it was hard with Hocus's hand on my chest.

"Sit tight, champ," he said. "There's a bus on the way. In case you don't know it, the back of your head looks a little pulpy right now."

I looked at him to see if he'd deliberately made the pun, but he didn't seem to notice it.

"Want to tell me about it while we wait?" he asked. I gave him what I knew and he said, "The last time I saw you—which was just hours ago—you didn't look up to a mad dash down ten flights of stairs and a tussle with a killer."

"I heal fast," I said, pushing his hand off my chest.

"I'll bet you didn't see this guy's face, either," he said.

"You win," I said.

At that point the ambulance arrived, and I promised Hocus I'd show at his office as soon as I was fixed up. The attendants wanted to wheel me to the bus, but I insisted on walking. I always walked out of the ring under my own power, even after a loss.

"Hey, Jacoby," Hocus called as I reached the door.

"Yeah."

"Twice in one night. You're making some pretty bad friends over some old books."

"Yeah," I said, looking at Steinway, "but not as bad as his."

Chapter Seventeen

They stitched my head, told me I'd have a headache for a few days and—ha, ha—take some Extra-Strength Tylenol for it. I told them that if it was all the same to them, I'd stick with aspirin. After that I went to the Seventeenth Precinct to give my statement to Hocus.

"It was odd," I said, "but there was no doorman when I got there."

"Yeah," Hocus said, "he wasn't around when we got there either, but we found him."

"Where?"

"Curled up in the basement with a bottle. Seems he was an ex-alkie who decided to choose tonight to become an ex-ex-alcoholic."

I leaned my head back and bumped it against the back of the chair. I reacted with a start, even though it didn't particularly hurt.

He leaned sideways behind his desk to look at the bandage on the back of my head and said, "You got a bald spot now?"

"Not too bad," I said. "They just had to cut it short to put a few stitches in." I put my hand up to the bandage and said, "When I take it off I'll be able to comb my hair over it until it grows back in."

"If it grows back in," he said. "You're close to thirty, Jacoby; it don't grow in so fast anymore when you start to get old."

"As long as you still got yours, I'll consider myself safe," I told him. I stood up slowly so my head wouldn't roll off and said, "Do you have any aspirin in your desk?"

"Yeah, I think so," he said. He opened a drawer and brought out a small tin. He took out two and handed them to me, and I swallowed them using half a cup of lukewarm coffee that was still on his desk. "Thanks. I'm going to get some sleep, if I can."

"Sure. Listen, let me know if you turn up anything, okay?"

"Turn up what?" I said. "My client's dead. I've got no reason to keep on looking for those books, and murder is out of my league."

"You sang a different tune a few months ago," he reminded me.

"That was personal," I said. "This one is all yours, Hocus, and you're welcome to it."

"Well, I just hope your friend in the car feels that way, too," he said. He dug out his wallet, took out a five-dollar bill and handed it to me. "Here."

"What's this for?"

"I've had enough excitement for one night. Take a cab home."

I made a face, but kept the five.

"Before I leave, what's the story on Steinway?"

"I don't have an autopsy report from Dr. Mahbee yet, but it looks like he was shot at close range with a large-caliber bullet."

"Mahbee wasn't at the scene," I said, remembering that there was a man examining the body when I woke up, but I hadn't recognized him.

"No, but Mahbee will do the autopsy. Go on home, huh? Or wherever it is you're sleeping these days."

"Yeah, I'm going. Thanks, Hocus."

"Yeah, sure, champ. Take care."

When I got out in front of the station house there was a cab dropping someone off. Taking that as an omen, I fingered Hocus's five in my pocket, hopped in the cab, and told him to take me to Bogie's. The bar was still open when I got there, but I used the private entrance instead, not really wanting to talk to anyone. My head was aching too much, as were my knees, not to mention my pride—and my wallet, now that my client was dead. When I got into the office it all crashed in on me and I lay down on the cot fully dressed and fell asleep.

Chapter Eighteen

In the morning I took a shower and stiffly made my way to my office. I called all of my contacts and told them to send me their bills. I held off on phoning Hank Po and calling him off Jimmy the Dime because there was still a decision I hadn't made yet.

I had already decided that there was no longer a reason for me to pursue Steinway's collection. My client was dead and no one was paying my way. However, I was still pretty interested in who had tried to run me down in front of Bogie's, and Jimmy the Dime Denton might be the man who could tell me.

With the morning mail came that second check from the deceased Aaron Steinway. I took it out and looked at it, and decided to let Po keep on looking for a while. The check covered the fees for the contacts and P.I.'s I had used, with a little bit left over, and I decided to put that towards finding Jimmy the Dime.

As far as finding Steinway's killer, I had been involved with murder only once before, but then it had been personal. My best friend was the victim, and my brother was the accused. This time there were no such circumstances. I figured to just stay away from the case and out of the way of the cops who were working on it.

I played my answer machine back and found another message from Tracy, who simply said that it would be nice if I called her. The fact that there was no message—drunken or otherwise—from my brother, Benny, reminded me that I had gotten him a job with Willy Wells at the Forty-second Street gym. I thought it might be a good idea to make sure he showed up for work on his first day.

I took Steinway's check to the bank and left most of it there, then took the subway to my old apartment. If Benny was drinking, he'd most certainly be passed out at this time of the morning. When I used my key to enter, I found him lying on the sofa bed on his back, fully dressed, snoring.

"Let's go, Benny," I said, shaking him.

"What?" he asked without opening his eyes. "Whozat?"

"It's Miles, your brother. Remember me?"

He opened his eyes and looked at me, then closed them and said clearly, "What do you want?" Apparently, he wasn't as far gone as I had first thought.

"Come on. It's time to get up and go to work."

"Work? What work?"

"I got you a job."

"A job?" he asked. He opened his eyes and said, "What kind of a job?"

"You're working for Willy Wells."

"Wells?" he said, as if he couldn't believe it. "That old man hates my guts."

"Nevertheless, you've got a job. Take a shower and let's get going."

He sat up in the bed with moans and groans, swung his feet to the floor, and began to dry-wash his face with his hands.

"Come on, Benny," I said. "You'll feel better after a shower. Apparently you didn't drink all that much last night."

"Nobody would give me credit," he said, getting to his feet.

"Not even Packy?"

"You took care of that, didn't you?" he said.

"I also got you a paying job, so let's hurry it up."

As Benny went into the bathroom and turned on the

73

shower, I did some mental subtracting. I had been intending to give him fifty bucks to hold him until his first payday, but after his remarks about nobody giving him any credit, I decided to cut it in half, to twenty-five. I didn't want him thinking he could afford to spring for a few drinks every night. Twenty-five bucks would keep him on a tight leash—I hoped.

I opened the bathroom door once and peered in to make sure he was in the shower, and he shouted, "Shut the damned door!" from beneath the water. I had caught a glimpse of his paste-white body, with its ripples of excess flesh, and it made me even more determined to get myself back into some kind of shape. It was going to be club sodas and salads for a long time to come.

It took a little more pushing, but I finally got Benny dressed and looking fairly presentable, and then took him uptown by subway and left him at the gym.

As I was leaving I heard Willy Wells saying, "All right, get a bucket," but I didn't stay for Benny's reaction.

I found a pay phone and dialed Tracy's number, but there was no answer. I decided not to let the day end without seeing her and talking to her. I wanted to examine my own feelings while I was with her and see if I was ready for any kind of a closer relationship—emotionally speaking, that is. There wasn't much more we could do to get closer physically.

I started back to my office and on the way stopped at a Charles & Co. and bought a bottle of club soda. Seated behind my desk, I opened the center drawer and drank the club soda while staring at the letter from Julie.

I reached for the letter once, then slammed the drawer and dialed Tracy's number again. Still no answer. Just to have something to do, I dialed Hank Po's number, but there was no answer there, either.

I called Knock Wood Lee then, to tell him that I was no longer on the missing-pulp-magazine-collection case, and Tiger Lee answered the phone.

"Hello, Lee."

"Hello, Jack. Wood can't come to the phone right now, I'm afraid."

"That's okay, Lee, just tell him I'm off that magazine case."

"What happened? Did you find them?"

"My client got killed last night."

"Oh, I'm sorry. Are you going to look for his killer?"

"That's the police's job," I said. "I'm off the case altogether. I've got no client, no fee, and no desire to find those magazines for myself."

"What about the killer?" she asked. "He cost you a bundle by killing your client, didn't he?"

"He sure did."

"Doesn't that make you want to find him?"

"I can't afford to pay my own way on a case, Lee. Besides, murder is police business."

"You didn't feel that way a few months ago," she said, sounding like Hocus.

"That was personal. Just give the message to Wood, okay?"

"Sure, Jack, sure, but I still think you're breaking some kind of a private-eye code."

"Lee, have you been reading books or watching old movies?" I asked her. "I'm the kind of private eye who works when he gets paid—and those times are too few and far between for me to start going out and working for nothing."

"Whatever you say, Jack. I'll pass on the message. Come up and see us, huh?"

"Yeah, soon. Thanks, Lee."

I hung up, drained the bottle of club soda, and thought about what she had said about a "private-eye code."

Vengeance is Mike Hammer's, not mine.

Chapter Nineteen

A week went by uneventfully. No new cases came along, no one tried to run me down. About the only thing that happened was that the stitches were removed from my head. The money Steinway had paid me ran out, and I had gotten into the habit of earning my keep at Bogie's by being a "catch" bartender, relieving the regulars when they needed a break, and filling in on days when they couldn't make it, or were off.

Seven days after Steinway's death I was behind the bar when in walked the last person I would have expected to see: Laura Brackett.

Wrapped in her half-length fur, and draped liberally with glittering jewelry, she looked grossly out of place as she entered and approached the bar. Business was light with only some late diners and after-dinner drinkers, so she was easily the center of attraction.

"Hello, Mrs. Brackett," I greeted her.

"You look surprised, Mr. Jacoby," she said, looking amused. Her dark hair was swept up over her head, revealing a long, graceful neck and small, delicate ears.

"Can I get you something?" I asked her.

"A glass of white wine, please."

Setting it in front of her, I asked, "You didn't come down here all alone, did you, Laura?"

She picked up the wine and said, "I have a car waiting outside. You needn't worry about me, Miles.

"I have a reason for coming, Miles," she confided. "Is there somewhere that we could go and talk?"

"Sure," I said. "Let me arrange for a relief for a while."

She nodded and sipped her wine.

I called over one of the waitresses and asked her to get Billy for me. When Billy came out of the kitchen, I indicated Laura Brackett sitting at the far end of the bar and said, "Can you cover for me for a few minutes?"

"Potential client?" he asked, grinning. "It looks like she'll be able to afford your prices, too."

"Yeah, maybe," I said. "I won't be long."

"That may depend on her," he said.

I approached Laura Brackett and said, "Let's go this way," pointing to the front door.

"Outside?" she asked.

"There's another entrance to my office," I said, "unless you'd rather go through the kitchen."

She made a face and said, "Uh, no, outside is fine. May I?" she asked, holding up the glass of wine.

"Of course."

We went out the front door and as I was unlocking the one next door, someone called her name from the street. We both turned and saw a man standing just outside a chauffeur-driven limo.

"Laura, are you finished here yet?" the man asked. For some reason he looked familiar to me, but I couldn't quite make out his face under the streetlights.

"Not quite yet, darling," she called back. "Be a love and wait in the car, Carl."

The man put his hands on his hips, then gave an exasperated shrug and got back in the car.

"Do you think he'll wait?" I asked.

She looked at me, grinning like a Cheshire cat, and said, "Oh, he'll wait."

I believed her. I opened the door and led her down the hall to the door of the office. When I unlocked that one, I allowed her to precede me, and closed the door behind us.

"This is your office?"

"Actually, it belongs to the restaurant, but the owner lets me use it."

"How... economical. You are still a private detective, aren't you? I mean, you haven't given it up and become a bartender?"

"No, I haven't given it up," I said. "Tending bar is just something I do to help out."

"I see."

She put down her glass of wine on the desk and removed her fur coat. Beneath it she was breathtaking. The gown she wore plunged low between her creamy breasts, which were larger than I had thought when I first met her. Although she looked like she would have been a good model, she was too big breasted to have been a very successful one. However, I didn't know very many men who would have complained.

She picked her wine up, walked over to the shelves of "spirits," and began to study the labels.

"Mrs. Brackett, there was something you wanted to discuss with me," I reminded her.

She continued to walk around the room until she came to the cot. She sat down on it and ran one hand over the blanket, asking, "Is this where you sleep?"

"For now," I said, "until I can find someplace better."

Her eyes met mine boldly for a moment, but when I didn't look away she laughed softly and stood up again.

"Could we get to it, please, Laura?"

"I want to hire you," she said, finally getting to the point of her visit.

"To do what?"

"I think you know," she said. "I want you to find that collection for me. I will pay you to find it for me."

"Mrs. Brackett, even if I find it, the collection belongs to Mr. Steinway's estate."

"You let my lawyer worry about that," she said. "I'll pay you double your daily fee to find those books for me."

I hesitated because looking for that collection again meant getting involved in a homicide investigation. My license was still too new to take a chance on losing it.

"Miles?"

"There's a homicide investigation going on, Mrs.

78

Brackett," I told her. "I'd have to clear it with the police before I accepted the case."

She frowned at me and said, "You're certainly not like the private eyes of the pulps, are you?"

"They don't have licenses to worry about," I said, "and I do."

"Oh, I suppose," she said. "Do you anticipate any problem with the police?"

In the morning I'd call Hocus and make sure he had no objections to my continuing the search for the missing collection, but I thought I knew him well enough to predict that he wouldn't, as long as I stayed away from the homicide case—which was just fine with me.

"No," I answered, "I don't anticipate any problems."

"Good," she said. She went to her fur, reached into a pocket, and came out with her checkbook. "Then I'll write you a retainer. Would a thousand dollars be all right?"

"For a start," I agreed. "Uh, do you always carry your checkbook in your coat pocket?"

Facing me, she leaned on the desk to write the check, giving me an unobstructed view of her breasts.

"Where would you have me carry it?" she asked and, looking up at me while still bent over, she added, "Between my breasts?"

She straightened up with a grin and handed me the check.

"I'll trust you to cash it only after you've cleared your position with the police," she said, "and to call me and let me know that you're definitely on the case."

"I'll let you know, Mrs. Brackett," I assured her.

She walked up close enough to me for her scent to tease me and said, "If you do decide to accept, Miles, one stipulation will be that you will have to call me Laura."

In her high heels she was as tall as I was and I looked straight into her eyes and said, "I'll let you know."

She left her wineglass where it was on the desk, picked up her fur coat, and draped it negligently over her shoulder. She walked to the door and from there said, "I'll be waiting for your call."

"Good night, Mrs. Brackett. Have a pleasant evening."

She smiled broadly and said, "I usually do," and swept out.

I waited a few moments until I was sure she was gone, then held up her check and looked at it. It seemed I wasn't quite through with that pulp collection after all.

For some reason, right at that moment, I thought of the still unopened letter from Julie sitting in my desk drawer.

Chapter Twenty

"You want what?" Hocus asked in surprise the next morning.

"I want your okay to keep looking for Steinway's book collection," I said again, leaning both of my hands flat on his desk.

"After a week?"

"A week ago I didn't have a client anymore," I said. "Now I do."

"Who?"

"Laura Brackett," I answered, because there was no harm in it.

"The partner's wife," he said, raising his eyebrows. "Is she a looker, or what?"

"Yeah, great," I said. "How about it?"

"What are you asking me for?"

"Because I don't want to lose my license."

"You know, you are the weirdest—are you going after the books or the killer?"

"The books. I don't want any part of the killer."

"Well, then, what are you worried about? You go after your books, and we'll keep after the killer, and never the twain will meet, okay?"

"I didn't know you were into poetry," I said, standing up straight.

"I had to impress a girl once," he answered. He opened a drawer of his desk and took out a large brown envelope. "If you're back on the case, you'll want this," he said, handing it to me.

"What is it?" I asked, taking it.

"It's that police report you asked me for, on Steinway's house," he said. "You never picked it up."

I opened the envelope, slid the computer printout sheet out, scanned it briefly, and then put it back and closed it again.

"Thanks, Hocus."

"Sure," he said. "Get out of here now and let me get back to work."

I started for the door, but he called to me before I reached it.

"Uh, hey, Jacoby."

"Yeah?" I said, turning my head.

"Uh, while you're looking for those books, if you happen to trip over the killer. you'll let me know, won't you?"

I turned around so I was facing him squarely, planted my hands on my hips, and said, "You don't believe me, do you?"

"About what?" he asked innocently.

"About not wanting to go after the killer," I said. "Hocus, I've had enough of that. I almost got killed last time!"

"I remember," he assured me. "All I'm saying is that if you happen to bump into the guy—"

"You'll know where to go looking for him," I interrupted him, "because I'll be going in the opposite direction."

I left the squad room and headed for the stairs, and just about ran headlong into a detective who did not count me among his favorite people.

"Jacoby," Detective Vadala said. "What the hell are you doing here?"

"Uh, just making a report, Detective Vadala," I told the dapper detective. I'd met Vadala during my investigation to clear Benny of killing Eddie Waters, and we hadn't gotten along very well. In the interim, things had not improved.

"Well, if you're finished with your business..."

"I'm on my way, friend," I said, starting down the steps.

"Don't call me your friend!" he shouted after me.

I never did know whether he just didn't like private detectives, or if it was me personally, but then I was never that intent on finding out.

Chapter Twenty-one

"Terrible thing," Walter Brackett said. "When the police told me what happened to Aaron, I couldn't believe it."

We were in his office—or rather, the offices of Steinway & Brackett, except that there was a man there scraping Aaron Steinway's name off the door. Brackett's shock over his partner's death didn't seem to affect his revamping the business.

After some heavy thinking about how to proceed, I had decided that the best thing to do would be to go over all of the old ground again, talk to the same people, and see if there wasn't something else they could tell me. I had called Hank Po off Jimmy the Dime's trail earlier in the week, then called him that morning to ask him to be on the lookout again.

The first person I had decided to see was Brackett, which may have had something to do with the fact that he was the most accessible.

"What happens now?" I asked Brackett.

"I don't know for sure," he said, contriving to look confused. "I'll have to consult with my—our—the firm's attorneys."

"Naturally you'll come into his half of the business," I remarked.

"I suppose," he said, staring at the man who was wiping Steinway's name off the door.

"What about his personal property?"

"His daughter, I guess."

"His daughter?" I asked. I thought back to the first day I'd met Steinway and said, "I thought he told me he wasn't married."

"He wasn't," Brackett said. "But he had been, once."

"And he had a daughter."

"Right."

"Where is she?"

"I have no idea. She was going to school somewhere in the Midwest, then she was in Europe. I don't know where she is now."

"How will you get in touch with her?"

"That'll be up to Steinway's lawyers," he said.

"Which one?"

"I don't know. Not the firm's lawyer, but one of Aaron's. He had a platoon of them. One of them probably knows where she is."

I made a mental note to talk to Heck Delgado about that.

"Are you working on Aaron's murder, Mr. Jacoby?"

I shook my head.

"Murder is police business, Mr. Brackett," I said. "I'm looking for the pulp collection."

"Really, Mr. Jacoby, Aaron is dead. Do you seriously intend to go on looking for his collection?"

"I have a client, Mr. Brackett. I do what my client pays me to do."

He frowned and said, "Who is your client?"

"I'm not at liberty to say," I answered. "Have you spoken with anyone about the missing collection since it was stolen?"

"Aaron and my wife," he said, "but no one else."

"Not Michael Walsh?"

"Walsh was Aaron's client."

"I thought you were partners?"

"In name only," he replied. "We each had our own client list."

"I see. Did any of your clients know that Steinway was leaving town that week?"

"One or two might have, I suppose."

"Did any of them know about his collection?"

"I wouldn't know."

"Did you ever mention it to any of them?"

"Why should I?" he said, as if I was crazy. "The less I hear about those books, the better."

"Have you spoken to your wife about them lately?"

He examined me for a few moments with a look of mild annoyance on his face, and then the look deepened and he said, "You're a detective, Jacoby. You know I haven't spoken to or seen my wife for some time now. But you have, haven't you?"

"What does that mean?"

"It means you're young, in reasonably good shape, and some women—like my wife—might even find you attractive."

"Look, Brackett," I snapped, "if you're having problems hanging on to your young wife—" I stopped myself before I could go any further and took a deep breath. "Look, Mr. Brackett, I didn't come here to discuss your marriage."

"No," he said, drawing his back straight, "of course not. Uh, I'm sorry I didn't mention my, eh, problems before but I don't like airing my dirty laundry in public."

"No one does," I said.

"Except for my wife," he said tightly.

I decided to leave before he started accusing me of holding the microphone while she did her broadcasting.

"Listen, Mr. Brackett, I'd appreciate it if you'd try and find out if any of your clients knew about the collection. I'm sure you have some kind of interest in seeing that it's found—even if it's just to have your partner's estate settled properly."

"I'll, uh, I'll see what I can do," he said. I gave him my office number, and Bogie's number, and left.

Outside I found a pay phone and called Heck Delgado's number. His phone was answered by a very nervous-sounding young girl who told me to hold on and she'd see if the "doctor" was in.

When Heck came on the line I said, "Oh, she's a winner, that one is."

"She's only worked for doctors in the past," he explained. "Working for a lawyer is something new and she's a little nervous."

"A little, huh? Listen, can I come up there for a few minutes? Do you have time?"

"I'll make the time," he said. "Come ahead, I'll have some coffee waiting."

"Great. See you in a few minutes."

The trains were running well for a change and it wasn't much more than a few minutes later when I arrived in Heck's reception room, looking at a very nervous, kind of plump, but not unattractive young secretary.

"My name is Jacoby," I said.

"Do you have an appointment?" she asked.

"Sort of," I said. "I just called and Heck told me to come on up."

"Oh, that was you...on the phone?" she asked.

"Yep, that was me."

"Oh, what I said about the, uh, doctor—"

"What's your name?"

"Holly."

"I understand, Holly. Heck—Mr. Delgado explained it to me."

"Oh, I see. I'll tell him that you're here."

She announced me over the intercom and he told her to send me right in.

He had two coffees sitting on his desk, one of which was black, for me.

"What can I do for you?" he asked. "Do you need some work?"

"Actually, I'm working again," I answered.

"Well, that's good news. Something I can help with?"

"I hope so. I'm looking for Steinway's collection again."

"I thought you stopped looking when he died," he said.

"I have a client again."

He raised his eyebrows in surprise, but said, "I won't ask you who, but I hope it's a paying client."

"Oh, it is," I said.

"Well, then, what can I do to help?"

"You were one of Steinway's attorneys," I said.

"That's right. I did work for him on and off."

"Do you know anything about his daughter?"

He hesitated just long enough for me to know that he did.

"Heck, I'm not asking you to reveal anything confidential," I said. "I just heard the old man had a daughter."

He nodded to himself, then said, "Yes, he does. Her name is Erica Steinway. He sends her money when she needs it—or rather I send it."

"Then you know where she is."

"I have an idea, yes," he said. "Why?"

"Well, chances are, she's going to inherit—"

"Not necessarily," he broke in. "She and Steinway were not on the best of terms."

"But he was sending her money."

"And he may have provided something for her in his will, but I doubt that she will inherit."

"Has she been notified about his death?"

"I am working on that."

"If she comes to town in response to it, I'd like to talk to her. Maybe she'd have some ideas about the collection."

He nodded again and said, "I doubt that, too, but all right, if she comes to town I'll put you together with her."

"Okay, thanks," I said, standing up. I was heading for the door when an off-the-wall thought struck me. It wasn't something I had ever thought about before, and I wondered why not.

I turned and said, "Heck."

"Yes?"

"This girl outside, Holly—"

He smiled and said, "She will not last, although she tries."

"I just had a thought I should have had long ago," I said. "You go through secretaries like...like—"

"Suffice it to say that secretaries do not last long in my outer office," he offered. "Go on."

"I have just the girl for you," I said.

"A girl friend of yours?"

"An ex-almost employee."

Before I had a chance to say her name, it dawned on him and he said, "Missy?"

"Exactly. She's working in a temporary service right now, but I know she'd welcome a steady job."

He stood up while he was thinking about it, then said, "If she is as good a secretary as she is lovely..."

From someone else's mouth that might have sounded a bit lecherous, but not with Hector Delgado's Ricardo Montalban accent. Heck had all the good looks of a young Ricardo, and then some, and in ten or twenty years he'd be ready to step right into "Fantasy Island." His mention of Missy's loveliness was a simple statement of fact.

"Tell her to call me—if she's interested, that is."

"She'll call you," I said. "I promise. Boy, this is really going to be something."

"What is?" he asked, looking puzzled.

"Well, I've always wondered why you go through so many secretaries," I said. "Is it them or is it you?"

He smiled his charming smile and said, "Do you have an answer? I'd be interested as well."

"Not yet I don't, but once Missy takes the job—and we know what an excellent secretary she is—we'll find out."

"How so?"

"If you can lose a secretary like her," I told him, "we'll know it's been you all along. *Adios.*"

Chapter Twenty-two

I went back to my office and read the police report on Steinway's house, but it didn't tell me anything I didn't already know. Earlier, before going to see Walter Brackett, I had tried Laura Brackett's number and gotten no answer. I tried again and this time she answered, sounding as if I had woken her up.

"Mrs. Brackett?"

"Hmm, yes, what?" she mumbled into the phone.

"This is Jacoby, Mrs. Brackett. Are you all right?"

"Hmm? Oh, I'm fine."

"I'm sorry I woke you," I apologized. "I called earlier, but there was no answer."

"I'm a deep sleeper." She cleared her throat and I got a sudden vivid impression of her that stirred my hormones. "Have you called to say that you will take the case?" she asked, sounding a little more awake now.

"I've already started," I said, "but I haven't cashed your check yet."

"Well, then, do so," she said. "It's nice to know that you're so honest."

"It's a flaw I'm trying to correct," I said. "Listen, I'd like to come over in a little while and talk to you. Will you be home?"

"I intend to be in the rest of the day," she said. "I come alive when it gets dark. Maybe you'll have a chance to find out."

"Maybe. I'll try not to come by too late."

"Chicken," she said, and hung up.

I hung up my end thinking that maybe she was right. Maybe I was afraid to be around her when she came alive. She certainly was alive last night, in that low-cut gown.

I touched the drawer where Julie's letter was, then picked up the phone and dialed Missy's temporary secretary service. They gave me the number where she was—which was different from the last one—and I called her about working for Heck.

"For Heck Delgado?" she asked.

"Sure, why not? I don't know why one of us didn't think of it before."

"I don't know, Jack," she replied doubtfully.

"Why not? You've said yourself the guy's a dream-boat."

"I never said—well, maybe I did, once or twice," she admitted, "but that doesn't mean he'll be good to work for. I mean, he does go through secretaries like...like—"

"Suffice it to say that secretaries don't last long in his outer office," I said, paraphrasing the man himself. "But you're no ordinary secretary."

"Thanks, Jack, but—"

"Call him, Missy. He's waiting to hear from you. The two of you were made for each other—speaking from a business standpoint, that is."

"Of course," she said. "All right, Jack, I'll call Heck and talk to him about it."

"Good."

"How about you, Jack?" she asked. "Are you...all right?"

"You mean, did I open that letter?"

"That's what I mean."

"No, I never did."

"But you still have it, right?" When I didn't answer right away she said, "I know you, Miles Jacoby. I told you to throw that letter away."

"I know, I know," I said, feeling an odd sort of embarrassment. "Missy..."

"Never mind," she said, "it's none of my business. I'll call Heck, Miles. Thanks."

She hung up, but she had called me Miles, which meant she was pissed. I couldn't blame her. Ever since the time she found out that Julie was somehow involved with Eddie's death, she'd had nothing but contempt for her. She had flown into a fury the day she found out that Julie had left town, because that meant she couldn't get at her.

I hung up the phone, telling myself to call her again after she spoke to Heck.

Before leaving the office I made one more call, this one to Willy Wells. I talked to one of the fighters first, and then Willy came on the line.

"It's Jack, Willy."

"What's up, Kid. I got a boy in the ring now, I can't—"

"I just want to know how Benny's doing, that's all," I said.

Willy snorted into the phone and said, "Ask him, Kid. He quit two days after you brought him in. Ain't you seen him since then?"

"No," I said, "I haven't." I'd been avoiding Benny ever since I left him at the gym. So he quit the job, so what? He was a big boy. I'd done my part.

"Can I go now?" Willy asked.

"Huh? Oh, yeah, sure, Willy. Thanks for trying."

His voice softened and he said, "I'm sorry it didn't work out, Kid. Why don't you try remembering that you're his brother, not his mother?"

"Yeah," I said, "good advice. Thanks."

"You getting in shape?"

"I've dropped some weight," I told him truthfully, "and I've been working out."

"You working?"

"I'm working," I answered. "If things go right, I won't need a sparring job for a while."

"I hope you don't, Kid. Gotta go," he said, and he hung up.

I reached for my answering machine and turned it on. I hadn't listened to it for a couple of days; maybe there was a message from Benny. I turned it back and listened, but there was nothing, nothing at all on it.

I slammed my hand down on my desk and cursed Benny inwardly. Why the hell was he so bent on destroying himself? And why did it have to be me who was knocking himself out trying to stop him?

I dialed the number at the apartment, but there was no answer. He was probably passed out on the bed— or the floor—sleeping off a twenty-five-dollar drunk!

He hadn't even been smart enough to work for a week's salary, so he could go on a decent binge.

I called Packy's, but the big ex-heavyweight said he hadn't seen Benny in a week.

"I wouldn't serve him the last time he was in, Jack, and he got pretty mad."

"Tough," I said. "Thanks, Packy."

I didn't have time to worry about my brother, who was a grown man and should be able to take care of himself. I had a magazine collection to find, a client to see, and a fee to earn.

Chapter Twenty-three

"Oh, you did come early, didn't you?" Laura Brackett said in greeting.

"I have other stops to make, Mrs. Brackett."

"Laura, remember?"

"Laura," I said. "Can I come in, please?"

"Of course."

She was wearing a floor-length silk robe with a hood. It was a pullover and, with no buttons or seams, it was obvious that she wore nothing underneath.

We went into the living room and she asked, "Was I right on the phone? Are you chicken, or just careful?"

"As I said before," I replied to her teasing tone, "I have other stops to make. You *are* paying me to do a job."

"Yes," she said, becoming serious, at least for a moment, "I am. What have you found out?"

"Not as much as I hope to," I said. "Did you know Aaron Steinway's daughter?"

"No, I never met her."

"But you knew he had a daughter?"

"Oh, yes. Walter said she travels a lot."

"It's possible that she might inherit his property."

"Including the collection?"

"If it turns up, yes."

"She would probably sell then," she said, "don't you think?"

"I can't say, not having ever met her."

"But a young woman, a world traveler, what would she want with old pulp magazines?"

"That's what I asked myself when I met you," I said. "Is his daughter young?"

"In her twenties, I believe."

"Not much younger than you are," I observed generously.

"You can be sweet when you want to be, can't you, Miles?" she asked, curling up on the couch with her legs tucked underneath her. "Would you like a drink?"

"No, thanks."

"I have coffee made," she said, indicating an ornate pot and two cups on an end table near the couch. "Would you pour?"

"Sure."

I poured us each a cup and handed one to her. She took it the same way I did, black, no sugar. I seated myself in a chair across from her.

"Still careful," she murmured, raising her cup to her lips.

"Mrs.—uh, Laura, do you know a man named James Denton?"

"Denton?" she said, frowning. "I don't think I've ever heard the name. Why?"

"He made an offer to Steinway for his collection, and showed a large sum of money up front."

"But Aaron wouldn't sell?"

"No, that's not the point, though. I know Denton, and I know he'd never be able to come up with that kind of money on his own."

"You're saying someone gave him the money?" she asked. "He was acting on someone else's behalf?"

"That's the way it looks."

"But who, and why?"

"I'd say it was someone who had already tried, unsuccessfully, to buy the collection from Steinway. Perhaps they thought it was a personal thing, that Steinway simply wouldn't sell to them."

"By them you mean me, don't you?"

"Or your husband. Or maybe a man named Walsh."

"I don't know that name, either," she said, shaking her head.

"I wouldn't expect you to. Do you know Mr. Pulps?"

"The catalogue? Of course, but not the man behind it."

"No, he keeps pretty much to himself."

"You've spoken to him?"

"Yes, and I've seen his...stock. Very impressive."

"I'd love to see it," she said, eyes shining. "Are you going to see him again?"

"I expect to, yes."

"When?" she asked, leaning forward. "I want to go with you."

"You didn't hire Denton, did you?" I asked her.

She looked shocked and said, "No. I thought I answered that already. Who is he?"

"A snitch, a front man."

"A hood?"

"You could call him that, yes."

"How would I even know someone like that?"

I thought back a moment to the night before, and the man standing outside the limo. The man she had called Carl. He had seemed familiar, and I still felt that I knew him from somewhere.

"I don't know, Laura," I said. "You'd have to tell me that."

"I couldn't," she said. "I don't know him."

"All right," I said, standing up.

She put aside her cup and stood up quickly. Her feet were bare and she wasn't as tall as I was now as she came up to me.

"Will you take me with you when you go to see Mr. Pulps?" she asked, like a little girl. "Please?"

"I'll let you know," I promised.

"There'll be a bonus for you," she told me, touching my arm.

"Why do I get the feeling we're not talking about money here?" I asked.

"Would that be so terrible?" she asked, moistening her bottom lip with a quick flick of her tongue.

"Just unnecessary," I said after a moment. "I'll call you, Laura."

She took her hand off of my arm, let it hover inches above, and said, "All right, Miles."

We stood that way for a few seconds more, and then I cleared my throat and said, "Thanks for the coffee. I'll be in touch."

I left her standing there, which in itself was quite an exercise in willpower.

In the elevator I thought more about Jimmy the Dime, and who might have hired him. Laura had been convincing, but that didn't mean I believed her. Still, it could have been her husband, or Michael Walsh, who hired Denton.

Or someone else entirely.

Finding out who hired Jimmy the Dime would go a long way towards finding that collection.

If I could only turn up the Dime.

Chapter Twenty-four

I called Hank Po and we arranged to meet at a place he called Debbie's. It was a special hangout of his, and the first time I ever saw Debbie, I understood why.

It was actually a little no-name tavern on Tenth Avenue, just off Eighteenth Street, and two blocks from his loft apartment. Debbie was a gorgeous blonde who ran the place with her cousin, a beautiful strawberry blonde named Rosellen.

When I got there Hank was sitting at the counter/bar, talking to Debbie over a beer.

"'Lo, Hank," I said, clapping him on the back and taking the stool next to him.

"Jack, how are you?" he asked. "Good to see you."

"Hello, Miles," Debbie greeted me. "What can I get you?"

"Beer, light," I said. "How are you, beautiful?"

"Wonderful."

"I'll buy that," Hank said.

"You'll buy anything this lovely lady will sell you," I said, as she went off to get my beer. "When she comes back with my beer, let's go to a table for a few minutes, okay?" I asked.

"Sure, Jack."

Debbie brought the beer back and we excused ourselves.

"Private-eye talk, huh?" she asked.

"I'll send him right back," I promised.

We took our beers to a table by the wall and sat down.

"Hank, what's the story on Jimmy the Dime?"

"It's the weirdest thing, Jack," he said, hitching his chair closer to the table. "The man seems to have just dropped off the face of the earth. I can't get a line on him anywhere."

"That's odd," I said. "The one thing you can always count on with him is that he's always around. Now, all of a sudden, he's not."

"I can't explain it," he said, "I can only keep going over the same ground."

"Am I keeping you from anything?"

"Nah," he said, "things are quiet around the track."

Hank was a licensed P.I., but he worked as an investigator for the New York State Racing Club, investigating incidents of possible corruption in thoroughbred racing.

"Don't tell me racing is getting honest?"

"Watch it," he said, "you are talking about the sport for which I toil."

"Sorry. I appreciate your help, Hank."

"I don't see why," he said. "You're paying for it."

"Then that makes us even," I said, standing up, "because you're paying for the beer. *Ciao.*"

Chapter Twenty-five

My next stop was the Seventeenth Precinct, and I hoped Hocus was in.

He was.

"Busy?" I asked.

He looked up from his desk and asked, "How did you get past the front desk?"

"I'm starting to get pretty well-known around here," I said. "You'd be surprised what a few cups of coffee can get you in a police station."

On the way in I had dropped off a bag with four coffees at the front desk, for which several cops were eternally grateful—until next time, that is.

Now I put another bag containing two coffees on his desk and said, "Don't worry, I didn't forget you."

His eyes lit up and he reached into the bag to draw one out.

"Who's the other one for?"

"You don't think I'd let you drink alone, do you?" I asked, taking the remaining cup out.

"What about my partner?" he said, inclining his head toward Detective Wright's desk, where his partner sat, massaging his stomach.

"Coffee's bad for his ulcer."

He took the top off the coffee, took a deep, grateful swallow, and then pinned me with a cop's special suspicious stare and asked, "To what do I owe this special treatment?"

"We're friends, aren't we?" I said.

"Since when?"

"Let me put it another way," I offered. "What have you got on Steinway's murder?"

He leaned his elbows on his desk and asked, "I thought you weren't interested in the murder case."

"I'm not—that is, I'm not interested in working on it, but it might be connected with the missing collection, don't you think?"

"Possibly," he admitted. "We're coordinating with the police in New Hyde Park on the burglary, but they haven't come up with anything."

"Mmm," I said, nodding my head. "Uh, Hocus, have you seen or heard from Jimmy Denton lately?"

"Jimmy the Dime? I haven't spoken to him in weeks, why?"

I explained about the lists that Steinway had furnished me, and about Jimmy the Dime's connection with my investigation into the missing collection.

"Why didn't you tell me that before?"

"The magazine collection isn't your case," I said. "I'm sure the detectives out there got all the same information I did from Steinway—if they were doing their job, that is."

"What makes you think they weren't?"

"I didn't say they weren't," I argued, then added, "Steinway seemed to feel that way, though."

"I'll get in touch with them and see what they have," he said grudgingly. "What did you get from the Dime?"

"Nothing. We can't turn him up; that's why I asked you if you've seen him."

"What do you mean you can't turn him up?"

"Just that. I couldn't find him; now I've got a friend on it, and he can't find him. The man has disappeared."

"Or somebody made him disappear. Denton would never get his hands on that kind of money by himself. He was fronting for someone."

"Exactly, but who? We won't know that until we can find him."

"All right," he said. "There is some kind of a connection between your case and mine, there's no denying that. Off what you've told me, I'll put Jimmy the Dime on the teletype and see if we can come up with him."

"Great," I said, "and if you do, you'll let me know."

"Coffee can only buy so much," he warned, but before I could protest he said, "but goodwill buys more. You gave me the info, so I'll let you know when we find him."

"If," I said.

"When."

I stood up and dropped my empty cup into the wastebasket behind his desk.

"If, when," I said, "whatever. I just hope we find him in one piece."

"Any reason to believe we won't?"

"What's the one thing that stands out about Jimmy the Dime?" I asked.

He shrugged and said, "He's always around, like dogshit on the sidewalk."

"Right."

He made a face and said, "I see what you mean."

"Well, I'll let you get to work," I said, backing towards the door. "Don't forget, Hocus, let me know when you pick him up."

He looked at me sourly and said, "If."

"Whatever," I replied, and backed out the door, waving.

Chapter Twenty-six

Back at my office I opened the top drawer and took out the Mr. Pulps catalogue, ignoring the item right next to it. I dialed the phone number on it, hoping to save myself another trip out to New Jersey, but it apparently wasn't going to be that easy. There was no answer. I tried to remember if he'd had a phone on his desk in the basement, but couldn't. Maybe the phone was upstairs and he was downstairs. I'd try again later.

Next I dialed Michael Walsh's home number, and spoke to a servant. She said that "the mister" was not at home, and that I could try him at his New York office. She was nice enough to give me the phone number, and the address, which was at Madison and Thirty-third. In keeping with my new physical-fitness program, I walked it—briskly.

When I got to the building I realized that I didn't know what company Walsh worked for. I checked the directory, hoping that his office was large enough for him to rate a space on it. Apparently, it was. His office was on the fourteenth floor, Suite 1412.

When I got there all it said on the door was: Michael Walsh, Insurance. I went in and told the fiftyish secretary who I was, and that I wanted to see Walsh.

"Do you have an appointment?"

"Uh, no, I don't, but if you tell him I'm here, I'm sure he'll see me," I said, although I wasn't really all that sure, at all.

As it turned out, he was willing to see me.

"You can go in, sir," she said, pointing to a door.

"Thank you." I approached the door, knocked, and went in.

"Mr. Jacoby," Walsh said, standing behind his desk. "Is there something I can do to help you?"

"I hope so, Mr. Walsh," I said. I walked up to his desk and took note of the fact that he did not offer to shake hands. In fact, his hands were tightly clasped in front of him.

"I'm still looking for Aaron Steinway's collection, and I was wondering if you had heard anything."

"I don't understand," he said. "Aaron is dead; you can't still be looking for the collection for him."

"I have another client."

"Who?"

"I'm not at liberty to say, Mr. Walsh."

"It's his partner, isn't it?" he said. "He wants the collection, too."

"What do you mean, he wants it, too?" I asked.

"Uh, I mean he also made an offer to Steinway for it."

"Steinway told you that?"

"He did, and he also told me that no matter who made an offer, he wasn't interested in selling."

"I see."

"Well, is it?"

"Is what it?"

"Is Walter your client?"

"Mr. Walsh, I didn't come here to talk about my client," I said. I frowned then, as I recalled something Brackett had said, and asked him, "Do you know Brackett?"

"Not personally," he said. "I dealt with Steinway."

"Why did you call him Walter, then?"

"Because Aaron did."

"I see."

He unclasped his hands and thrust them deep into his pockets. Neither of us had taken a seat.

"Tell me, why would you think I'd hear something about the collection?" he asked.

"Oh, you're a collector. I just figured if they showed up on the market, you'd hear something about it. Have you?"

"Nothing."

"If you did hear about it, what would you do?"

"What do you mean?"

"I mean, would you call the police, call me...or would you just go ahead and buy it?"

"I, uh, I don't know...what I'd do, Mr. Jacoby," he stammered. "I guess that's the most honest answer I could give you."

It probably was honest. It would have been just as easy to lie and say he'd call the police right away if someone came to him with the collection.

"I appreciate your honesty, Mr. Walsh," I said. "I also appreciate your seeing me."

"That's quite all right," he said, taking his hands out of his pockets. "I should have offered you something—coffee, a chair—please, sit down."

"No, that's all right," I said, "I have to be going anyway. Mr. Walsh..."

"Yes?"

"I hope that if you do hear something, you will call me, or the police. If the collection is recovered, there is always a chance you could buy it from his estate. That would be a lot better than buying it hot."

"Hot," he said. "You mean, stolen?"

"Right."

"No, no, I agree," he said, "I really do."

"Okay," I said, getting ready to leave. "Thanks for your time."

"No problem," he said. "Anything I can do to help."

"This is a nice office," I commented.

"Oh, uh, thank you," he said, finally coming around the desk.

"Yeah, what company do you work for?"

"I, uh, don't work for any one company," he explained. "I look around for the best policy for each individual person, and it doesn't matter what company it comes from. I'm more valuable that way, don't you think?"

"Sure, it sounds like a good idea," I said. "Anyway, thanks a lot for your time. I'll let you get back to work."

"I am kind of busy..." He hesitated a moment, then stepped forward and extended his hand.

"Let me know if you find it," he said, shaking my hand. "I'd be very interested to know the particulars."

"Sure," I said. "Why not? Have a good day."

"Uh, yes, you too. Thank you."

I left, bade good-day to the lady at the desk, and took the elevator back down.

The thing that bothered me about Walsh was the same thing I had wondered about when first meeting him.

Why was the man so nervous all the time?

Chapter Twenty-seven

Having gone without lunch, I went to Bogie's and had an early steak-and-salad dinner while sitting at the bar. When I finished I asked Billy if I could use his phone.

"The call is to New Jersey."

"I'll add it to your rent," he said. "Coffee?"

"Please."

He handed me the push-button handset and went off to get the coffee. I took the folded Mr. Pulps catalogue out of my jacket pocket and called Leon Battle again, but he was still not answering his phone. If I didn't get ahold of him by morning, it was going to mean another trip out there. I tapped my fingers on the bar, wondering if I should take Laura Brackett along for the ride.

Maybe.

I stood up, reached over the bar and hung up the phone, and Billy came back with two coffees.

"Mind if I join you?"

"Be my guest—since I'm yours. Oh, by the way, dinner is on me," I said, indicating that I'd like to pay for this one.

"You're not tending bar tonight, are you?" he asked.

"No."

"Well, then, I'd expect you to pay for it."

"Oh. Well, good," I said, "I want to pay for it."

"Good," he said. "What's happening with your case?"

"Not a hell of a lot," I said. "I haven't been able to find anything I'm looking for, magazine or man." I sipped my coffee and then remembered something.

"Billy, you collect books, don't you?"

"That's right, but not pulp magazines, so I'm not your man. I didn't steal them."

"Maybe you could tell me why someone would, though."

"There could be lots of reasons," he said, "and they could apply to collecting almost anything."

"Name one."

"I just enjoy reading the books, and then keeping them, watching them pile up and push me out of my apartment."

"Oh, I see."

"Seriously, pulp collectors probably do it to hang on to the past, if they're old enough, and to read some pearls of the past, if they're not."

"Well, you certainly have a way with words."

"Are you, uh, going to tell me who that lady was who came by last night?"

"Laura Brackett, Steinway's partner's wife."

"And your new client."

"Right."

"That's what I thought."

I looked at him and said, "Good guess."

"I'm not so dumb as you think I am," he said, grinning.

"In that case, tell me what you would do if you thought a client was coming on to you."

"A client?" he asked. "You mean, that client who was here last night?"

"That's the one."

"Why is she coming on to you?"

"I don't know," I said. "It's either my good looks, or because she wants me to take her to New Jersey with me to see umpty-million pulp magazines in one place at one time."

"It must be the magazines."

"Thanks, I knew you'd help."

"I'm a married man," he reminded me. "You don't want to know what I would do. That wouldn't help you at all."

"Yeah," I said, staring at the cold remnants of my coffee.

"Another one?"

"Yeah." I handed him the cup and he went and refilled it.

"Have you heard from—" he began, then stopped and stared into his cup.

"What?" I asked. "Have I heard from who?"

"Forget it."

"Come on, friend," I said, "ask."

"I was going to ask you if you, uh, heard from Julie," he said, shrugging his shoulders. "Dumb question, huh?"

"Not so dumb."

"You mean, you have heard?"

I nodded. "I got a letter."

"Jesus," he said. "What'd she say?"

"I don't know. I haven't read it . . ."

"Yet?"

"What?"

"It sounded like you were going to say 'yet.' Do you still have the letter?"

"Um, yeah, in my desk. I've had it for a little over a week."

"Are you going to read it?"

"I don't know, Billy," I replied. "I guess if I wasn't, I wouldn't still have it, huh?"

"I guess not."

I finished the coffee and said, "I'm going to go in the back and try that Jersey number again. I'll see you later, huh?"

"Sure, later."

I went through the kitchen to the back office and dialed the number in New Jersey again, but there was still no answer. I guess that pretty well wrapped things up. In the morning I'd rent a car and drive out to Battle's house in Parlin.

I picked up the phone and called Laura Brackett.

"I'm sorry to call so late, Laura," I said.

"Late? It's not late, Miles," she said.

109

I looked at my watch and saw that it wasn't yet nine o'clock.

"No, I guess it's not."

"You just caught me. I was on my way out."

"I'll let you go, then," I said. "I just wanted to tell you to be ready tomorrow morning at nine."

"For what?" she asked, sounding puzzled.

"We're going to New Jersey."

"Oh, you darling," she said. "Miles, thank you."

"That's all right," I said. "Just bring gas money. Have a nice evening."

"Miles—" she started, but I hung up, feeling pissed at myself for some unknown reason.

My hand was still on the receiver, so I picked it up and dialed Tracy's number.

Chapter Twenty-eight

"What's wrong?" Tracy asked me. "You're acting very strange, Jack."

It was almost eleven, and we were in her apartment on Christopher Street, just walking distance from mine, lying in bed.

"I don't know, Tracy," I said. "I just feel like there's something inside of me, waiting to explode."

"Tension," she said. "What we just finished doing is supposed to relieve tension."

"I don't know what it is," I went on. "Maybe it's this case. Ever since I saw Steinway that first day—"

"Ever since you got that letter from Julie, you mean," she said. I turned my head sharply towards her, and she had a very determined look on her face.

"Jack, I don't know why that letter should affect you and me, but it has. Have you read the damned thing yet?"

"No."

"Well, read it, damnit, or get rid of it," she snapped. "We're friends, but I don't want you sitting around here feeling guilty, especially right after we've finished in bed."

"Tracy," I said, reaching over and taking her hand, "we are friends…"

"I know that, Jack," she said, putting her head on my shoulder, "and we could be more than friends if we could get a few things settled, but the first thing you've got to do is take care of that letter, either by reading it or burning it."

I squeezed her hand and then stared straight ahead.

"You know I'm right," she said. "Julie is still with you, Jack, in more ways than just that letter. You've got to settle that for yourself."

"You're probably right," I said, knowing that she was. "You're really very wise."

"I'm not so wise," she said, freeing her hand from mine and bouncing off the bed. I watched her taut, round breasts bounce as she shrugged into her robe. "If I was I wouldn't be…"

"Wouldn't be what?" I asked.

She stared at me for a few seconds, then shook her head and said, "Never mind. Want some coffee?"

"We talk about my problems, but not yours, huh?"

"First take care of your problems," she said, "and then we can work on mine…together. Okay?"

I smiled and said, "Okay."

"How about that coffee?"

"I'd love some."

"Are you going to stay the night?"

"If you don't mind."

"Bite your tongue," she said. She went to her small kitchenette and started the coffee.

Being in her little apartment with her made me think of my own apartment—or Benny's apartment—and of Benny.

"How's Benny?" she asked with her back turned.

"What are you, a mind reader?"

She turned and said, "Sometimes," with a small grin, "but usually not at the right times. How is he?"

"I don't know," I said. "Willy Wells said he quit that job I got for him after two days."

"And you haven't seen him since?"

"No."

"And you feel guilty."

I hesitated, then admitted, "Yes."

"Why don't you call him?" she asked, "or walk over there now?"

"It's late," I said. "Besides, if he's drunk, he won't make sense, and if he's passed out, the phone won't wake him up."

"Then go and see him tomorrow. At least get that off your mind," she suggested.

"I'm going to New Jersey in the morning," I said. "Maybe later, when I come back."

"Sure," she said, and turned back to the stove. She knew I was making excuses not to see him.

"I will use your phone, though," I said. "To call Jersey, if that's all right with you."

She waved a hand without turning or speaking, and I took that as an okay.

I dialed the number in New Jersey for Battle, and when there was no answer, I started to worry. How much time could the guy spend in his basement, and if he spent that much time there, why didn't he have a phone down there?

I hung up and she came over with two cups of coffee and asked, "No answer?"

"No answer," I said, taking one cup from her. "Curious."

"Is that where you're going tomorrow?"

"Yeah."

"Well, then, you'll find out what the story is tomorrow," she said, seating herself on the bed. "Don't think about it tonight, Jack. Don't think about anything tonight—Benny, old books...Julie. Finish your coffee, I'll give you a rubdown, and you can relax. Maybe we can relieve some of that tension that's built up inside of you, for a while."

I smiled at her and touched her lovely face.

"One way or another?" I asked.

She smiled and said, "That's right, friend. One way or another."

A little bit later Tracy whispered, "Jack?"

"Hmm?"

"Are you awake?" We were lying back to back.

"Barely."

"I got a call today from my agent," she said. "He says I've got a part in a legit feature film if I want it."

"That's great, Trace," I said, wishing I could muster more enthusiasm for her.

"I'd have to go to California, though...for a while."

"Oh. When do you leave?"

"I haven't decided yet if I want to," she answered. "I just thought I would let you know I was considering it."

"Oh, okay," I said. "Let me know what you decide, okay?"

"Sure," she replied. "Get some sleep now."

"You, too. 'Night."

I guess she had wanted me to roll over, grab her, and tell her not to go, but I wasn't prepared to do that. That would constitute some kind of a commitment, and I wasn't in any condition to handle something like that right now.

I hoped she understood.

Chapter Twenty-nine

Having been the route once before did not keep me from getting lost on the way to Mr. Pulps's house in Parlin, New Jersey.

"Any minute now you'll run out of gas, hmm?" Laura said, smiling coyly.

"I think we turn right here," I said, ignoring her remark.

"You know, since I am paying for it, you could have gotten a bigger car."

"I'm sorry, they were all out of limos," I said. "For that you'll have to call your friend Carl."

"Ooh, but you sound jealous."

"Who is the guy, anyway?" I asked.

"Just a friend," she replied. "He was a client of Aaron's, and I met him in the office one day."

"Steinway's client?" I asked. "Not your husband's?"

"Oh, heavens, no," she said. "Walter is frightened silly of Carl."

"Why is that?"

"Carl is a very . . . imposing man. He's very sure of himself. People like that have always intimidated Walter."

"You said 'frightened.'"

"Are we going the right way?"

"Yes," I said, recognizing a small stone church.

"Yes, Walter is usually intimidated, but with Carl it goes a little deeper."

"What does he do?" I asked. "What's his last name?"

"I don't think that while I'm with you I should talk about my, uh, other friends."

"I see."

"What about you?"

"What about me?"

"Do you want to talk about your other friends?"

"Is this conversation supposed to indicate to me that you consider us friends?"

"Well, we could be . . . couldn't we?" she asked.

"You're my client, Laura."

"What if I wasn't your client?"

"That sounds like a question that could get me fired."

"Don't be silly," she scolded me. "All I'm saying is that maybe we could get together after the case is over, when I'm no longer your client."

"I don't see married women, Mrs. Brackett."

"Well, who knows," she said, "that may end soon as well."

"Here it is," I said. We came around a bend in the road and the house was up ahead.

"My God, it's falling down," she said.

"Not quite," I said, pulling up in front.

I got out, walked around the car, and opened the door for her. She stepped out with a whispered thank-you, and we climbed the front steps to the door.

I rang the bell, waited a few moments, and when there was no answer rang again.

"Maybe he's not in," she suggested.

"Maybe," I said, reaching for the doorknob.

"Are you going to pick the lock?"

I turned the knob and the door opened.

"No," I said, pushing it wide. "Besides, I couldn't if I wanted to. I don't know how."

"But you're a private eye."

"I was a fighter before I was a private eye," I said. "I missed that part of my P.I. education. Hello!" I shouted into the house.

No answer.

"Would he leave the house and not lock the door?" she asked.

"This isn't Manhattan, you know," I said.

"Yes, but all those pulps."

"Come on," I said. We went into the house and I closed the door behind us.

"My God, this place looks—"

"All of his money goes into the basement," I said. She looked at me oddly and I added, "That's where all the books are."

"Oh."

We looked around the first level and there was no sign of Battle.

"Not a dirty dish or glass," I said. "Something's not right."

"And you tried to call him?"

"All day yesterday."

"Should we look upstairs?" she asked.

I thought a moment, then said, "No. We'll look downstairs first."

She followed me down the hall, back through the kitchen again, to the basement door. As I reached out to open it she put her hand on my arm.

"What?"

"Don't you have a gun?"

"Yes."

"Where is it?"

"In my office," I said, and opened the door. I felt around the wall on either side and found the light switch. I turned it on, looked down the steps, and saw enough.

"Stay here," I told her.

"I want to see—"

"Stay here!" I said in a firmer voice.

She subsided, and I started slowly down the stairs.

At the foot of the stairs I could see that a bookshelf had been overturned, and books strewn about. As I got closer to basement level I saw that more than one shelf had been overturned. When I finally got to the bottom of the stairs, I realized the full extent of the damage.

Every set of shelves had been overturned, probably using the domino effect of one following the other. The basement was literally knee-deep in old books.

"Jesus," I said under my breath. I waded through

117

the books until I reached the part of the basement that Battle used as his office. I had almost expected to find him there, slumped over the desk, but all I found was that the desk itself had been overturned, and his file cabinets opened and emptied on the floor.

I heard a sharp intake of breath behind me, and turned to find Laura standing there with her hands covering her mouth.

"I thought I told you to stay upstairs," I said.

She looked at me through frightened eyes, and then moved one hand away from her mouth and pointed.

I looked where she was pointing and saw what had frightened her. Sticking out from beneath the shelves and piles of books was an arm, a man's arm, looking as if it had been detached and thrown among the books. Unfortunately—or fortunately, depending on how you looked at it—there was a body attached to it, buried beneath the books.

We had found Leon "Mr. Pulps" Battle.

Chapter Thirty

I had to take Laura back upstairs and sit her down with a glass of water before I could go back down, dig up the body, and make sure it was Leon Battle. After that I called the police and waited with Laura for them to arrive.

Two tan-uniformed officers arrived in a radio car and, after verifying that there was a body in the basement, one of them stayed in the living room with us while the other radioed for a homicide team.

"All those books his?" the cop with us asked.

"It would make my life a lot easier if they weren't," I told him, and he frowned and then shrugged.

When the homicide detectives got there they were introduced as Detectives Abel and Seidman. Both were tall and slender, but Abel's hair was prematurely gray while Seidman's was brown.

"Shall we go downstairs?" Seidman asked.

"By all means," I said. "Uh, the lady can stay up here, can't she?"

They looked at each other and Abel said, "Sure." He looked at one of the officers and said, "Stay with her."

"Where do you think she's going to go?" I asked him.

He looked at me, smiled, and said, "Nowhere. Would you show us the basement, please?"

"This way," I said. I squeezed Laura's hand and then showed them the way.

When we got to the base of the steps, Abel looked around and said, "My God," in a matter-of-fact tone.

When we waded to the point where Laura had stood when she first saw the arm, I pointed it out and Seidman said, "Jesus, that's what I call being into heavy reading."

They both moved in closer to the body and I stayed where I was.

"What did you touch?" Seidman asked.

"Just enough of the books to identify the body."

While Seidman bent over and moved some of the books out of the way, Abel turned to me and asked, "Did you have any reason to suppose that the body would not be that of the owner?"

"No," I said. "I just...wanted to be sure."

The second uniformed man had come down with us and was standing at the base of the steps. Now he looked upstairs, then said, "The lab boys are here."

Abel and Seidman looked at each other and shook their heads. Standing up straight, Seidman said, "They're not going to find a damned thing down here."

"Tell them to come down," Abel told the officer. "Mr. Jacoby, would you wait upstairs? The fewer people down here the better."

"Sure," I said. I went up the steps, passing the lab boys on their way down.

"Can we go?" Laura asked as I entered the living room. She looked at me, and then at the cop.

"Not yet, Laura. I just have a few more questions to answer."

She gave me a sorrowful look and I said, "You wanted to come, remember?"

"You certainly do show a girl a good time," she said. She looked at the officer and asked, "Could I make some tea?"

He was about to say yes, but I said, "That might not be a good idea."

"Why not?" he asked, a beat before she could.

"Because," I told them both, "the body is in the basement, and in order to get it out of the basement they have to—"

"—carry it through the kitchen," she finished for me. "Never mind, I'm convinced. Tea is not such a good idea."

"Tea sounds like a wonderful idea," a voice said from behind us. We all turned and saw Abel and Seidman. It was Abel who was speaking. "I'll make some," he finished, and went back into the kitchen.

"Can we go?" Laura asked Seidman.

"I still have a few questions for Mr. Jacoby, Mrs. Brackett," he said, very courteously. "It won't be long."

He turned to me and said, "The main question is, What brought you out here?"

"I think this can all be made much easier, Detective Seidman, if you would call Detective Hocus at the Seventeenth Precinct in Manhattan. He can explain my connection with Leon Battle, and also a possible connection between this murder and one he's working on."

He studied me for a few moments, then said, "Why don't you just give me a brief rundown of what you did when you got here, and maybe we'll call it a day."

Detective Abel came out of the kitchen with two cups of tea, one for Laura and one for himself, and while they drank it I gave Seidman just what he asked for, a "brief" rundown of our actions prior to calling the police.

While I was finishing my story the M.E. arrived with his men and they were shown downstairs by Seidman.

Laura finished her tea and Abel took the cup from her.

"Thank you," she said.

"My pleasure, Mrs. Brackett." It struck me that New Jersey cops were no different from New York cops when there was a beautiful—or even reasonably good-looking—woman around—although I had never seen one of New York's finest whip up a cup of tea.

Seidman returned from the basement and told me, "I've called for a stenographer to be brought out here. He'll take your statement again, and then you can go. It'll save you a trip to the station house."

"Thank you," I said, somewhat surprised at the special treatment.

"While I was in the kitchen I also called your De-

121

tective Hocus, just to check you out. He said you were a little gung ho, but okay. I'll call him later and get the full story."

I gave Hocus a little mental thanks as well. If anyone had saved us a trip to the station house, it was him.

When the steno man finally arrived, he had to step aside at the door for the M.E. and his men, who were taking the late Mr. Pulps out in a body bag. Following that he took my statement, and Laura and I were finally released.

"We have your phone numbers if we should need to talk to either of you again," Seidman told us. "Thank you both for your cooperation."

"Thank you both for your courtesy," Laura said, shaking hands with both men.

"Excuse me," I said, because both detectives were looking at Laura, not me.

"Yes?" Seidman said, tearing his eyes reluctantly away from Laura.

"How was Battle killed . . . if you don't mind my asking?" I asked him.

The two men exchanged glances, and Abel shrugged and tossed the ball to Seidman.

"I guess there's no harm," Seidman said. "From the way it looks, he was stabbed with a sharp instrument, possibly a knife, a letter opener, something along those lines."

I nodded, frowning to myself.

"Thanks."

"I take it that doesn't match the method in your New York murder?" Abel asked.

"No," I said. "There the man was shot at close range."

"Well, both were done in at close range," Seidman said, as if that should be some consolation to me. "I'll talk to your Detective Hocus when I get back to the station house."

"Thanks," I said, and we left.

When we got into the car I said, "Laura, I'm sorry if all of that was difficult for you."

"Well, after the initial shock it was quite educational," she said, looking at me. "Seeing how it's all really done, I mean."

"Were you surprised?"

"I was surprised at how polite and courteous the detectives were," she admitted.

"Yeah," I said, starting the engine, "so was I."

Chapter Thirty-one

I dropped Laura off in front of her apartment house and resisted—yes, that's the right word—her invitations to come upstairs with her.

"I have some more work to do," I said, "and I have to return the car."

"Trying to save me money?" she asked.

"What's the matter?" I asked. "That doesn't fit your impression of a private eye either? I don't pad expenses, Mrs. Brackett."

"I didn't mean to imply that you did," she said, opening the door. "Please keep me informed about your progress?"

"Sure," I said. "I'll call you."

"I hope so, Miles."

I watched her go into her building, and then took the rental car back. After that, I went over to see Hocus at his office.

I dropped a bag of coffee containers off at the desk and started for the steps to the second floor.

"Hey!" somebody yelled. I turned and saw an officer I didn't know standing behind the desk looking at the bag I'd dropped off.

"Yes?"

"What's that?" he asked, pointing to the bag.

"Coffee," I said, and started for the stairs again.

"Hey!"

"Yeah!"

"Where do you think you're going?"

"I'm going up to the squad room."

"Not without me calling first," he said, shaking his head.

I walked back to the desk and said, "You're not a regular desk man, are you?"

"No," he said. "I'm just relieving the regular guy for a meal." He picked up the phone and asked, "Who do you want to see in the squad?"

"Hocus."

He dialed three digits then said, "Detective Hocus, please." When Hocus came on the line the young cop said, "There's someone down here to see you." He waited a moment, then said, "What? Oh, uh, just a minute." He covered the receiver with his hand and asked, "What's your name?"

"Marciano," I told him, smiling.

"His name's Marciano," he said into the phone. He listened, then said, "Okay." He hung up and said, "You can go up."

"Thanks."

I started to walk away, then went back and grabbed the bag with the coffee a split second before he did.

"Hey," he said.

"Sorry," I said, and hurried up the steps to the second floor.

I walked to Hocus's desk and put two bags of coffee on his desk.

"What's that?"

"And you're a detective?" I asked him. "It's coffee."

"Why so much?"

"The kid on the desk talked himself out of his."

"Oh."

He took one out for himself and I carried one over to his partner's desk.

"That's bad for his ulcer," Hocus yelled to me. Wright gave him a nasty look, but I said, "It's okay, it's Sanka."

Wright smiled and picked it up from his desk. I went

125

back to Hocus's desk and said, "I heard somewhere that people with ulcers can drink that stuff."

I sat down and took a coffee for myself.

"I hope the rest of it doesn't go to waste," I said.

"Not up here," Hocus assured me. "The rest of these animals will smell it in a minute."

I looked around at the other desks, two or three of which were occupied, and in a moment heads started turning and noses sniffed the air.

"Come and get it," Hocus yelled, and in a second his desk was cleared of coffee cups.

"See?" he said.

"I see."

"I just got off the phone with Detective Seidman, from Jersey," he told me.

"Thanks for vouching for me."

"He said that you said I'd tell him how his murder connects up with mine."

"Did you tell him?"

"Sure, I told him," he answered. "I told him that I didn't have the foggiest notion how they connected."

"What'd you say that for?" I demanded.

"Jacoby, what connects the two?" he asked patiently. "Suppose you tell me, and then I'll be more than happy to call him back and tell him."

"Come on, Hocus," I complained, "don't play dumb on me."

"I'm not," he insisted. "You explain it to me."

"You know that working for Steinway is what put me onto Battle in New Jersey. First Steinway is killed, and then Battle. You don't call that a connection?"

"It connects your missing magazine case with Battle," he said, "but not necessarily with the man's murder. And it doesn't necessarily connect his murder with Steinway's. We've got three cases here, Jacoby," he informed me, "a burglary in New Hyde Park, a killing in Manhattan, and a killing in New Jersey."

"And they all involve magazines," I added. "Look, Hocus, you're working with the police in New Hyde Park—"

"I'm in contact with the police out there," he corrected.

"So stay in contact with the police in New Jersey, too," I suggested.

126

"I intend to," he said, grinning tightly. "Now do you have any other advice for me?"

"No," I said glumly, "I don't." I stood up and went to lean over his desk and throw away my empty coffee carton, but he took it and did it for me.

"What about the method?" I asked.

"What about it?" he said. "Steinway was killed at close range with a forty-five. According to the detectives in New Jersey, your man Battle was stabbed."

"Both were killed up close," I said. "Maybe by someone they knew?"

"Maybe," he agreed, "but not necessarily by the same someone."

"Hocus," I began, wondering if he was deliberately giving me a hard time for some reason.

"Prove it to me, Jacoby," he said, "or stop chewing on my ear. Thanks for the coffee."

"Anytime," I said. "By the way, have you come up with anything on Jimmy the Dime?"

"Now there you're dead right," he admitted, pointing a pencil at me. "The man has vanished—but we'll turn him up, sooner or later."

"I hope sooner," I commented, "because later might be too late."

Chapter Thirty-two

I went to my office and sat down behind my desk, somewhat dazed. The murder of Leon Battle was a shock, and, no matter what Hocus said, I felt that the two killings had to be connected to the missing pulp magazines. I didn't know what Mr. Pulps had known about the missing books, or what he had to do with the fact that they were missing, but whatever his connection with the whole business was, it had gotten him killed.

I opened the bottom right-hand drawer, where Eddie had always kept his .38 Colt revolver, and stared at the gun. I had put it back in that drawer after clearing Benny of the murder charge and had not taken it out since. There had not been a "Max the Ax" in my life during the past three and a half months to cause me to take the gun out again, but with two murders, one attempt on my life, and a lump on the head during the past week and a half, maybe it was time.

The mere fact that I was sitting there contemplating taking that gun out and strapping it on made me wonder if I wasn't over my head in this thing.

I took the gun out, with the shoulder holster, and placed it on the desk. I pulled the phone over towards me and dialed Knock Wood Lee's phone number. When

Lee answered I simply asked if Wood was in and had time to see me. She told me to come ahead, the beer would be cold.

Wood had recently moved out of his loft apartment in Chelsea and into a building in Little Italy, a block from Umberto's Clam House. Wood owned the building, and the restaurant beneath his apartment.

That corner in Little Italy was a crossroads of sorts, with Italian and Chinese establishments, as well as heavy Italian and Chinese traffic. At the right time of day you can hear strains of Italian music coming from one window and Chinese tonalities coming from another.

Wood had bought the building, and knocked down the walls of three apartments to make one large apartment for himself and Tiger Lee. Most of his business was done between Chinatown and Chelsea, and this put him in the middle of his territory.

Lee answered the door, looking—if possible—lovelier than ever. Her long, very black hair was parted more towards the right side now than the middle, and she was wearing a silk dress covered with dragons. She was much more full-bodied than most Chinese women and proud of it.

"Hello, Jack," she said, pecking me on the cheek.

"Hi, Lee. You look fabulous."

She smiled and said, "You talk nice. Wood is inside. Would you like a beer?"

"Light beer, if you have it."

"Coming up. Go on in."

I went ahead into Wood's sitting room and found him seated in his favorite chair. Wood was almost twenty-five now, about an inch taller than Tiger Lee's five three. He was a holder of black belts in both karate and judo and had much more confidence than you would normally find in a small man.

"Well, well," he said when I walked in, "my favorite private eye. How are you, Jack?"

"Fine," I said, extending my hand to him.

Instead of taking my hand, he reached past it to pat me down, touching the .38 in the shoulder holster under my left arm.

"Fine, huh?"

"Well," I said, seating myself across from him, "maybe a little scared, too."

"From what I've heard, you have some reason to be," he commented. He looked up as Lee entered the room carrying three bottles of beer by the necks. He accepted one from her, and, after handing me one, she perched on the arm of Wood's chair.

"What have you heard?" I asked.

"People are dying over these books of yours," he said. "First your client—your first client—and now this man in New Jersey with the two names."

"Leon Battle."

"Otherwise known as Mr. Pulps," Lee supplied.

"Right."

"And then there was the attempt on your life," Wood pointed. "Yes, I'd say you had some reason to be scared."

"Now that we've agreed on that," I said, "why don't you tell me what you've heard."

"About?"

"About Jimmy the Dime, about Aaron Steinway's collection. Tell me what you know, Wood, what all your 'ears to the ground' have told you."

"Ah," he sighed, taking a deep pull on his bottle. I looked at Lee, but she was inspecting something on the ceiling. I looked back at Wood, and he shrugged his shoulders at me and said, "Nothing."

"Nothing?" I asked. "You don't know anything? You?"

"I know, I know," he said, waving his hand, "I can't believe it, either, but the lid is on tight, Jack. Tighter than I've ever seen it before."

"Who could put the lid on that tight, Wood?"

"Oh, a few people—but only a few."

"Then I guess those are the people I should talk to."

He frowned at me and said, "Jesus, Jack, you're not only scared, you're scared stupid. You can't get in to see those people."

"Can you get in?" I asked. "Can you get me in?"

"Two very difficult questions," he said.

"Let me get something clear," I said. "We're talking Mafia, right? You've got Mafia connections, don't you?"

"We're talking some pretty powerful people, Jack," he said, putting it differently, "and I know some people

130

who know some people. Why don't you take the night off and let me see what I can find out."

"A night off," I said. I looked at my beer, which I hadn't yet touched, and then took a deep swallow. As the cold brew worked its way down, I thought that a night off didn't sound too bad. The death of Leon Battle had been a shock, more of a shock than I cared to admit.

"You'll call me tomorrow?"

"I'll call you tomorrow," he promised. "If you're looking to relax tonight, I can have one of the girls—"

"That's all right," I said, interrupting him. "I can find my own way of relaxing." I drank some more beer and then put the bottle aside.

"Find out what I'm dealing with here, Wood," I said, standing up. "I'll owe you a big one."

"And I'll collect," he said, "along with all the little ones you still owe me."

I grinned and said, "Right. Thanks for the beer."

"Lee?" he said.

"I'll see you out," Lee said, standing up.

She took my arm and walked me to the door and, as always when I was around her, I entertained certain thoughts...

"Why don't you let Wood help keep your mind off things, Jack?" she asked.

"By sending me one of his girls?"

"They're top notch," she assured me.

"They would pale by comparison to you, Lee," I said. "If I can't have the best—"

"As I said before," she commented, opening the door, "you do talk nice." She kissed me on the cheek—something more than the peck she'd greeted me with—and said, "Have an enjoyable evening."

"I'll try," I said. "Thanks, Lee."

She closed the door gently behind me and I walked to street level, where it was starting to get dark. If nothing else, my visit to Wood had told me one thing I'd wanted to know.

I was almost certainly getting in over my head.

Chapter Thirty-three

With the unfamiliar weight of the .38 underneath my arm, it was a little difficult to "relax." The weight of the gun was a reminder of impending doom, and I really didn't need a reminder.

I'd been scared when I went to see Wood, and after the visit I was even more scared. The prospect of getting involved with the "big guys" was not a comforting one, but why would they be interested in a pulp magazine collection?

I took the train up to Bogie's and claimed a spot at the bar.

"Dinner?" Billy asked over my shoulder.

I thought a moment, then said, "Maybe later. I need to get loose, first."

"Breaking training?"

"Just a few lights," I promised.

"Everything okay, Jack?"

"A few things have come up," I said. I went on to tell him about the trip to New Jersey, and the demise of Leon Battle.

"I guess that must have been a shock for Mrs. Brackett," he said when I was done.

"For me, too," I said. "I'm not one of her pulp detec-

132

tives who gets up in the morning and goes to bed at night with dead bodies."

"No, of course not," he agreed. "You've got every reason to be shocked."

"Yeah."

"And scared."

"Yeah, that too," I admitted. Ed brought me a cold light beer and I swallowed half of it very quickly.

"What are you going to do?" Billy asked.

I shrugged, then said, "I'm still waiting for some information to come in. When it does, I'll make a decision."

"I hope you make the right one," he said, stepping down from his stool and putting his hand on my shoulder.

"Yeah, so do I, Billy."

He patted my shoulder, then went off to do his work. I finished my beer and asked Ed for another one.

Just with Steinway and Mr. Pulps both being killed, it looked as if I were in over my head; but if the people involved were the ones Wood had been referring to, I was in even deeper than I'd thought—maybe too deep to get out.

I hoped not.

I took the second beer into the back office with me and sat at the desk, drinking it slowly. The big mystery to me was how all of this could have started with a missing collection of books. Was that really something for two people to die over? Was there something else involved here that I wasn't aware of? And if there was, who would know?

Maybe the only person who'd come after me to keep me on the trail of the missing books.

Laura Brackett.

She had offered me money and implied another form of payment was available as well. Did she want the books badly enough to go that far?

Or was there something in the books? There was a thought. Suppose it was not the books themselves, but something that was in one or more of them.

A code, a secret code—and all of the people I was

dealing with were agents for different foreign powers who were after the code.

Sure, how did that sound?

Like I needed something a little stronger than beer.

Chapter Thirty-four

Instead of having a stronger drink, I decided to go over and talk to Laura Brackett again. Maybe, after the shock of finding Leon Battle's body, she was ready to talk—if, in fact, there was anything further to talk about.

I called her from Bogie's and she told me to come right up.

When she opened the door she was wearing another silk lounging robe, likewise with very little on beneath it.

"So you decided to take me up on my offer," she said, smiling coyly.

"What offer was that?" I asked.

"To find out how I come alive when the sun goes down."

"Actually, I just wanted to talk to you."

"Well, that's fine," she said, backing up so I could enter. "We could start there."

We walked into the living room and she asked, "Would you like a drink?"

"No, thank you."

"I'm working on one," she said, indicating the glass on the end table by the couch. She was a little unsteady

135

on her feet, and her eyes had a slightly glazed look to them, so I figured she had been working on more than one.

"Sit down," she invited, and I sat in the chair directly across from her.

"You're so unsociable," she complained. "There's so much room on this couch."

"I don't want to get sidetracked," I said.

"Well, at least you've admitted the possibility," she replied. "What did you want to talk about?"

"Steinway's collection."

"What about it?" she asked, reaching for her glass. She missed it on the first try, almost knocking it over, but grabbed it before any of the contents could spill.

"I want to know what's so important about it, Laura."

"I'm a collector," she said. She raised the glass to her lips and took a long swallow.

"What I'm getting at, Laura," I went on, "is, What's so important about a collection of books that would cost two men their lives?"

"You think that Aaron and Mr. Pulps were killed because of the collection?" she asked, frowning.

"That's the only thing that connects them," I pointed out. "Is it really the books that are so important to you, or is it something else?"

"What else could there be?" she asked.

"Something...inside?" I suggested.

"Shame on you, Miles," she replied, wagging her finger at me as if I were a disobedient child. "You lied to me."

"What do you mean?"

"You told me you didn't read pulp fiction," she answered. "Something inside the magazines? Like what, a code?" She laughed, throwing her hand out and sloshing her drink on herself. She didn't seem to notice. I didn't say anything because, in the shape that she was in, the booze did more good for her outside than in.

"Then you want the collection for no other reason than what you've said?"

"No other reason," she repeated. She peered owlishly at her watch and said, "I'm supposed to get dressed. I'm going out."

"Do you think you should?" I asked.

"Why shouldn't I?" she demanded.

"You've had quite a bit to drink."

"You sound like my husband now," she said, in disgust. "Walter was more like my mother than my husband. That's why I like Carl."

"Carl?" I asked. "The fella in the limo..."

"Carl treats me the way a man should treat a woman," she went on, ignoring me. She put her glass down and got unsteadily to her feet. "I've got to get dressed for Carl."

"I've got to go, anyway," I said, but she continued to act as if I weren't there. I stared at her, wondering if she were in shock from discovering Leon Battle's body.

The doorbell rang at that point.

"That'll be Carl," she said, over her shoulder. "Would you let him in on your way out, please?" She continued walking and disappeared into her bedroom.

I opened the door and stood face to face with her Carl. He was a big man, over six feet, and well built without being muscular. He looked like he would have made a good light heavyweight.

"You're Jacoby," he said. "The P.I."

"Yes."

"Where's Laura?" he asked.

"She's in the bedroom, getting dressed," I answered. "She's been through a lot today. I think an evening here at home would be better for her."

"Is that so?" he asked. "Are you a doctor, too?"

"No," I replied. "I'm just offering an opinion—but a doctor might not be a bad idea, if you can get one this late."

We eyed each other for a few moments, and I felt an even stronger sense of familiarity, now that I could see his face, but I still couldn't put my finger on it. Something about the eyes, maybe, the heavy eyebrows, the broad forehead...

"If she needs a doctor," he said, finally, "I'll get one for her, no matter what time it is."

I believed he could, too.

I stepped past him into the hall and said, "Tell Mrs. Brackett that I'll be in touch."

"Sure," he said, stepping into the apartment. "But

137

make sure it's about business, huh, friend?" he added grimly.

"Don't worry, friend," I replied. "I'm not your competition. Have a nice evening."

I walked down the hall to the elevator and it wasn't until after I pressed the down button that I heard the door to the apartment close.

When I got back to Bogie's, Billy Palmer approached me immediately and said, "You had a call."

"From who?" I asked, thinking that if it was Wood, he had gotten the information I needed pretty quick.

"Heck Delgado." I was surprised. "He said he was calling from home, but that he wouldn't be in for you to get back to him. He said you could call him at his office in the morning."

Maybe he wanted to talk about Missy, but if that were the case, why would he call from home? More than likely it was about Steinway's daughter. Maybe she was in town, and he wanted to put us together, as he had promised.

"Okay, Billy, thanks."

"My pleasure," he said. "I'd rather get those kinds of calls than the others—girl friends looking for boyfriends, wives looking for husbands...."

"Sounds like we could pretty much be in the same business," I pointed out, and we both laughed.

"How are you doing?" he asked.

"Eh," I said, "I'll know better tomorrow."

He asked if I wanted a drink, but I told him I was going to turn in. It had been a bitch of a day, and the sooner I got it behind me, the better I'd like it.

Chapter Thirty-five

The phone in the office rang early the next morning, which was unusual. It was 9:30, and Bogie's was not yet open, so I staggered out of bed and snatched the instrument up on the fourth ring.

"Yeah, hello," I mumbled hoarsely.

"Jack, is that you?" Heck's voice asked.

"Yeah," I croaked. "Hang on a second."

I put the phone down on the desk and shuffled into the bathroom, trying to clear my throat. I turned on the cold water, washed my face, rinsed out my mouth, then swallowed a mouthful from my cupped hands to clear my throat further.

Back on the phone I said, "Okay, I'm back."

"And alive this time," he added. "Do you always sound like that in the morning?"

"So don't marry me," I said. "What's up?"

"You said you wanted to meet Erica Steinway."

"That's right."

"She'll be in my office at twelve noon," he said. "Why don't you drop by?"

"I'll do that, Heck," I said. "Thanks. I was going to call you later."

"I figured I'd save you the trouble," he said. "I will see you later."

I hung up and considered going back to sleep, but I was past that point now. I showered, dressed, left by the front door and went to get some breakfast at a McDonald's on Eighth Avenue. I conveniently forgot my diet for that morning.

After breakfast I took a long, leisurely walk across town and then uptown to my office, fairly confident that no one was going to try and run me down in broad daylight.

In my office I opened some mail, put some bills aside "to be paid—sometime," and listened to my answering machine. There was only one message and it was from Benny. He sounded sober, but shaky, and said he had to talk to me. The message had come in the day before. I still hadn't seen or spoken to him since finding out he'd quit the job at the gym. Maybe if I responded to his message and talked to him, I could get him to go back. That is, if I could get Willy Wells to give him another chance.

That was personal stuff, though, and it was later for that. It was already eleven o'clock, and I was due at Heck's at twelve. I hung around the office awhile longer, waiting for the phone to ring, hoping Knock Wood Lee would call, and then I started walking downtown to Heck's office.

Missy smiled at me when I walked in, and I smiled back, very pleased that she was there.

"Good morning," she greeted me.

"I almost feel like Cupid," I said, planting my hip on the edge of her desk.

"Well, don't," she said. "It's not a permanent situation yet."

"Why not?"

"I haven't quit my job with the temporary service," she explained. "Heck simply called them and asked that I be sent here for two weeks."

"Why do it that way?"

"Because, Cupid," she said, "we have to see if we're compatible."

"What's to see? He needs a good secretary, you're a great one; what could be better than that?"

140

"We have to make up our own minds, Jack," she said. "Do you want to go in, or do you want me to tell him you're here?"

"Is the lady here?"

"Yes, she's in with him now."

"You better announce me then."

She depressed the switch on the intercom and said, "Mr. Delgado, Miles Jacoby is here."

"Does he have an appointment?" Heck's voice asked.

Missy made a haughty face at me and I shook my head and shrugged my shoulders.

"No, sir, but he says it's very important."

There was a pause, and then he said, "All right, send him in."

"He'll see you, sir," she said, properly.

"Done just like a good little secretary," I said, cupping her lovely chin. "I'll see you later."

"No, you won't," she said.

"Why not?"

"Because when you get a look at Erica Steinway, you won't be looking at me anymore."

"Impossible," I said.

"You'll see," she answered. "I know you, Miles Jacoby. You'll see."

"I'm very anxious to," I admitted, and opened the door to Heck's office and walked in.

"Hello, Miles," he said, rising from his chair. I knew that only moments before he had been apologizing to the young lady for the interruption.

"Nice of you to see me without an appointment, Heck," I replied.

"What are friends for?" he asked, smiling. He looked at the girl, whose back was to me, and said, "Miss Steinway, I'd like you to meet a friend of mine. Miles Jacoby, Erica Steinway."

She remained seated and I walked around so that I could see her.

"It's a pleasure to meet you," I said, and when I looked at her I knew that Missy was right. Erica Steinway was about twenty-two, and she was probably the most classically lovely woman I had ever seen. Her hair was red, and long, and her eyes were . . . what, turquoise?

"Mr. Jacoby," she said, putting out her hand.

141

"I'm sorry about your father," I said.

"Oh," she said, surprised. "Did you know my father?"

"I, uh, was working for him at the time of his death."

"Really? What is it you do, Mr. Jacoby?"

"Miles is a private investigator," Heck broke in, "and a very good one. I sometimes use him myself, and I recommended him to your father."

"What did my father need a private eye for?" she asked.

"I'd like to talk to you about that, Miss Steinway," I said. I looked at Heck and asked, "Could we all have lunch together . . . on you?"

He laughed and said, "I'd like to, but I have another appointment. Why don't you take Miss Steinway to lunch?"

"And why don't you two stop the act?" Erica Steinway asked. "If there's something you want to talk to me about, Mr. Jacoby, then by all means let's go to lunch . . . on me." She turned to Heck and said, "Can we finish our business later?"

"Come back right after lunch," he said. "I have the afternoon free."

"What a coincidence," she said sweetly, "so do I. Mr. Jacoby?"

The lady had a definite take-charge attitude. I didn't know if I liked that or not, but I accepted it because of the setup we'd perpetrated on her.

On the way out I very deliberately looked at Missy and she just as deliberately stuck her tongue out at me, all of which was taken in by Miss Erica Steinway.

"A close friend of yours?" she asked in the elevator. I didn't like her tone.

"Yes," I said, "an *extremely* close and good friend. I don't have that many, Miss Steinway, and I resent it when people make the wrong assumptions about them."

She stared at me for the duration of the elevator ride, and just before the doors opened she said, "I apologize."

"Apology accepted," I said. "How hungry are you?"

"Not very. Is there a Blimpie's nearby?"

"As a matter of fact, there is."

"Blimpie's is one of the things I missed while I was in Europe."

"They don't have Blimpie's in Europe?" I asked, feigning horror.

"McDonald's abounds," she said, "but if there was a Blimpie's there, I missed it. Do you mind?"

"No, not at all. There's one a few blocks north."

"Which way is that?"

I pointed and said, "It's that—oh, hell, just follow me."

When we were seated with our sandwiches and coffee, she asked, "So, what did you do for my father?"

"He hired me to find his pulp magazine collection," I said. "Someone had broken into his house while he was out of town and taken it."

"How?"

"I don't know."

"What about the police?"

"They don't know, either."

"And my father's murder," she said. "Does it have something to do with those books?"

I hesitated, then said, "I think so."

"What do the police think?"

"They're not admitting to any connection between the two," I said.

"Are you trying to find his killer?"

"No," I said, shaking my head. "That's a job for the police. I am still looking for the magazines, though."

"Why? Did he pay you that much that you think you still have to earn it?"

"The money he paid me was gone a long time ago," I said. "I have another client."

"Who?"

"Someone who wanted to buy the collection from your father. He wouldn't sell. They want me to find it."

"If you do, you can't give it to them," she said.

"No. It would be part of your father's estate. Depending on who inherited, they would try and buy it from that person. Will it be you?"

"I don't know," she said. "Mr. Delgado is supposed to read me my father's will. I suppose I will inherit. We didn't see each other very much, but there were no real...insurmountable problems between us."

"That's good."

143

"I guess it is," she said. "I must admit I do feel guilty about not having been here."

"There's no need for that," I assured her.

"I know," she said. "Do you think you can find the collection?"

"I haven't had much luck so far," I admitted. "And there was another man killed."

"Who?"

I explained about Mr. Pulps, and that I believed that his murder might be connected to her father's, and to the missing books.

"They haven't admitted to a connection," I continued.

She put her half-eaten sandwich down and asked, "Who is the detective in charge?"

"Detective Hocus. He works out of the Seventeenth Precinct."

"Do you know him?"

"Yes. He's a good cop."

"I'd like to meet him. Can you introduce me?"

"Of course."

"When?"

"I'll have to pin him down," I said. "And you still have to talk to Heck. Where are you staying?"

"I'm using my father's apartment while I'm in the city."

"Have you been out to the house yet?" I asked.

"No."

"I'll walk you back to Heck's office, and call you when I've set up a meeting for you with Hocus. Okay?"

"Fine. Thank you."

"No problem."

"I appreciate your taking the time to talk to me," she said. "I'm sorry if I seemed rude, or cold, earlier."

"There's no need to apologize," I said. "And my reasons for talking with you aren't entirely unselfish."

"Oh?"

"No. I wanted to see if you knew anything that might help me find your father's collection."

"I don't really know anything about any part of his collection," she admitted. "Even as a child I wasn't anywhere near it. I came to hate it. I don't guess I really care if you ever find it."

"Does that mean you'd sell it if I found it?" I asked.

She stiffened and said, "Why, are you empowered to make an offer?"

"Don't get tense on me, Erica," I said. "It was just a question."

She relaxed and said, "Again, I'm sorry. I guess this whole thing has just been something of a shock."

"I imagine it would be," I said. She hadn't touched her sandwich for a few minutes, and her coffee was gone, so I said, "Are you finished?"

"Yes."

"I'll walk you back then."

"What will you do?"

"I'll go and talk to Hocus, and then see if some information I've been waiting for has come through yet."

"I see," she said, as we stood. "About the collection?"

"Having to do with it, yes."

As we were walking back she said, "It's rather hard to believe that two men could die over an old collection of books."

"Yes," I agreed, "it is. Very hard."

When we got back to the office, Missy told Erica she could go right in, but the girl turned to me first.

"I'll expect your call, Mr. Jacoby."

"I'll phone you as soon as I can, Erica," I promised.

When she went into Heck's office, I looked at Missy. She was smiling knowingly.

"What are you smiling at?"

"You."

"Why?"

"Because this is the first time you've looked at me since you and she came back from lunch."

"You're nuts," I said. "Can I use your phone?"

"Be my guest," she said, still smiling.

I called the Seventeenth Precinct Detective Squad and Wright, Hocus's partner, answered.

"How'd you know we were looking for you?" he asked.

"I didn't," I said. "What's the matter?"

"Hold on," he said, and in a moment Hocus came on the line.

"Jacoby, those New Jersey cops found another stiff you might be interested in."

"Another one?" I asked. "Where?"

"The same place," he answered. "They finally got

145

around to having somebody go down in that basement and clear away all the books. They found another body underneath it all."

"Jesus," I breathed. "Killed the same way?"

"Yeah," he said sourly, "the same way as Steinway, close up with a forty-five."

"You see, there is a connection," I said.

"Save the I-told-you-so's, Jacoby," he growled. "There's another connection that you ain't going to like so much."

"What's that?"

"The I.D. on the new stiff."

"Well?" I prodded. "Are you going to make me ask?"

"Who you been looking for all this time?" he asked.

"Oh, shit," I said, realizing what he meant.

"Yeah. Your buddy, Jimmy the Dime, bought it under a bunch of books in Jersey." He snorted and said, "I'll bet you it was the first time he's ever been out of New York, too."

"They didn't happen to find Jimmy Hoffa under all those books, too, did they?" I asked.

Chapter Thirty-six

"Goddamnit!" I snapped, pounding my fist on Hocus's desk.

"Hey, easy," he snapped, "that's city property."

"The whole thing was supposed to be tied up when we found Jimmy the Dime, and now look," I complained.

"You should be happy as a pig in shit," Hocus said.

"What the hell for?"

"Well, you been crying all along that the two murders were connected with the magazine collection. This means you were at least half right."

"What do you mean half right?"

"Denton ties your collection to the killing in New Jersey," he said. "Why else would he be out there?"

"Yeah, but was he buying or selling?" I asked. "We've got to get an expert up there to look those books over and see if he can find out if Steinway's collection is there."

"You know anybody?" he asked.

"No, but I know somebody who might," I said, thinking of my P.I. friend in San Francisco. If he could give me a name, and somebody could discover that Steinway's collection was in that basement, then my job would be over.

"Can't see the forest for the trees," Hocus said, half aloud.

"What?"

"I was just thinking," he said. "Where's the best place to hide a book?"

"In a library," I answered, seeing what he was getting at, "and that basement made a damned good hiding place for those books."

"How is anybody going to be able to tell Steinway's books from the rest of them?" he asked.

"Steinway had his stuff indexed," I said. "That should make it a little easier. Why don't you call New Jersey and tell Seidman or Abel that we're going to send someone over there to take a look. Maybe we can stop them before they make it harder than it already is."

"Right."

"Oh, yeah, another thing."

He was in the act of reaching for the phone and when I spoke he stopped and said, "What?"

"Steinway's daughter is in town, and she'd like to talk to you."

"To me? What for?"

"You're the detective in charge of the investigation into her father's death."

"Gave me right up, didn't you?"

"Oh, you won't mind talking to this young lady, Hocus," I said. "She is something to look at."

"Oh, yeah? Bring her in then."

"When?"

"In the morning. I've got to get some paperwork done on this thing now, and I do have other cases."

"Okay," I agreed, standing up, "but make that call."

"Yes, captain," he said. "Anything else, captain?"

I turned to go and saw Wright sitting at his desk, holding his hands over his stomach.

"Is he okay?"

He looked over at his partner and said, "It's been acting up on him lately. Kicking him back is what it's doing, the way he eats."

I shook my head and said to him, "I'll have Miss Steinway here early tomorrow morning."

"Not too early," he said. "And bring coffee."

"Don't I always?" I said. I looked at Wright again and added, "And I'll bring some milk for him."

"He won't drink it if it doesn't have coffee in it," he said.

"Then he's got a death wish," I said. "See you tomorrow."

"For your sake, Jack, I hope that collection turns up in Leon Battle's basement."

"Why's that?"

"Because I'd hate to see you end up there, or someplace else," he said.

"That's a comforting thought."

"I hope you've got a license for that piece you're carrying," he said, "especially if you have to use it."

"I've got a license," I said, shifting my shoulders uncomfortably.

"You'll get used to it," he said, "if you carry it long enough."

"I hope not," I said. "I won't be carrying it that long."

"Will you be able to hit what you shoot at?"

I'd thought about that myself, more than once.

"I hope so," I said, "because if I use it, it will mean my life depends on it. That's the only time I'll use it."

"Yeah," he said, looking inside his head at something only he could see, "that's the only time any of us want to use it." He looked at me again and said, "Just walk carefully. With a little luck, your end will be over soon."

"Yeah," I said, "with a little luck...I just hope it's good."

Chapter Thirty-seven

I went back to my office and called my friend, the Lone Wolf P.I. of San Francisco, and asked him if he knew of an expert who would come to New York and New Jersey in the interest of finding Aaron Steinway's collection.

"My client would pay his way, naturally," I added.

"Why don't you let me make a few calls, Kid," he suggested. "If I come up with somebody, I'll give them your number and have them call you direct."

"That sounds fine," I said. I also gave him the number at Bogie's, in case I was out of the office when the call came.

After that I listened to my answering machine and found a message from Knock Wood Lee asking me to call him, which I did immediately.

He answered himself, which was a sure sign of trouble.

"Wood? Where's Lee?"

"She, uh, went away for a while."

"Went away?"

"Yeah. Listen, I've got that information for you, but I can't give it to you over the phone. You'll have to come over here."

"When?"

"Right now."

"Wood, are you all right?"

"I'm fine," he said levelly, "just fine. I'll be waiting for you."

He hung up before I could ask any more questions.

Something wasn't right. Lee wasn't there to answer the phone, and Wood didn't sound like himself. I had the feeling I would be walking into some kind of a setup if I went, but if that was the case and Wood was in trouble, then it was probably my fault.

There was only one way to find out.

I thought about calling for some backup, but that would have slowed me down. I wanted to get over there as soon as possible. The only thing I did before leaving was switch from the shoulder holster to the belt holster, and I clipped it behind my back, underneath my windbreaker.

I took a cab and had him drop me a block from Mott and Hester, Wood's corner. I walked the remaining block, looking up at Wood's windows. I thought I detected some movement at one of them, but I couldn't be sure.

When I got to Wood's street-level door and found it unlocked, my stomach began to flutter the way it always used to before a fight. That was okay, though. That had never bothered me, because I knew it wasn't nervousness, and it wasn't even fear. It was anticipation.

I only wished that this time I knew what to anticipate.

Halfway up the steps I started to reach behind me for the gun, but I forced myself to stop. I told myself this was the feeling-out period, the first round. Just keep your eyes open, Kid, and see what develops.

When I got to the top of the stairs I rang the bell.

"It's open," Wood's voice called out.

That meant bad trouble. Wood's door was never open.

I took a deep breath, fingered the doorknob, and then pushed the door open.

"Wood?"

"In here," he called from his sitting room.

Said the spider...

I flew in.

151

"Easy, Jack, just stand easy," Wood said from his favorite chair. "These gentlemen want to talk to you for a few minutes."

I looked around. There were four, and all of their hands were clasped in front of them, which meant they were...relatively empty. At least there were no guns in sight.

"Friends of yours, Lee?" I asked.

He snorted and said, "Hardly."

"You all right?"

"I'm fine," he said. "I went after that information you wanted and opened up a can of worms pretty quick." He made an all-encompassing gesture with his eyes and said, "These are what crawled out."

There was a man on my right and one on my left. The one to my left took a step towards Wood and said, "Hey—"

There was a man on Wood's right and left, and the one to his right pinned my man with a hard stare and said, "Step back."

The first man stopped cold and then stepped back. Since the man on Wood's right was obviously in charge, I looked at him and said, "You want to talk to me?"

"In a moment," he said, unclasping his hands and holding up one finger. He laid the hand on Wood's shoulder and said, "Why don't you take a walk, Wood."

"Why don't you take your hand off my shoulder before I detach it at the wrist," Wood replied.

The other man lifted his hand as if Wood's shoulder had suddenly caught fire, then stopped himself.

"This is my home, DeLauro," Wood said, calling the man by a name unfamiliar to me.

DeLauro, a tall, slender man in his thirties, slowly moved his hand away from Wood and reclasped both his hands in front of him before responding, "All right, Wood."

He turned his head and addressed himself to me.

"We have been sent to talk to you, Mr. Jacoby, about a matter that concerns you, and my...principal."

"Your boss," I said, but he ignored me. "All four of you?" I asked.

"Oh, no," DeLauro said, "these are just my friends. They came along for the ride, as it were."

I looked at the other three men, who were of a comparable age and type to DeLauro, and then said, "You got ugly friends, Mr. DeLauro."

"Well," he replied, "fortunately none of them are anticipating entering a beauty contest in the near future."

"Why don't you say your piece and leave," I suggested.

He moved his right hand again, this time pointing one finger directly at me.

"You are making it very hard for me to be civil," he warned.

"Fuck civil," I said. "Get to it."

The man was frustrated. His orders clearly called for him to talk, and that was all.

"You are to stop searching for Aaron Steinway's missing book collection, and you are to stay away from Mrs. Laura Brackett."

That one threw me.

"Whoa, hold on a second, let's back up," I said. "I'm confused enough wondering what your people are doing getting involved with a pulp magazine collection, but what's this about Laura Brackett?"

"It's very simple," he said. "Stay away from her."

"The lady happens to be my only source of income at the moment," I said. "Staying away from her is like telling me to stop living."

"That could easily be arranged as well," he said.

"You know, that could be construed as a threat," I pointed out.

"Well," he said with a barely restrained grin, "we were instructed to take stronger measures if you refused."

"Not in my home," Wood said.

"Shut up, Wood," DeLauro told him.

Wood had been sitting like his namesake since I arrived, staring straight ahead of him, so that when his eyes flicked over to me, it alerted me. I was barely a beat behind him when he made his move.

It was like watching a kung fu movie, only live. Suddenly, in a flurry of motion and with a wild yell, both of his hands flew out from his body, catching each of the men next to him in the stomach. I would have

153

liked to watch further, but I had a couple of fellas of my own to take care of.

I pivoted to my right, threw a stiff left jab and then a straight right across that put one of my men down. I turned to face the other, but Wood was already there. He jabbed stiffened fingers into the man's middle, folding him up.

"Here," Wood said to me, and we both backed off and watched DeLauro and his friends pick themselves up. To avoid any further contact, I reached behind me and took out the .38.

One of DeLauro's people looked at him and said accusingly, "I thought you said he didn't carry a piece."

"That's what I was told," DeLauro said, keeping his eyes on me. "This is a mistake, Jacoby."

"The only mistake here is you and your friends, so move on," I said. I was holding the gun down at my side, but it was making its presence known.

"This is not the end," DeLauro said, and he followed his men out.

We looked out one of Wood's windows, watched the four men cross Mott Street to their illegally parked car.

"You want to tell me what that was all about?" I asked.

"You asked me to find out who had the lid on. I asked around, and they showed up here about an hour and a half ago."

"Where's Lee? Is she all right?"

"She's fine. When they came I sent her for a walk."

"Who sent them?"

"They work for Carlo Caggiano."

"Senior or junior?" I asked. Carlo Caggiano, Sr. was the top mob man in New York City, but junior was pushing.

He shrugged and said, "They didn't say. I'd say junior. Senior's men are not so brash as these were, and DeLauro has been seen with Cagey Carl."

"Oh, shit," I said softly, as I realized something.

"What?"

"Carl," I said. "Laura Brackett's Carl."

"Carl, Jr.?" he asked.

"I knew he looked familiar," I said. Carlo, Sr. had been in the newspaper many times, and junior had the

154

same eyes, the same wide forehead. "I should have seen it before."

"You've seen Carl, Jr.?" he asked.

"Spoke to him yesterday, as a matter of fact. I was coming out of Laura Brackett's apartment as he was going in."

"Which would explain this visit," he said.

"But why involve you?"

"I involved myself when I started asking questions," he said. "They simply brought the two of us together in one place."

"Then you got a message too, today."

"Yes, to stop being such a big help to you."

"Then maybe you should," I suggested.

"And maybe I should take a slow boat to China," he added.

"Yeah," I said. I looked down at the gun in my hand and then returned it to the holster. I was very glad that the necessity to use it had not arisen.

"DeLauro was right about one thing, though," Wood admitted, sitting himself down in his chair.

"What was that?"

"The gun," he said, pointing at me. "It was a bad move."

"Did you want to go a few rounds with those guys?" I asked.

"The fact that you produced a gun makes you more dangerous to them," he pointed out. "You saw how surprised they were."

"Yeah, they were surprised," I admitted. "They knew that I don't usually carry a gun. Somebody told them."

"Obviously," he said. "And as far as going a few rounds with them, I was only waiting for you to arrive."

"For me?"

"Sure," he said, grinning. "Once you got here, the odds were even. You see, three's my limit."

Chapter Thirty-eight

I went back to my office to let it all sink in. Three dead men, and now the mob was involved, and man was I ever in over my head, or what? I mean, Carlo Caggiano, junior or senior, what the fuck was the difference? It was time for me to give everything I knew to Hocus and get the fuck out while I was still in one piece.

The phone rang and I jumped in my seat and broke into an instant sweat.

"Hello," I breathed into the phone.

"Is this Miles Jacoby?" a man's voice asked.

"Yes, it is."

"I was given your number by a mutual friend, Mr. Jacoby. I understand you need an expert in old pulp magazines."

"Uh, yeah," I said, scratching my forehead. "I did...."

"I also understand that you will pay expenses to New York," he went on.

"Uh, yes, that was the original—"

"I'd like you to know you don't have to do that," he said.

"I don't?"

"No. I live in Philadelphia, and I would be glad to drive to New Jersey on the chance that Mr. Steinway's excellent collection might be there. I was shocked to hear that it had been stolen, and I'd like to do what I can to help recover it."

"You would?"

"Definitely. When would you like me there?"

If he was willing to drive down himself from Philly, I wouldn't have to get in touch with Laura Brackett again at all, except to send her a final bill once the collection was found—and I still wasn't sure I would do that.

"What's your name, sir?" I asked him, picking up a pencil and pulling over a pad.

"Stuart Kaminsky."

I wrote down his name, address, and phone number and told him that either myself or the police would be in touch with him to set up an appointment to meet him at the former home of the late Mr. Pulps.

"Of course, you'll need Mr. Steinway's index," I said.

"It would be a great help."

"I think I can arrange that," I said. "We'll be in touch, Mr. Kaminsky. Thank you very much."

"This is an opportunity I could not pass up, I assure you," he said.

"You're a collector yourself, are you not?" I asked.

"That's right."

"May I ask what business you're in?"

"I'm a mortician," he said.

"I see," I said, instantly sorry I had asked. "Goodbye, Mr. Kaminsky."

"I'll wait to hear from you," he said, and I hung up.

I dialed the number of Steinway's New York apartment before I could change my mind, and Erica Steinway answered.

"This is Miles Jacoby," I said.

"Well, hello," she said. "You have good timing. I only just got in."

"I was able to arrange that appointment for you, with the detective in charge of the investigation."

"That was fast," she commented. "When?"

"In the morning. Would you like me to pick you up?"

"That won't be necessary," she said. "I can meet you there...if you're going to be there, that is."

"I'll be there," I said, because I had the impression

that she was asking me to. "How about ten o'clock?"

"That's fine."

"I also have a favor to ask."

"What is it?"

"Do you have the key to your father's house?"

"I have an extra key that Mr. Delgado gave me, yes. Why?"

"I need your father's index," I said. "The one that has to do with his pulp collection."

"That's no problem," she said. "I was going out tomorrow anyway."

"Good, then I can tag along, if you don't mind."

"I don't mind," she said. "I hope you don't mind my asking, but are you all right? You sound strange."

"I'm fine," I said. "I've just had a hard day, that's all."

"I hope that doesn't include lunch," she commented.

"No," I replied, "that in no way includes lunch."

"I'm glad."

There was an awkward silence, as if each of us was waiting for the other to speak.

"Well," she finally said, "I guess I'll see you in the morning."

"I suppose..." I began to agree, but let it trail off. "Uh, do you have any plans for dinner tonight?"

"I hadn't made any plans, no," she said. "I have very few friends in New York, and I've only arrived today."

"I know a very nice place," I said, "and this time it would be on me."

"Well, that sounds like an offer I could hardly refuse."

"I hoped you'd see it that way," I said. "I could pick you up—"

"Why don't we just meet there?" she suggested.

I checked my watch and saw that it was almost seven.

"Would eight o'clock give you enough time to get ready?" I asked.

"Plenty of time."

I gave her the exact address of Bogie's and said, "I hope you like good Italian food."

"I love it."

"I'll see you there, then."

"Thank you for the invitation."

"Thank you for accepting," I replied. "I'll see you in a little while. Don't dress up. I said the food was good."

Next I called Hocus.

"What's up?" he asked.

"I have an expert who is willing to go to Jersey and search through those books for Steinway's collection."

"So? What do you want me to do?"

"I want—I'd like you to call Seidman or Abel in New Jersey and make an appointment for my man."

"Why can't you do it?"

"Because I think they'll agree more readily if the request comes from you. They don't have to help me find the collection, you know."

"Neither do I, for that matter."

"Ah, but we're friends," I said.

That stopped him for a moment, and then he said, "Give me the information. I'll try to set something up."

I gave him everything I had on Stuart Kaminsky and thanked him for helping.

"Well, maybe it'll solve your case for you, and then I can go ahead and solve mine. I'll let you know what happens."

"And...we've got to talk again tomorrow. Erica Steinway is coming to see you at ten. I'll come at nine-thirty."

"What's the matter?" he asked. "You sound funny."

"Maybe so," I said, "but there's nothing funny about the way I'm feeling right now."

"All right, Jack," he said. "I'll see you at nine-thirty."

"Thanks, Hocus," I said. Hanging up I realized that, since I'd met him, that was perhaps the third or fourth time he'd called me anything but "Jacoby."

I also realized, maybe for the first time, that I didn't have any idea what his first name was.

Chapter Thirty-nine

I made sure I got to Bogie's first, arriving at 7:30.

"Hey, Jack," Billy greeted me. "Is everything all right?"

"Not really, but let's not discuss it now," I said. "I'm expecting a guest for dinner, Billy."

"A lady?"

"Yes."

"Mrs. Brackett?"

"No!" I snapped, and he stared at me curiously. "I'm sorry. No, it's not Mrs. Brackett, it's someone else. I'd like a good table, excellent service, and great food."

"In other words, you want the usual," he said.

"Exactly."

He patted my shoulder and said, "No problem, my friend. Put yourselves in my hands."

"When Karen sees this lady, she won't go for that at all," I told him.

"Figure of speech," he said, quickly, "just a figure of speech. Pick a table, and let me know when the lady arrives."

"Okay, thanks."

I took a table against the far wall, which was more

or less isolated from the other tables, and then sat at the bar to wait for Erica Steinway to arrive.

When she walked in Billy was standing at the other end of the bar, and I gave him the high sign. I went to greet her, and he was right behind me.

She was wearing a simple blouse and skirt, and her hair was down around her shoulders. She attracted every male eye at the bar.

"Hi," I said, taking both of her hands.

"Good evening."

I turned as Billy approached and introduced them.

"This is a lovely place," she said, following the introductions.

"Thank you. We have a table ready for the two of you, if you'll follow me."

He took us to the table I had picked out and held her chair for her.

"Thank you," she said.

"The waitress will be right with you to take your orders."

He was out of her line of view as he gave me the eye, which meant he approved.

"This is nice," she said when he left.

"Yes, it is."

"I take it you and the owner are good friends?"

"Very good friends," I said. "We have to be, he's letting me live in his back office for a while."

"Really? Why?"

"That's a long story," I said. "Let's save it for another time."

"If you wish," she said.

A waitress I didn't know came with a couple of menus and took our orders for drinks.

"May I inquire why you need my father's index?" she asked when we had our drinks.

"I have a man who might be able to go to New Jersey and pick out your father's collection, but he'd need that index to work from."

"I see. If the collection is there, then your job is over."

"Uh, yes," I said. I knew that even if the collection was not there, that my job was over. With the death of Jimmy the Dime, and the involvement of the Mafia, I didn't feel that I could stay involved in the search, or with Laura Brackett. I intended to heed the warning of DeLauro and stay away from both—only because I wanted to stay alive.

"Are you all right?"

She was sharp. She had picked it up on the phone, and now in my face.

"I have a confession to make," I said, and I went on to tell her that, even if the books were not found in Mr. Pulps' basement, I was withdrawing from the case—no matter how much Laura Brackett wanted to pay me—and I told her why.

"Then you're pulling out because you're frightened?" she said.

Not something a man wanted to admit to a lovely woman, but I said, "That's right."

She put her hand out and rested it on mine, and I looked up at her, having been staring at the tabletop the whole time I was explaining.

"Don't be embarrassed, Miles," she said. "May I call you Miles?"

"Uh, yes, sure," I said, having become flustered by her touch and her words.

"You have every reason to be frightened, and you would be a fool to continue. My God, in view of what's already happened, I'm amazed that you've kept on this far. More than that," she continued, "I'm impressed by the amount of courage it took for you to admit all of that to me. It couldn't have been easy."

I wondered if my gratitude for her words showed on my face.

"Thank you," I said, "doesn't seem sufficient somehow."

"And it's not necessary, either," she said. She removed her hand from mine and said, "Shall we order?"

"Why not?"

As we were doing so, Billy came rushing over to the table and said, "Excuse me, Jack, but there's a call for you."

"Who is it?"

He looked at Erica, then at me, and said, "It's Hocus. He doesn't sound good, Jack."

I looked at Erica and she said, "You'd better take the call, Miles. Go ahead."

162

I put down my menu and walked with Billy to the bar, where he handed me the phone.

"Hocus," I said.

"Jacoby," he said. "Uh, listen, I'm at your apartment—your old apartment."

"What are you doing there?" I asked. "That's not even your—"

"Jack, shut up and listen," he snapped. "You'd better get down here right away."

"Why, what's happened?"

I became aware of Erica's presence at my elbow, and I moved so that I could look at her. She smiled at me encouragingly.

"Hocus, damnit, what's wrong?" I asked when he didn't answer right away.

"Somebody...blew up your apartment, Jack," he said.

"What?" I asked, stunned. "My brother," I heard myself stammer, "w-what about my brother?"

There was another pause, and then he said, "We don't know, Jack. Uh, the fire department is still fighting the fire. He might have been inside, but we...we just don't know."

"I'm on my way."

Chapter Forty

Christopher Street was clogged with fire engines, police cars, crowds of people, and billowing black smoke when we arrived. I had tried to leave Erica at Bogie's with an apology, but she insisted on coming with me, and suggested that we not take the time to argue about it.

We caught a cab and promised him the world if he'd run every light in sight and still get us there alive. We made it—barely.

We found Hocus standing in front of my building, which was almost totally engulfed by flames.

"Jesus," I said, and Erica grabbed my arm and held it tightly.

"It was an old building," Hocus said, "and the fire spread very quickly."

"Anyone else—"

"The other tenants are accounted for."

"And my brother?"

He looked at me and I saw that his face was blackened by soot and smoke. I also noticed that his suit was in much the same condition.

"Jesus Christ, man, you didn't go in there, did you?" I asked him.

"It wasn't quite this bad when I got here," he explained, "and I had to—wanted to find out if you were inside. I got into the building, but I couldn't get into your apartment. I got most of the other people out, though."

"So you still don't know..." I said, letting it trail off.

He made a face, scratched his head, and said, "A couple of the other tenants said they saw your brother stagger in about an hour ago, in bad shape."

"Drunk," I supplied.

"Uh, yeah. Shortly after he got home, there was an explosion. Nobody saw him get out."

"Then he's in there," I said.

"Oh, Miles," Erica said, tightening her grip on my arm further.

"We're not sure—"

"Forget it, Hocus," I said. "They saw him go in and didn't see him come out."

I dry-washed my face with both hands, my eyes already smarting from the smoke.

"Hocus, could you get Erica—this is Erica Steinway, by the way, the lady I was bringing to see you tomorrow—"

They nodded to each other and I continued, "Could you get her somewhere where she won't have to contend with this smoke?"

"Miles," she started.

"Officer?" Hocus called out, beckoning to a uniformed cop.

"Go with him, Erica," I said gently. "I'll be along in a little while."

"Take the lady somewhere...cleaner," Hocus instructed the cop, using "cleaner" for want of a better word. "Get her some coffee."

She put her hands on my chest and the look in her eyes said more than any words could have.

"I'll see you in a while," she said, and followed the uniform away.

In spite of the situation, I couldn't help but think that this was just what I needed, extra complications in my life.

"Listen, Kid, why don't you just—"

"I'll stick around," I told him, staring up at the flames

as they shot out the window of my apartment. I only hoped that Benny was so drunk that he never knew what happened.

The guilt was the worst part of it all. Guilt over not having seen him or spoken to him in a while, but even more was the guilt I felt because he'd gotten killed because of me.

"It was meant for me," I said aloud.

"What?"

"That's supposed to be me up there," I said louder, "not Benny."

"What are you talking about?" he demanded. "We don't know what caused this yet. It could have been any one of a dozen things."

"Yeah," I said, "that's why when you called me you told me that some*body* had blown up my apartment."

"Uh, yeah, well, that's what comes from working homicide for so long. What I meant was—"

"We both know what you meant, Hocus."

"Jacoby—"

"Look, there's something I was going to tell you in the morning. Since we're going to be here a while, I might as well tell you now."

"What are you talking about?"

I told him about the incident at Knock Wood Lee's, and about finding out just who Laura Brackett's "Carl" really was.

"Shit," he said. "Cagey Carl? Are you sure?"

"I am now. I should have realized it much sooner; I might have been able to prevent this."

"You think Caggiano set this up?"

"What do you think?"

"I think if he did, the old man isn't going to like it," Hocus said. "I think maybe I should have a talk with the old man."

"You know Carlo, Sr.?"

"Oh, yeah, I know him. We know each other. I worked for him, years ago."

"You worked for Carlo Caggiano?" I asked, staring at him

"I was working undercover. This was before I was assigned to homicide. I was on the inside of his organization." His thoughts of those times were fond ones.

That was obvious by the look on his face. "I did him some harm, but I could never pin anything directly on him. That was one slippery old man."

"And junior?"

"Junior I don't know much about, but what I do know I don't like, and, from what I hear, neither does Carlo, Sr."

We both stared up at the fire again, watching the water from the fire hoses work futilely against the flames.

"I was going to dump the whole thing," I said then.

"The case?"

"Too many bodies, the Mafia, I figured I was in over my head."

"Sounds like a good decision to me," he said. "Let us handle it."

"Handle this?" I asked, gesturing towards the burning building with my right hand. "That's my brother up there, Hocus, not yours."

"If he's up there, Jack," he said. "Let's not jump to conclusions."

"He's up there, Hocus," I said, feeling it in my gut. "He's up there where I should be. Benny only wanted two things in his life, you know? First he wanted to be a champion, and when he didn't make it, he tried to make me a champion." I looked at Hocus and said, "I never made champion, and I guess I was never much of a brother, either."

"Don't let guilt get the best of you, Jacoby," Hocus warned me.

"I want to go and see Carlo, Sr. with you. Can you set it up?"

He stared at me for a few moments, then he said, "Let me see what I can do."

I nodded, and stared up at my brother's funeral pyre.

"They had me scared off, Benny," I told my brother, "but they should have quit while they were ahead."

I finally asked Hocus to have someone drive Erica back to her father's apartment, and then persuaded her to go.

"Will we still be meeting in the morning?" she asked, and then hurriedly added, "you don't have to, you know...."

"I'll be there," I assured her.

"Miles, I'm terribly sorry. I hope your brother was . . . not in there."

"Thank you, Erica," I said, no longer hoping for the same thing. I'd given it up already. "I'll see you tomorrow."

When she left I waited with Hocus and Wright until the fire department got the blaze enough under control for them to send a man into the apartment, wearing protective clothing and an oxygen mask.

"How'd you get down here, anyway?" I asked. "You're out of your element, aren't you?"

He frowned and said, "Not if you're right and your brother is in there." He looked at me then and said, "I got the call originally from one of the responding officers. He knew your brother, and he knew that I knew you."

"I'd like to talk to that officer," I said.

"What for?"

"I haven't seen Benny in a few days. Maybe he has."

"I'll put you together with him later," he said.

The fireman came out again, removed his mask, and began taking deep breaths. As smoky as the air outside was, it was nothing compared to what it must have been like inside, mask or no.

"Wait here," Hocus said.

As the fireman began to speak to the fire chief, Hocus approached them and began speaking. Another man, wearing a suit that was as smudged as Hocus's, also approached, and I assumed that he was a fire marshal; the shield pinned to his jacket was not NYPD.

They all spoke for a few moments, and then Hocus nodded to them and walked back to me.

"The marshals haven't been able to get a close enough look yet, so they can't tell what caused the fire."

"Hocus," I said, "what did the fireman say?"

He frowned and shifted his feet.

"Damnit, man, the shock to me would be if he wasn't there," I explained. "Is he in there?"

He hesitated, then nodded and said, "Somebody's in there. The body is pretty badly burned. The M.E. will have to make the final I.D., but—"

"—But who else could it be," I finished.

"I'm sorry, Jack."

"Yeah," I said, covering my mouth with my hand. I dropped my hand then and said, "Thanks, Hocus. I'm, uh, not going to wait until they bring the body out. I'll be in your office in the morning, you can give me the lowdown on the cause of the fire and all—if that's okay with you."

"Sure. Go home, get some sleep," he advised. "Don't do anything foolish tonight."

"Don't worry," I said, "I don't plan on doing anything foolish—not until at least tomorrow."

Chapter Forty-one

I took a shower when I got back to Bogie's, which by that time had closed. It was nearly three in the morning and I was exhausted, but I could not sleep. By eight o'clock I still had not slept, but I was covered with a cold sweat and took another shower before dressing. I could have taken ten showers and I still would have been able to smell the smoke from the fire that had killed my brother. Actually, my only hope was that the explosion had killed Benny, and that he had already been dead by the time the fire engulfed him.

I tried to have some breakfast in a diner, but my stomach wouldn't permit it. I left the food, paid for and untouched, drank the coffee, then left the diner and headed for the Seventeenth Precinct.

Hocus had left word at the desk to pass me through and he was waiting for me at the top of the stairs.

"You look like hell," he said. "You couldn't sleep?"

I shook my head; but he looked like hell, too, and I knew that he had not even had the opportunity to try and sleep.

"I've got coffee inside," he said.

"You're buying the coffee?" I asked. "I guess the M.E. verified it, huh? My brother's dead."

"Your brother is dead," he repeated.

I nodded to myself, then said, "Let's go get that coffee."

We went into the busy squad room, alive with the activities of a shift change. Detectives coming in and detectives going out, laughing as they fenced verbally. There was no reason for them to feel any sorrow just because I did—and come to think of it, the way I had treated Benny over the past months, what right did I have to feel any?

Yet I did. I felt something else, though, at the same time. I felt anger, but not a burning anger, the kind that makes you see red. What I felt was a cold, controlled anger and that scared me even more than anything that had happened since the case started.

"Jacoby," I heard Hocus call, and I became aware that it wasn't the first time he had said my name in the past few moments.

"What? I'm sorry."

"Just sit down, will you, before you fall down?" he said.

He sat behind his desk and I sat in front of it. I turned and looked at Wright, who was sitting at his desk, massaging his stomach.

"Drink your coffee," Hocus said. "We'll wait for your young lady to come."

"She's taking me out to her father's house, to look for the index that Kaminsky will need to identify the collection," I said.

"Good. I've already arranged with Detective Seidman in New Jersey to make an appointment with your man directly."

"That's good," I said absently.

"Damnit, man!" he snapped so suddenly that I jumped, yet he spoke softly enough so that no one else heard him. "It's not your fault!"

"Tell that to Benny."

"You saved him four months ago," he reminded me.

"Three and a half," I corrected him. "And that doesn't make the rest of it right. Is this what I saved him for, to die in my place?

"Suppose the explosion didn't kill him?" I asked. "He

had no idea why he was dying. If I hadn't saved him he'd be in prison now, but at least he'd be alive."

"That's crazy."

"Maybe it is," I agreed. "What did the fire marshal say?"

"A small incendiary device," he answered, "planted by someone who knew what he was doing."

"A pro."

"Yes. We're canvassing now, pulling in every torch man we know," he explained.

"Were you able to arrange a meeting with Don Carlo?"

"Tonight."

"With me along?"

"Yes, but you've got to let me talk."

"I can't promise I'll keep my mouth shut, Hocus," I said, "but I'll give it one hell of a try."

He looked past me at that moment and said, "Here's the lady, and she's early. That makes her pretty special, doesn't it?" he asked, standing up.

"She was special way before this," I said, but I didn't think he heard me.

Erica looked tired, but she wore it well.

"You look tired," I said, standing awkwardly as she approached.

"I didn't sleep very well," she admitted.

"Well," Hocus spoke up, "that puts you one up on us, Miss Steinway. I'm glad you could come today."

She looked at Hocus, said, "Thank you," and then looked at me again. "Miles?"

"It's all right," I said.

"Your brother?"

"He's ... dead."

She closed her eyes, then opened them and said, "I'm sorry."

"It's all right," I said again, inanely. "Erica, we're here to talk about your father, not my brother."

"Yes," she said in a low voice.

"Miss Steinway, I'd be glad to answer any questions you might have," Hocus said, "as the detective in charge of the case."

She switched her gaze from me to Hocus and said, "I, uh, don't have any questions ... really. I know you're probably doing your best to find out who killed him."

172

"Erica," I began.

"Thank you, Miss Steinway," he said. "That's very kind of you."

"Erica—"

"I've rented a car, Miles, so we can drive to the house. Can we go now?"

I looked at Hocus and shrugged helplessly. He would have answered any of her questions and done so honestly, but she had chosen not to ask.

"Meet me here at five," Hocus said to me, "and we'll go and see Caggiano."

"Right," I agreed. I took Erica's arm and said, "Let's go."

When we got down to street level she took the keys to her rented car and held them out to me.

"Will you drive?"

"Sure," I said, taking them.

"Can we not talk until we get there?" she asked. "I've got to organize my thoughts."

"I think that's a good idea," I said.

We drove the entire way in silence, and I used the time to do some organizing of my own thoughts as well.

Chapter Forty-two

When we got to Steinway's house in New Hyde Park, Erica handed the keys to me and I unlocked the front door.

Inside she said, "It's been years since I've been here."

"Did you grow up here?"

"No," she said, looking around. "After they were divorced, I lived with my mother, but I came here sometimes."

"How long ago were they divorced?"

"Oh, years," she answered, "ten or twelve, I guess. She died five years ago, and that was when I started traveling. I think my father preferred that to my coming to live with him."

"So he arranged for you to receive money whenever you needed it."

"Yes, through lawyers."

"Let's go to the room where he kept most of his collection," I suggested. "His index might be there."

"No," she said, "it would be in his den, on his desk, in a small file cabinet. I remember."

She led the way to his den and we went to his desk.

"Here it is," she said. It was a small desk-top, three-drawer file cabinet, with each drawer large enough for three-by-five index cards. We each took a drawer, and eventually met at the middle one, where we found the index cards for his pulp collection.

"Here are some rubber bands," she said, taking them from a desk drawer, and we wrapped the cards tightly together so I could drop them into the pockets of my windbreaker.

"I guess that's it," I said.

"Miles, could we talk?"

"Here's as good a place as any, I guess," I said.

"Here is the perfect place, as a matter of fact," she pointed out. "Do you still intend to stop working for Mrs. Brackett?"

"Yes," I said, "but my reasons are different now. She's involved somehow, and I don't want to have any responsibility to her as a client when push comes to shove."

"I'm glad to hear that," she said, "because I'd like to pay you to find out who killed my father."

"Let's sit down, Erica," I said.

We both avoided sitting behind the desk.

"Your father's murder is a police matter," I explained, "and they wouldn't take it too kindly if I started getting in their way."

"But you and Detective Hocus are friends."

"That's true, but remember I told you he's a good cop. He won't let friendship prevent him from having my license yanked if I get in the way."

"That doesn't sound very friendly."

"He's a professional, and he'll do his job. He'll catch whoever it was that killed your father."

"I'd feel much better if you were working on it," she said.

"Murder is not my game, Erica."

"You'll need some kind of income while you're working," she said. "I assume you are going to look for your brother's killer."

"That's different," I told her. "That is a personal thing."

"I understand," she said, and with her father dead she did understand. "My father and I weren't that close, but I think I know how you feel."

"Well, my brother and I weren't particularly close,

175

either," I explained, "but I suspect that we both feel the same things."

"Anger, sorrow...and maybe a little guilt?"

I nodded and said, "Try a lot of guilt. That explosion was supposed to kill me, not my brother."

"Miles, can I pay you to keep looking for my father's collection?" she asked then.

"That may not be such a long job," I pointed out.

"However long," she said. "Allow me to pay you for your time. You have to make a living."

She was right, and on top of that, it would help if I had some kind of an official status—as official as a private detective can have, that is—and that meant a client.

"All right, Erica."

"At your regular rates."

"Aw, shucks," I said, "I was going to double it."

"No, you weren't."

She should only have known what I was charging her father, which was just about double my regular fee.

"Let me write you a check now," she said. "How much would you need?"

I told her to write the check for one day's work and gave her the amount, but when she handed it to me it was for two days' work.

"Just take it and shut up," she said, putting her checkbook away.

"You're the client," I said, pocketing the check.

"You can also keep the car," she added. I would have objected except that I expected to be making another trip to New Jersey to deliver the index.

I looked at my watch and saw that it was after noon. I had to meet Hocus at five and I was wondering if I had time to drive out to New Jersey and deliver the index to Seidman or Abel before then.

"Maybe we'd better go back to the city," she suggested. "I know you must have a lot to do...and I know I've had enough of this house for the present."

"I'll drop you off at your apartment," I said, careful not to call it her father's apartment.

Again we didn't talk much during the drive back to the city, and when I dropped her in front of her building and got out, she said, "Will you call me?"

"As soon as I know something," I promised.

"Even if you don't," she replied. "Call me, Miles."

"I'll call."

I drove the rented car to my office and found out right away that having a car is not such a great thing in New York. I finally had to park it in a Kinney lot so I could go up to my office. Right after the drive to Jersey, I'd turn the car back in a hurry.

I went up to my office and started making phone calls. The first was to Hank Po, to tell him that we had finally found Jimmy the Dime Denton.

"But it hasn't helped you very much, has it?" he asked.

"No, it hasn't, Hank," I said. "A lot of things have been going on, but I really can't discuss them with you now. I just wanted to let you know that you could stop looking."

"All right, Jack," Po said. "Give me a call when you have time and we'll have a sit-down somewhere."

"Okay, Hank. Thanks for your help."

The next call I made was to New Jersey, asking for either Detective Seidman or Detective Abel.

"I understand that Detective Hocus has put you in touch with my expert," I said, when Seidman came on the line.

"Yes, he has. We've made an appointment for tomorrow morning, around eleven."

Well, that saved me a trip today.

"I have the index he'll need, so if you don't mind, I'll come by at eleven as well."

"Hell, I don't mind," he said. "Bring another lovely lady with you."

"Sure," I said. "I'll see you tomorrow."

I called Laura Brackett next, to call off our association. When she asked me why I was withdrawing from the case, I said, "You have some very nasty friends, Laura. Ask them."

"I don't know what you mean."

"Ask your friend Carl," I suggested.

"Carl? What's he got to do with you and me?"

"There is no more you and me, Mrs. Brackett, and that's what he had to do with it."

I was letting her think that I was completely withdrawing from the case, rather than just having switched clients. When she spoke to Carl, Jr., that's what she would tell him, and hopefully he'd be satisfied—for a while. Only time would tell if there would be another attempt on my life.

"I'm sorry, Mrs. Brackett, but I can't work for you any longer. I'll send you a bill."

"Don't bother!" she snapped, and hung up.

She hadn't argued all that much, so maybe she knew more than she was letting on. In any case, word would get back to Carl, Jr. that I had quit, and maybe that would keep him off my back for a while.

Chapter Forty-three

I was in Hocus's office at 4:45 and had to wait while he finished up some paperwork.

"What have you been up to?" he asked, putting down his pen and closing a folder.

"Just trying to get adjusted," I said.

"It's a whole new case for you now," he said.

"Yeah."

"Do you remember Hocus's number-one rule for being a good detective?" he asked.

I grinned and said, "Yeah, I remember." It was while I was trying to clear Benny of the murder rap that Hocus had told me about that rule. "Never investigate a case in which you are emotionally involved."

"You won't listen any more this time than you did last time, will you?" he asked.

"I did all right last time, didn't I?"

"Yeah," he said, standing up and taking his jacket from the back of his chair, "but there are exceptions to every rule. You ready to go meet Don Carlo?"

I stood up, took a deep breath, and said, "Yeah, let's go see the Godfather."

"He's not quite that, but he is a dangerous old man."

"And you and he are friends?"

Walking down the stairs he said, "Far from friends, but I pulled a fast one on the old man and he admires me for it."

"Where are we going to see him? At his home?"

"Little Italy," he told me, while we were leaving the building. "A men's club in Little Italy, with the Italian music playing, and all the old men sitting around talking about boccie ball and the old country."

As he started his car I asked, "Where's Wright?"

"He's working on something else right now."

He drove downtown and parked illegally on a hydrant on Hester Street in Little Italy. We were only two blocks from Knock Wood Lee's place. Not knowing if Hocus knew it or not, I kept the information to myself, but I found it disconcerting.

When we got out of the car I could hear the Italian music filtering down the block, but couldn't tell from where.

"Where to?" I asked.

"Follow the music."

He followed the music, and I followed him to a plain storefront that looked as if it had been boarded up. Hocus knocked on the door and when it was opened he showed his shield and said, "Hocus to see Mr. Caggiano."

The old man who answered the door flicked his eyes over to me, then back to Hocus, who said, "He's with me."

"Wait," the man said, closing the door.

"He didn't ask if you wanted to see junior or senior," I pointed out.

"Are you kidding? Junior wouldn't be caught dead down here. You'd most likely find him at Club Fifty-Four."

The door opened and the same old man appeared.

"Come," he said, swinging the door wide.

Hocus stepped inside and I followed. We were immediately braced on either side by two men.

"Easy," Hocus warned me. "Just give them your gun."

I watched as he turned his over, then pulled mine from the belt holster and presented it as well.

There were more than a few elderly men sitting around the room, and a small bar in one corner. The four men who had braced us were younger than the others, but they were still over forty. All eyes in the room were on us, and conversation was suspended for as long as we were there. The Italian music was coming from speakers set in the ceiling, and there was also a lone speaker outside, above the front door.

"This way," the old man who had answered the door said, and we followed him to a stairway leading up.

Walking alongside Hocus, I whispered, "You been here before?"

He shook his head, then said, "But I've met him in other places like it. Relax."

The old man took us into a room where there were five men. Four of them were standing in different parts of the room and their eyes fell on us as we entered. They were all between forty and fifty years of age.

The fifth man was sitting in a large, overstuffed armchair, and the chair was made to look even larger by the man's emaciated condition.

"Don Carlo," Hocus greeted him.

"Mr. Hocus," the old man replied in a reed-thin voice.

I was shocked by the old man's physical condition. The photos in the newspapers had always shown him as a large, robust man, but obviously they were using old photos. The man sitting in front of me was tall, but he was so thin that his clothes, though probably altered, still hung on him like rags. His skin had a decidedly unhealthy sheen to it, and his hair—what there was of it—was snow white.

I was willing to bet that an up-to-date photo of Don Carlo Caggiano had not appeared in the newspapers in nearly ten years.

"You are Mr. Jacoby?" the old man asked.

"Yes, sir," I said. In spite of his present condition, the man still had something—a presence—that commanded respect.

"The private eye."

"I prefer private investigator."

"I understand from Detective Hocus that you have had some dealings with my son."

"That's not exactly true," I said. After having been warned by Hocus to let him do all the talking, I was surprised that the old man was talking to me. "I've seen

181

your son twice, met and spoken to him just once, very briefly."

He nodded, then looked at Hocus.

"Why have you come to me?" he asked the detective.

"Jacoby was, uh, warned off a case of his by four men led by a man named DeLauro."

"DeLauro," the old man repeated, as if trying to place the name.

"When Jacoby indicated to them that he wasn't about to be warned off, his apartment was blown up."

"Has that been verified?" he asked.

"By the fire marshals, yes. A professional job."

"I see." Caggiano looked at me and said, "You seem unharmed."

"I wasn't in the apartment at the time," I replied, "but my brother was."

"And how is he?"

"He's dead."

"Unfortunate." He looked at Hocus and said, "Continue, please."

"DeLauro is one of your son's boys, isn't he?"

"I believe my son has a friend by that name, yes."

"We'd like to find him."

"Ask my son."

"I thought we would ask you first."

The old man turned his head to look out the window at the street below, then said, "I should have stayed in Italy."

He looked at Hocus again and asked, "Do you think my son blew up your friend's apartment?"

"I don't think you did it," Hocus answered.

"I would have no reason to," he said. "What reason would my son have?"

"He's involved in a case Mr. Jacoby is working on, and maybe one that I'm working on."

"What kind of cases?"

"Burglary and murder," Hocus said. "Maybe four murders."

Don Carlo closed his watery eyes and said, "I'm very tired. If you have questions concerning my son, you should ask them of my son."

"I just wanted to talk to you first, Don Carlo," Hocus

explained. "I wanted you to know that I'm looking for Carl, Jr."

"I do not think he will be hard to find," the old man said.

"Let's go," Hocus said to me.

"That's it?" I asked.

"Let's go," he said again, and I followed him out. We retrieved our guns and left the men's club.

"What did we find out?" I asked Hocus as we walked to the car.

"That the old man's not involved, and that he won't interfere if we get into an altercation with junior."

"He said all that?"

"Between the lines." He winked, and we got in his car.

Chapter Forty-four

When I got back to my office there were all kinds of messages on my machine, and it wasn't hard to figure out what had prompted them. Missy, Heck, Packy, all of whom had undoubtedly heard about the commotion on Christopher Street last night. I didn't return any of the calls because I wasn't ready to start accepting condolences yet.

Likewise, I refrained from calling Erica Steinway, because I had enough problems, and she was just too damned understanding and beautiful.

I touched the middle drawer of my desk, then left it closed and walked out of the office. There was nothing left to do but have some dinner and turn in. In the morning I had to drive to New Jersey, and Hocus was going to arrange for Benny's body to be moved to wherever I wanted it, as soon as I decided where that would be.

I walked across town to Bogie's where, over dinner, I explained to Billy everything that had happened.

"This changes the whole case for you," he said when I had finished.

"Yeah, it's personal now."

"Like it was that last time."

"I'm still in over my head, Billy, but I intend to learn fast," I said. "At least I don't have Don Carlo Caggiano to contend with."

"You're not even sure you have Carl Jr. to contend with."

"I'm sure he's involved with Laura Brackett," I said, "and almost dead sure he's involved with the book collection. Now the question is, What's his connection with the books?"

"Laura Brackett," Billy suggested. "Maybe by getting her the books he gets her, and he doesn't want you interfering. Maybe he sees you as competition for her."

"Put that way, it sounds like a contest between me, Carl, Jr., and Walter Brackett. Whoever finds the collection wins."

"Is Laura Brackett still your client?"

I shook my head. "I withdrew from the case."

"So you're working on your own, with your own money?"

"What money?" I asked. "No, I've got another client."

"That makes three so far on one case. Is that a record?"

"I'll look it up," I answered, "tomorrow. Right now I think I'm going to turn in."

I called the waitress over and paid the check. Billy stood up and said, "Karen and I are sorry about your brother, Jack. If there's anything we can do..."

"I know, Billy," I said, putting my hand on his shoulder. "Thanks."

"What about funeral arrangements?"

"Hocus said I could have the...body tomorrow, but first I've got to decide where to have it brought."

"Would you like me to look into a few places for you?"

Since I had to go to New Jersey in the morning, that wasn't such a bad idea.

"I'd appreciate it."

"Sure," he said. "I'll be glad to."

"Thanks. Good night."

I walked back through the kitchen to the office, thought about a shower, and then just decided to wash up. I'd shower in the morning, then go out and rent another car for the drive to New Jersey.

I went to sleep with my thoughts alternating between Benny, and Erica Steinway. I thought about her to avoid thinking about him.

And vice versa.

Chapter Forty-five

I got to Seidman and Abel's station house at 10:30 and asked for either of them. A young patrolman in a tan uniform directed me to their office on the second floor.

"Good morning, Mr. Jacoby," Seidman said as I entered.

Their squad room was the same as Hocus's, only on a smaller scale. I hadn't brought coffee with me, but what I saw—empty coffee cups all around—told me I could have, and built up some goodwill.

"Good morning, Detective Seidman." I looked around, saw a few men, but not Abel. "Where's your partner this morning?"

"He'll be along. So, I assume, will your expert."

"I certainly hope so."

"Do you have the index?"

I took out the three banded groups of index cards and dropped them on his desk.

"I'll need them back."

"I won't need them," he assured me. "Can I get you some coffee?"

"Thanks."

Abel arrived at a quarter to eleven, and my expert, Kaminsky, five minutes later. He looked more like a college professor than a mortician, and he kept rubbing his hands together as we talked about the collection. When I handed him the three packs of cards that comprised Steinway's index, he began to stroke them lovingly.

"Shall we get on with it?" Abel asked.

"By all means," Kaminsky said.

"Are you coming along, Mr. Jacoby?" Seidman asked. "I expect this will be at least an all-day affair."

"I might be able to help," I said, then had a thought and voiced it. "In fact, why don't I drive him over there, and then you two can stay here and catch up on whatever work you have on your desks?"

They exchanged glances and I said, "You're finished with the house, aren't you? No more prints to be taken, no more bodies to find."

"Yes, we're quite finished," Abel said. He looked at Seidman again, who nodded, dug into his pocket, and came out with a key.

"Here's the key to the front door. Just remember to lock up when you leave—whenever that is."

I took the key and said, "Don't worry. I'll call you when we're done and let you know what we came up with."

"Well, you can do that, sure," Seidman said, "even though whether you find the collection or not doesn't have much bearing on our case."

"Wait a minute," I said. "If we do find the Steinway collection there, that could mean that Battle and Denton were killed because of it."

"I suppose, but that's just one possible motive," Seidman said. "We have to keep an open mind."

"I guess you do," I said, deciding not to try and convince them. I was sure that the collection was the key, the common denominator behind all of the murders, and I was going to act on that assumption even if the police—in New York *and* New Jersey—were not.

"Could you use a hand, Mr. Kaminsky?" I asked.

"You saw the basement, Mr. Jacoby," Seidman spoke up, then turned to Kaminsky and said, "You will be needing help, Mr. Kaminsky. Take my word for it."

"I will gladly accept all the assistance I can get, but I would like to get started," the man said impatiently.

"I'll give you directions to the house from here," Seidman said, and I listened attentively while he did so.

"Okay, let's get going," I said to Kaminsky. "We've got a lot of work ahead of us."

Kaminsky nodded to the two detectives and we went out to the street.

"Do you have your car with you?" I asked.

"Yes, I do."

"Well, why don't we leave it here and go in mine," I suggested, and he agreed. There was nothing that he needed from his own car, so we climbed into mine and followed Seidman's instructions. We arrived at the house fairly quickly, and I parked the car out of sight behind it.

"The house itself is not very impressive, is it?" Kaminsky said as we got out of the car. "I mean, it's large enough...."

"Nothing about the house is impressive," I assured him. "Mr. Battle spent all of his money on his basement."

"Where he has all his books?"

"Where he had all of his books, yes," I said, correcting him. "Let's go inside, shall we?"

"By all means."

We went inside and I led him to the basement. His reaction was divided. He was delighted at some of the books he saw—pointing them out as he tiptoed among them—but he was horrified at the condition they were in. That is, that they were haphazardly strewn about the basement floor.

"This is ghastly," he complained, but in the same breath he said how wonderful it was to find this or that particular copy of Black Mask or Doc Savage, or whatever.

"Uh, don't you think we should get started?" I asked him as he picked up magazine after magazine until they started to pile up in his arms.

He stared at me over the stack of books he was holding to his chest and said, "Of course, of course. Where can I put these down?"

"Right there," I said, pointing to his feet.

"Yes, of course." He put the books down gingerly, and we got down to the business at hand.

Since he had a general idea of what the magazines looked like, I held the index cards and began reading aloud from them while he waded among the rubble.

Once we got into it, it began to go fairly quickly, and when I started reading and looking, the pace increased even more. We were up to a snail's pace now, zeroing in on tortoise.

After we'd been there for a few hours I thought I heard a noise and said, "Wait a second."

"What's wrong?" he asked from a squatting position.

"I thought I heard something."

"Mr. Jacoby," he said, and his voice sounded strange, "what is this?"

"What?" I asked, looking up at the ceiling, straining with my ears.

"This," he said, a bit more forcefully.

"Shhh," I said, looking at him in annoyance, and I saw what he was talking about. He had found the spot beneath the books where Leon Battle had been lying, and there was a large dried bloodstain on the floor.

"That's blood."

"Blood?"

"Quiet," I cautioned him, because now I was sure I had heard footsteps. Someone was moving around upstairs.

"Mr. Jacoby, I was under the impression that the owner of this house—Mr. Pulps—had simply, er, died."

"He was killed, Mr. Kaminsky," I said.

"Here?"

"Right here," I whispered. "There's someone upstairs," I added, "and I think we'd better be a little quiet."

"You mean he was murdered?" he asked in a whisper, "down here?"

"Yes. I'm going to shut the light."

He started to reply, but there was a sound upstairs like someone moving furniture and he clamped his mouth shut as his eyes opened wide.

"Are you telling me that whoever killed him might be upstairs at this moment?" he asked, pointing up.

"It's very possible," I answered. "Why don't you stay down here and I'll go up and check?"

"Shouldn't we call the police?"

190

"I would, but there's no phone down here," I said. I couldn't resist the dramatic flair of producing the .38 from the belt holster, but it seemed to bring the point home to him.

"I'll keep very quiet," he assured me.

"Good. Keep the light off until I come back."

"You, uh, will come back, won't you?"

"With a little luck," I said, and moved for the stairway.

From the amount of noise being made, there was no longer any doubt but that there were people upstairs, and they were apparently under the impression that they were alone in the house. They were making no effort to conceal their presence.

When I got to the top of the steps I felt silly and put the gun away. It would take something extreme to make me use it anyway. For all I knew, there could have been a couple of kids in the house, thinking it was deserted, or perhaps some kind of a large animal—a dog—had gotten in and was merely bumping into things.

In any case, I opened the basement door slowly until I had a crack to peer through, but I couldn't see anything from there. I did, however, hear the sounds more clearly, and a murmur of voices.

It didn't sound like a dog, or like kids.

I took a deep breath, eased the door open wider, and slipped through. From the sounds I surmised that whoever they were, they were in the living room, and they were looking for something.

"What the fuck are you looking under the cushions for?" an annoyed voice asked aloud. "We're looking for a lot of books, not just one. You ain't gonna find the fuckin' things under a seat cushion, you *gavone*."

"You call me that again, Rocco, and I'm gonna fix your face for you," a second voice said.

"You? You couldn't fix your cock."

"Rocco, I'm warning you...."

"Look, DeLauro ain't gonna like it if we come out here and get into a fight and break up the place, okay? So let's just keep looking."

"What's upstairs?"

"How the fuck I know what's upstairs? I never been here before. What's always upstairs? The bedrooms."

"Maybe we should go up and check."

"Maybe you should go upstairs and I'll go downstairs. I'd like to get outta here and get home in time for the Knick game."

"Fucking nigger sport," the second man complained.

"Hey, asshole, my kid brother plays basketball in college, so don't be calling him no nigger, okay?"

"Could we get this over with?"

"Go ahead upstairs, I'll check the basement," the first man said. I heard the second man pounding up the stairs to the second floor, and number one was muttering, "Basement stairs probably in the back, or in the goddamn kitchen. Where's the kitchen?"

I actually don't know if I would have made my presence known to the two of them, but since one was now heading for the kitchen, it didn't really matter all that much.

I pressed myself against the wall and as he came through the doorway from the dining room into the kitchen, I hissed, "Don't move."

He stopped and stiffened, then put his hands up shoulder high and said, "Be cool, fella."

"Oh, I'm cool, friend," I said. He could have been one of the men in Wood's place with DeLauro, but I wasn't sure. They'd all seemed interchangeable.

"Why don't you tell me what you're doing here?" I said.

"I couldn't do that, friend," he said. "That could cost me my job."

"Then I'll tell you. DeLauro sent you out here to search the house for Aaron Steinway's pulp magazine collection. Isn't that right?"

"You're tellin' it."

"Yeah, I am, I'm telling you to call your friend down, tell him you couldn't find anything in the basement, and then the two of you haul ass back to Manhattan and tell DeLauro that Jacoby was here and chased you home."

"Jacoby."

"Yeah, maybe we met once before, but I wasn't noticing faces then," I said. "Oh, and make sure DeLauro tells his boss, Carl, Jr., that I send my love. Also, tell Carl I'd like to talk to him, if he can find the time."

192

"Hey, pal, I don't know what you're talking—"

"Just deliver the message to whoever sent you here," I said. "Now get going."

"You know," he said, lowering his hands a bit, "you talk pretty tough. You got something to back it up?"

"Like what?"

"Like that gun you were carrying at that chink's place," he said. "You got that piece with you, Mr. Private Eye?"

"I don't need a gun for garbage like you, friend," I told him.

He started to turn around slowly, testing me. He was tall, over six feet, and beefy, and he thought his beef would pass for muscle. He had a smirk on his face as his eyes met mine, and when he threw his right I was more than ready for it.

I caught his punch on my left forearm and threw a right into his considerable breadbasket. He folded over and "whoofed" as the air rushed out of him.

"You ought to work on that belly, friend. It's much too soft, and I didn't even hit you that hard."

I bent over and took the gun out of my holster. Holding it against his nose I said, "Was this what you were looking for?"

His eyes widened, but I didn't know if it was from the effort to catch his breath, or from the sight of the gun. I patted him down and removed a gun from his shoulder holster. It was a .45, just the kind of gun a man his size would carry.

"I'll keep this," I said. "When I see Carl, Jr., I'll return it to him. What he does with it is his business."

He tried to say something, but he hadn't recovered his breath enough to carry it off.

"Okay," I said, "let's straighten up now. Call your friend down and get lost, and don't forget my message."

"You're a dead man, Jacoby," he said, finally straightening himself up.

"You know, it would be just as easy for me to turn you over to the cops out here."

"We'd be out in an hour."

"Sure, but think how embarrassed you'd be, and how angry DeLauro would be, not to mention Carl, Jr. Oh, and then there's Don Carlo—I had a nice chat with him the other day. I don't think he's too happy about the friends junior keeps. I think it's time for you to go, don't you, Rocco? There's a good boy."

I turned him around roughly and shoved him through the doorway into the dining room. His friend made it easy at that point by coming downstairs, saying, "Ain't shit up there. Hey, what's the matter with you?"

"My belly hurts," Rocco grunted, still rubbing it where I'd tapped him. "Come on, let's get the hell out of here."

"What'd you find in the basement?"

"I'll tell you in the car."

"Rocco, you okay—"

"Fuck, Richie, let's get in the goddamn car, okay?"

"Okay, okay," Richie said. They started for the front door with Richie complaining, "Jeez, you don't have to get so..." and then they were outside.

I moved to the front window and watched them get into their car, which they had parked right behind mine, and drive away. They must have thought that my car had belonged to the dead owner. Apparently, it never dawned on them that someone else might be in the house. Obviously, they knew the owner was dead, but I was puzzled now. If Carl, Jr. had had Battle and Denton killed, why hadn't his men looked for the collection then? And how did they expect to tell Steinway's books from the rest?

Feeling pretty good about the way I'd handled the whole thing, I holstered my gun and started back for the basement to let Kaminsky know everything was okay.

I didn't stop to think twice about the hole I'd put myself in with Carl, Jr. instead of turning the two men over to the cops. Sending a message back to Don Carlo's little boy had been a spur-of-the-moment decision, and now I had to live with it.

At least, I hoped I'd get the chance to.

194

Chapter Forty-six

It took some convincing to get Kaminsky to stay and finish his job, but by nightfall we were done and the answer was no.

"None of Steinway's books are here?" I asked.

"Oh, there are some books here that match his index," he said, "but I doubt that they're from his collection. They're not all that rare."

"So you're saying that they were probably here anyway."

"That's right." He started putting his jacket back on and said, "I'm quite sure that none of Mr. Steinway's books are here."

"What if the collection has been split up?"

"I doubt it," he said. "That collection is only worth something to another collector, and then only as a collection."

"So wherever the collection is, you're sure that it's still in one piece."

"Uh, so to speak, yes. Do you think we could leave this place now? I'm anxious to get back to Philadelphia."

"Yeah," I said, "I'm kind of anxious to get home myself."

"Shall we call the police?"

"No, I'll drop you off by your car and go inside and tell them what we found," I answered. "Let's get going."

I went up the stairs first, just in case Rocco and Richie had come back, but the house was empty—and safe—and we went out to the car and retraced the route to the station house without incident.

After seeing a rather nervous Mr. Kaminsky off, I went into the precinct and found Detective Seidman, once again sans partner.

"Well, all done with your inventory?" he asked.

"Yeah," I said, throwing the key on his desk, "and it was a bust."

"Didn't find your books, huh?" he asked, picking up the key and putting it in his desk. "Too bad. Guess your case is still open."

"All our cases are still open," I said, "and I think when we close one, we'll close them all."

"I guess that remains to be seen."

"I know," I said, "you and Hocus need a lot of convincing."

"We're cops," he said, as if that explained it.

"Well, thanks for the keys, anyway," I said. "I guess I'll get back to the city."

"Let me know if you find anything concrete that connects our cases," Seidman said. "Like I said before, we keep an open mind."

"Sure. Good luck."

On the way down the steps I passed Detective Abel, and wished him luck as well.

"Same to you, Jacoby," he said.

Outside, as I was walking to my car, I saw another car pull away and thought that it looked familiar. As I climbed behind the wheel of my rented vehicle, it dawned on me just where I'd seen that car before.

In front of Leon Battle's house, with Rocco and Richie driving away in it.

I knew I hadn't been tailed from the house, and they weren't waiting at the station house to tail me home, because they'd left first.

So what the hell were two of Carl, Jr.'s men doing at the Parlin, New Jersey, Police Department?

Chapter Forty-seven

When I got home it was too late to turn the car in, so I went straight to Bogie's and sacked out until nine in the morning, then returned the car and went to my office. On the couch in my office I caught another few hours sleep and woke up when the front door was kicked in.

"What—" I croaked, coming awake and face to face with Rocco and Richie.

"Hi, shamus," Rocco greeted with an evil grin on his face. As I struggled to get up off the couch he took a step forward and kicked me in the stomach. While I was nose to nose with the floor, trying to breathe, he said, "I owed you that one, Jacoby. Mr. Caggiano got your message and was only too happy to grant your request. He'll see you—as soon as you can drag yourself away."

He and Richie laughed at his little pun, but I was too busy throwing up to appreciate his humor.

They finally got tired of waiting for me to announce that I was ready. They picked me up and carried me to my office's small bathroom. I washed my face and mouth and had barely dried myself when they grabbed me and started for the door.

"Wait a minute," I protested.

"We don't have a minute," Rocco informed me, tightening his grip on my right arm.

"But I forgot something."

"You'll have to do without it."

I thought about my gun in the bottom drawer of my desk, and hoped that I could indeed do without it. At that point Rocco remembered that I had his gun and went through the desk until he found it. He glanced at mine briefly, but left it.

They "escorted" me down to a dark limousine where a driver sat with the motor running, and "helped" me into the backseat, keeping me between them.

"Go," Rocco told the driver.

Aside from the initial kick in the stomach they didn't try to rough me up. I figured their orders were to bring me, not to hurt me, but Rocco felt that the debt had to be paid.

"Where are we going?" I asked.

"You'll know when we get there," Rocco said. "I'd advise you not to talk, because it's taking all I got not to take you apart right here. Don't make it any harder."

The driver went up to Eighth Avenue, then turned north and drove all the way up to Seventy-fifth and West End. We pulled up in front of a restaurant called Goings On, and the driver turned off the motor.

"Let's go," Rocco said. He opened the door on his side and slid out. I followed, with Richie right behind me. So far neither man had shown a gun, but I knew they each had one, and they knew I didn't.

We went into the restaurant, which was on two levels. We walked through the first level, then went up four steps to the second. At a large table in the back of the room sat Carl, Jr.

There were some early luncheoners, but they were well spread out, and none had been given tables within earshot of Caggiano's.

Rocco and Richie walked me to the table, where Carl, Jr. sat reading the *New York Times*.

"You're a little far uptown, aren't you, Carl?" I asked, not giving him the first opportunity to speak.

"The old man may like it down there with the old wops, playing boccie ball and listening to music, but that's not my style," he said. "I felt it was time for a move up." He looked up from his paper and said, "Thank you for joining me for lunch."

"I didn't have much of a choice."

"Sit down," he said. When I did he added, "As I understand it, the choice for this meeting was yours."

"A little advance notice would have been nice."

"Oh, and I thought you'd appreciate the promptness of it."

"Yeah," I said, rubbing my stomach.

"Order whatever you like. Everything is good, and it's on me. As a matter of fact, I own the place."

"I'm not very hungry."

Carl, Jr. looked up at Richie, and then at Rocco, who looked away.

"That's all, boys. Go and sit at your table."

The two men backed away, and sat at a table far enough out of earshot, but close enough for safety's sake.

"I hope they didn't rough you up," he said, sounding sincere. "I told them no rough stuff."

"Rocco just paid a debt," I said. "No big deal. He had it coming."

A waiter came over and said, "What would you like today, sir?"

"Would you like me to order for you?" Carl, Jr. asked.

"Just some soup," I said. "My stomach's a little jumpy."

He ordered lobster for himself and told the waiter to bring me some French onion soup.

"We have some talking to do," he said when the waiter had left.

"I guess we do."

"I'm going to talk first," he said, "and it might do you a world of good to listen. Okay?"

"Okay."

"Number one, I warned you away from Laura Brackett because I intend for the lady to be my wife. Number two, I warned you away from searching for Steinway's damned books because if I get them for her, I think she'll marry me."

"What about her husband?"

"That's over."

"So you're telling me that you don't know where the books are."

"That's right."

"And you didn't kill anyone?"

"That's right."

"Including my brother?"

He stared at me for a few seconds, then said very deliberately, "That's right. Look, Jacoby, I don't want to be the object of a vendetta. It will interfere with my business. I did not have anything to do with blowing up your apartment. If I had wanted you dead, you'd be dead."

"Do you have any ideas?"

"About what? The books?"

"My brother."

"Look, you'll pardon my bluntness, but I don't give a rat's ass who killed your brother, but I do want those books. I'll pay you to find them for me."

"I don't give a rat's ass about the books," I said. "I want my brother's killer."

He digested that a moment, then said, "All right. I'll keep my ear to the ground. If I come up with anything about your brother's murder, I'll give it to you."

"I guess I can go that far on the books," I agreed.

"Laura must not know that you're still looking for them, though," he said. "I want you to give them to me, and I'll give them to her."

"After which she'll be eternally grateful and marry you," I finished.

"That part is none of your concern," he said, then raised one eyebrow—I hate people who can do that!—and said, "Or is it?"

"It is not," I assured him.

The waiter brought lunch, and as soon as I smelled the onion soup I decided to stay and eat it.

"Let's talk fee," I said.

He took an envelope out of his inside breast pocket and laid it on the table, then began to attack his lobster.

"There's more than enough there for a retainer," he said.

It struck me that I must have been coming close to the record for clients on one case—four, by this most recent count.

I started to reach for the envelope, but he said, "Take it and look at it at your leisure, Mr. Jacoby. I guarantee you won't be disappointed."

"I'm sure I won't be," I said. I folded the envelope in half and put it in the pocket of my windbreaker.

"Not to ruin your appetite," he said then, "but I should warn you that I expect you to make me the same guarantee. Your future health may well depend on it."

Boy, there was an appetite enhancer for you.

Chapter Forty-eight

After lunch, Carl, Jr. had his driver take me back to my office, without his twin bully-boys, Rocco and Richie.

Before I left he said, "You can reach me here or leave a message anytime, Jacoby. The phone number is in the envelope. Do you have any leads as to the whereabouts of the magazines?"

"Not a one," I said. "The few I did have didn't pan out. There's something you should know, though, Mr. Caggiano."

"What's that?"

"Retainer or no retainer," I said, "my first priority is to find my brother's killer. If it's you, I'll be coming after you."

He grinned at me and said, "I'll be right here, Mr. Jacoby—but you won't find that the case, I can assure you."

"For your sake, I hope you're right," I said.

"Funny," he replied, "I was going to say the same thing to you."

In the car I asked the driver, "Could you drop me off somewhere other than my office?"

"I was told to take you wherever you wanted to go," he replied.

That was perfect. I gave him a street corner in the Village on which to drop me, and when he'd pulled away and driven out of sight, I walked the block to Packy's.

"Jack," he called out when I walked in.

"Draw me a beer, Packy, will you?"

"Sure, Kid," he said. When he brought it he said, "Geez, Kid, about Benny—"

"I know, Packy," I assured him. "I know."

"How're you doing?"

"Oh, considering it should have been me up there instead of him, I'm doing just fine."

"Jack—" he started to scold me, but I didn't give him the time.

"Had he been coming in here, Packy?"

He hesitated, then said, "I know you told me not to serve him, but yeah, he was in here most every day. He blew that twenty-five you gave him and then I started giving him credit. I'm sorry, Jack...."

"Forget it, Packy. How much did he owe you?"

The big man shrugged and said, "I forgot to keep count."

"Come on, Packy."

"Forget it, Jack. When's the funeral?"

"Oh, shit," I said, putting my hand to my forehead. "I forgot all about—I'm suppose to make arrangements to have his body picked up."

"Want me to do it?"

"No, I've got somebody checking out funeral arrangements, I've just got to get on it. There's been so much happening."

"You ain't looking for his killer, are you, Jack?"

"Yeah, I am."

"Let the police—"

"One way of looking at this, Packy, is that I'm looking for *my* killer. That bomb was meant for me, and now I've got to find the guy who had it planted before he can try for me again."

"Very unselfish of you," he said wryly, because he didn't believe that was my number-one reason.

Someone else came in and bellied up to the bar, and Packy went to serve him. I took the opportunity to take out the envelope Carl, Jr. had given me and check out the contents. The amount on the check was five thousand. That would keep me going for a while; and something struck me as ironic.

If it turned out that Carl, Jr. was the man behind Benny's death, then he was financing his own funeral.

Chapter Forty-nine

I called Billy Palmer from Packy's, intending to start making plans to have Benny's body moved from the morgue, but his reply surprised me.

"Plans have been made already, Jack."

"What do you mean? By who?"

"It was Missy's idea. She called here looking for you, and when I told her that I was checking funeral homes, she asked me to allow her to make the arrangements. She called Hocus and got his okay to have Benny's remains picked up."

In doing that, Hocus had stuck his neck way out, but he knew Missy was a friend of mine, and he knew that I was going to be preoccupied.

"I hope..." Billy started, and I knew he was wondering if he'd done the right thing.

"It's all right, Billy. You made the right decision, and I thank you for it. I guess I've got a few of my friends to thank."

"I'm glad I was able to help," Billy replied.

"I'll see you a little later. Thanks again."

As soon as I hung up I dialed Heck's office, and Missy answered.

"Missy, I called to say thank you. I didn't expect—"

"I know you've got your mind set on one thing, Jack," she said, interrupting me. "I wanted to help, and so did Detective Hocus. He was very nice."

"He can get like that sometimes," I said. "Missy, where and when will the, uh—"

"The funeral and burial will be at the same place as Eddie's was, Jack. I didn't think you would mind."

"No," I said, feeling a little stunned, "I don't mind. Thank you, Missy."

About four months ago Missy had been convinced that Benny had killed Eddie, but she had helped me in my investigation anyway. When I found out that Benny was innocent, she was very upset. I think she saw this as a way of finally making it up to me—and having him buried in the same place as Eddie was like icing on the cake. The only one who might not have appreciated it was Benny himself. He had never liked Eddie, because he thought that working for Eddie was keeping me from reaching my potential as a boxer.

"It'll be tomorrow morning, Jack, at ten o'clock."

"All right, Missy. I don't know how to—"

"Forget it," she said. "We're friends."

"Yes," I said, "we are. I'll see you tomorrow."

"Heck wants to talk to you. Hold on."

I hung on for a few moments, and then Heck's voice came at me over the line.

"Jack, I can't tell you how sorry I am about your brother."

"I appreciate that, Heck. Thank you. What's up?"

"I'm reading Aaron Steinway's will today. I thought you might want to be here."

"Who'll be present?"

"Just his daughter. You could act as a witness."

"What about his partner?"

"Separate arrangements were made through their corporate attorney. I will act jointly with that attorney in the disposition of their business. There's no reason for Brackett to be here. Will you come?"

"Only if it's okay with Erica," I said.

"Uh, Erica...has already consented," he said. "You and she...got along, did you?"

"We did," I said. "She's okay. What time do you want me?"

206

"At three."

"I'll be there, Heck. Thanks."

I hung up and called Hocus next.

"I wanted to thank you for what you did."

"What'd I do?"

"Don't get cute. You released my brother's body to Missy. You went out on a limb."

"No further than Dr. Mahbee did. He signed your brother out."

"I'll send him a box of cigars or something."

"What about me?"

"You'll get paid back," I told him. "Count on it."

"Promises, promises. How did things go in Jersey?"

"That depends."

I told him the whole story without holding anything back.

"You know you could have had those two goons arrested," he said when I finished.

"Sure I know it, but then who would have brought me this morning's invitation?"

"Uh, what invitation is that?"

So I told him about my "invitation" with Carl, Jr., leaving out the part about the kick in the stomach.

"He hired you?"

"Yep."

"That doesn't make sense."

"Maybe he just wants me working for him instead of against him," I suggested.

"But why would he even bother? If he tried to kill you before, he could simply try again."

"If it was him."

"What? Did I hear you right?"

"Yeah, well, maybe I'm giving him the benefit of the doubt," I said, defending myself. "He did sound awfully convincing this afternoon."

"You think Carl, Jr. is lovesick and is trying to win the lady's heart?"

"It happens to all of us, Hocus," I said. "Who knows, it may have even happened to you, once upon a time."

"Don't bet on it."

"Anyway, I guess you know the funeral is tomorrow, in Queens."

"Same place as Eddie Waters's, right? I remember. I'll be there, Jacoby."

"I appreciate it...and everything else."

"Let's hang up before one of us gets sloppy," he said. "See ya."

I hung up and kept my hand on the phone, wondering who else I had to call. I played back my answering machine, but the only messages on it were from the people I'd already spoken to.

With one exception.

Erica Steinway.

She had left a message asking that I call her at my earliest convenience. I tried to think of a few reasons why I couldn't call her right at that moment, but when I came up empty I picked up the phone and dialed her number.

"Erica, it's Miles."

"Hello, Miles. How did it go in New Jersey?"

"It didn't."

"The collection wasn't there?"

"No, it wasn't."

"That's too bad. Uh, has Mr. Delgado spoken to you about the reading of the will?"

"Yes, he has. I told him that I would attend as long as you consented."

"And I did."

"So I'll be there."

"Good, I'm glad. I'll, uh, see you at three then?"

"At three," I agreed, and we hung up.

I felt like a jerk. She had obviously been waiting for some kind of an invitation, most likely dinner, but I hadn't asked—and the reason I hadn't asked was in my desk drawer.

The presence of the letter in my desk was making me very gun shy when it came to other women. Even my relationship with Tracy, which was once a very comfortable, yet informal one, was beginning to change. Now there was Erica, and I felt myself drawn to her, but pulling away.

Maybe it was time for me to put the past where it

belonged, behind me. Tearing up that letter would be the first step in that direction.

So, naturally, I left the letter in the drawer where it was, took the .38 from the bottom drawer, and left the office as if it were on fire.

Chapter Fifty

When I walked into Heck's outer office, Missy came over, kissed my cheek, and gave me a powerful hug.

"I'm sorry," she said, and I could feel her tears against my own cheek.

"Thanks for everything, honey," I said, hugging as good as I got. She felt good, up tight against me like that, and I wondered why I had never set my sights on her as a . . .

"They're both inside, waiting for you," she said, pulling back and looking at my face. "Let me know if there's anything else I can do, okay?"

"Sugar, you've done more than enough," I said. I kissed her softly on the mouth, then went into Heck's office.

"Jack—" he said, rising quickly when he saw me.

"Sit back down, Heck," I told him. "I appreciate it, but I've had more than enough sympathy."

I walked to where Erica was sitting and put my hand on her shoulder. She covered mine with hers and looked up at me.

"I'm glad you came," she said.

I gave her shoulder a light squeeze and said, "Do you want to get on with it?"

"I want to get it over with," she said.

"Heck?"

"We might as well begin."

I sat down and Heck opened and read Aaron Steinway's will.

There were no surprises. Except for the business, he had left everything he had—money, stocks, house, and he specified the pulp magazine collection—to his only child, his daughter, Erica Steinway, to keep or dispose of in any way she saw fit.

"'Not being a man given to shows of emotion,'" Heck finished reading, "'I hope this will make up for the attention she did not receive while I was alive.'"

He put the document down and looked at Erica.

"It's all yours, Miss Steinway."

"Attention," she said, shaking her head. She looked at me and added, "He never said anything about love, though."

"I don't think he could, Erica," I said, "and he knew it. Maybe he did what he thought was the next best thing."

"Sure," she said.

Heck folded the will up and put it away, then asked, "What will you do now that you're a wealthy young lady?"

"I don't know," she said. "I guess I'll have to find out just how wealthy I am first."

"I have the name and address of your father's personal accountant," Heck said. "I'll have my secretary give it to you."

"What about the business, Heck?" I asked. "Do you think she'll get any of that as well?"

"I doubt it," Heck said, and then looking at her he added, "and I don't really think she'd want it, anyway."

"I've no desire to take over my father's business affairs," she said. "His partner can have it all."

"Well," I summed up, "I guess that means that Walter Brackett pretty much made out like a bandit, doesn't it?"

The question—rhetorical though it was—hung in the air for a short time before Erica said, "Do you think he killed my father for the business?"

"I don't know," I said. I switched my glance from one

to the other and said, "Maybe I've been wrong all this time. Maybe your father's murder had nothing to do with the pulp magazine collection."

"I'm sure the police have already acted on that assumption," Heck said. "I'm sure Detective Hocus has worked the case from all angles."

"You're telling me to leave it to Hocus," I said to Heck.

"That is what I am telling you, Jack, yes," he said. "You have said time and time again that murder is not your game."

"I know that, Heck," I replied, "and it isn't. But this is different. Benny's death is tied to Erica's father's death."

"Do the police—does Hocus feel that way?"

"Hocus is a cop; he deals in hard facts, physical evidence," I explained.

"I understand that," he told me. "As an officer of the court, I also deal in facts and evidence."

"Well, I'm not a cop and I'm not an officer of the court, and I feel that the two deaths—and the two in New Jersey—are all tied together."

"With the missing books."

"Right."

"But you just admitted that maybe Aaron Steinway's murder had nothing to do with the books."

"I'm confused, Heck," I admitted, standing up, "and I'm groping around for answers."

"Then maybe you need help."

"Maybe I do," I said. "I'm still new to this business—fairly new, anyway." I scratched my head and said, "Maybe I've got to lay it all out for somebody and see what they come up with. Maybe I'm too close."

"Don't look at me," Heck said, holding his hand up, "I'm not a detective."

"No, I guess not," I said, "you're just a damned good lawyer."

"Why, thank you very much." He touched his intercom and said to Missy, "Would you get Miss Steinway the name and address of her father's accountants? Uh, Boffa and Donohue, I believe the name of the firm is. Thank you."

212

"Come on, Erica," I said, taking her by the elbow, "I'll walk out with you."

She stood up and extended her hand to Heck, who rose and took it.

"Thank you for everything, Mr. Delgado," she said. "You've been very kind."

"My pleasure, Miss Steinway. If I can be of any other assistance, please do not hesitate to call upon me." He executed a very elegant little bow from the waist, of which I was very envious, and then we went out to Missy's desk to get the address of the accountants.

"Thank you," Erica said to Missy, putting the piece of paper with the information in her bag.

"You're welcome," Missy said, in a very professional tone. I had the distinct impression that she didn't care too much for Erica Steinway.

She looked at me and said, "Jack, I'll see you tomorrow. I'll be there early."

I leaned over to kiss her and said, "Thanks, honey."

"Watch yourself, huh?"

"I promise," I assured her.

We left and rode down in the elevator in silence. When we got to the street I said, "Would you like to get some coffee, or something strong?"

"Coffee, I think," she said. "I need to have a clear head in order to digest all of this."

"Yeah," I agreed sourly, "so do I."

Chapter Fifty-one

When we were settled in a nearby luncheonette named after a Greek philosopher, with coffee in front of us, she looked at me thoughtfully and said, "She cares for you, you know."

"Who?"

"Mr. Delgado's secretary."

"Missy? We care for each other," I said. "We lean on each other, cry on each other's shoulder."

"Do you love each other?"

"Probably, in a way," I said.

"Like brother and sister? Lovers?"

"Friends."

"Why not lovers?" she asked, staring at me curiously. "She's a lovely girl."

"Yes, she is," I agreed, "but if we became lovers, who would we go to when we needed someone to talk to?"

She thought about that a moment, then shook her head and said, "I'm not sure I understand that."

"I'm not sure I do, either," I said, "so why don't we just add it to the list."

"I'm sorry, I didn't mean to pry."

I touched her hand and said, "You weren't, Erica. I've just got a lot on my mind—as you must."

"Yes," she sighed, "I suppose I do. I have no idea of how large my father's fortune is, Miles. What will I do with all of that money?"

"Not to mention his holdings."

"Stocks, and things like that?"

"Yes."

"I suppose I could just sell them. I have no interest in business. I guess with the cash he had, if I convert his holdings to cash, I'd be set for life. I could continue to travel..."

"Do you want to do that?" I asked as she trailed off.

"I don't know what I want to do," she said. "It's all I've really done, actually. I don't have a profession, and my father always sent me enough money so that I wouldn't have to work."

"Working might be a totally new experience for you," I suggested. "Some people like it."

"Most that I've known don't," she said.

"Most haven't had the advantages you've had," I pointed out, "but I don't think we're here to talk about this."

"What are we here to talk about?" she asked. "You and me?"

"No," I said quickly—too quickly.

She frowned and said, "I thought that perhaps...you felt something, too."

"I did," I said, then, "I do—but I can't..."

"You're not making any sense, Miles."

"That's my problem," I said. "Lately I can't make sense out of anything. Not your father's death, not my brother's, not my...feelings."

"I understand," she said. "First things first."

"You want to know who killed your father, don't you?"

"I suppose I...should, shouldn't I?"

"And I should find out who killed my brother while trying to kill me," I said.

She touched my hand and said, "I guess we'll just have to take care of what we should do, and then talk about what we want to do."

I looked at her hand resting on mine and wondered if I'd be able to decide what I wanted.

I hoped so. At least, I thought I knew what I didn't

want. I didn't want to let my brother's murderers get away, I didn't want to remain a slave to some emotions from my past, and I didn't want to remain a slave to a sealed envelope in a desk drawer.

I guess knowing what you don't want is the first step towards knowing what you do want.

Chapter Fifty-two

The funeral had a small but somewhat surprising turnout. The people I expected—Hocus, Missy, Heck, Packy, even Erica—all attended, but there were a couple of people I hadn't expected.

"Jack," Willy Wells said, taking my hand and shaking it. "I'm sorry about this."

"Thanks for coming, Willy."

"Benny and I had our differences, but this—" he said, shaking his head.

"I appreciate it, Willy. Thanks."

"That's okay, Kid. Anything I can do to help."

The other attendee who surprised me did not show up at the funeral home but at the cemetery, which was where I had first met him, when he attended Eddie Waters's funeral.

"Well, look who's here," Hocus said, spotting the man first. I looked away from the grave and saw who he was talking about.

"That's a surprise," I said.

"I've got a strong feeling of déjà vu," Hocus said.

"I know what you mean."

When the ceremony was completed, people started heading back to the city.

Heck and Missy came over and said, "We're giving Erica a lift back to the city, Jack."

Heck added, "I think there's someone here who wanted to talk to you."

I looked in the direction he was indicating and there was the second surprise attendee at the funeral, walking over to us now.

"Hector," he said, greeting Heck and shaking hands.

"Walker," Heck said, greeting Walker Blue in return.

Blue turned to me and I tried to hide my surprise at seeing him there.

"Jacoby, you have my condolences," he said, extending his hand.

Walker Blue and I met for the first time after Benny was arrested for Eddie Waters's murder. He was tall, with a long-jawed face and neatly trimmed, gray hair. He looked good for a man in his early fifties.

I took his hand and shook it, saying, "Thank you for coming, Mr. Blue." There was something about the man—much as there was about Don Carlo Caggiano—that commanded respect, but he surprised me once again.

"Just call me Walker, Miles," he said. "Can I give you a ride back to the city?"

"I, uh—" I started, and looked around, but Heck and Missy were walking towards Erica, and Hocus had gone. "Sure, Walker, I'd appreciate it."

"This way to my car."

For some reason I expected him to have a chauffeur-driven limo, but he was driving his own car, a Mercedes. Blue was perhaps the highest-priced independent investigator in the business, and very probably the best.

Once we were on the highway I spoke my mind.

"What's this all about, Blue?"

He kept his eyes on the road and said, "I understand you're having some problems with a case."

Then it dawned on me.

"Did Heck put you up to this?"

"He did mention your problem to me, yes." When I didn't say anything he said, "He is just trying to help you."

"I realize that."

"Look, Hector and I are friends, but that's not the only reason I agreed to talk with you."

218

"Oh, no?"

"I've had some dealings with the Caggiano family," he said, "both senior and junior. I wouldn't mind helping pin something on them."

"I see."

"Also, I don't like what happened to your brother. I realize it was meant for you, and I like that even less."

"I'm touched."

"We're in the same business, Jacoby."

"Bad for business if one of us gets bumped off?" I asked.

"Something like that," he said. We drove in silence for a few moments and then he said, "Hector tells me you're smart, Jacoby. I believe him, but your brother was killed, and you may be too close to this case to see the obvious."

I was still hesitant to talk to Blue, of whom, despite my acknowledgment of his status, I had had an almost unreasonable dislike since meeting him. His superior attitude rubbed me the wrong way—probably because he'd earned the right to it.

"I'll tell you one more thing, Jacoby," he said, "and then we'll just forget it; I'll tell Hector I tried."

"What is it?"

"Some years ago I lost my wife," he said. "She was murdered, blown up in a car with a bomb that was meant for me. I tried to solve that case for months, but it wasn't until I talked about it, to a friend, that I was finally able to find her killers." He hesitated, then said, "We're not friends, Jacoby...but I know how you feel. I'd...like to help you, if you'll allow me to."

I looked at his profile, which was stony as his eyes remained straight ahead, but his tone was sincere, and I believed him.

I started talking, laying it all out for him, starting with Steinway's hiring of me to find his book collection.

"What do you think?" I asked when I'd finished the story.

"I think your instincts are good," he said.

"You think it all connects?"

"Like you, I feel it."

"I knew it," I said with feeling.

"Take it easy," he cautioned me. "Just because we feel it doesn't make it so."

"No, but I feel a whole lot better about it."

"As far as your investigation has gone," he added, "I don't know that I would have done it any differently. I might have been able to find Jimmy the Dime for you if I'd known—"

"How?" I asked, interrupting him.

"I think I have better contacts than you have, Jacoby," he said, "only because I've built them up over a longer period of time."

"If I could have found Jimmy before he was killed..."

"No sense in that now," he said. "Have you considered that the pulp magazines might be a coincidence?"

"But you just said you felt there was a connection."

"So I did," he said, "but suppose the connection is not the magazines?"

"Then what could it be?"

"Find that out, and you may solve your case."

Chapter Fifty-three

Walker Blue dropped me off in front of my office and our parting was somewhat awkward. I had no illusions about why he had offered me his help. On a scale of one to ten, his reason for wanting to help me carried about a three, while his personal reasons—wanting to see Caggiano brought down, and a favor to his friend Heck—carried at least tens.

"I'll get in touch with some of my contacts and see what I can find out," he said as I opened the door to get out. "Maybe we can discover where Jimmy the Dime was the whole time you were looking for him."

"You don't think he was in Jersey?"

"Just because he died there doesn't mean he was there all along," he pointed out.

"I guess not." I got out, then stuck my head back in and said, "I owe you, Walker."

"You don't owe me anything," he said. "If I come up with any information, I'll pass it on to Hector."

"That's fine," I said. "Thank you again."

"No problem," he said, then I shut the door and he pulled away.

When I got up to my office I called Erica Steinway right away and made a date for dinner. I told her I'd pick her up at seven. She asked if we could go back to Bogie's again, and I gladly agreed.

"I'm comfortable there," she said, "and I know you are."

"Billy will be glad to hear it," I said.

"A-are you all right?" she asked. "I mean, after this morning."

"I'm fine," I assured her. "We'll talk later on. I need your help."

"You've got it."

"We'll talk about it, okay?"

"Okay."

I hung up, and sat back in my chair to go over what Walker Blue had said. Other connections, other common denominators in all the cases, other than the magazine collection.

What else connected Aaron Steinway to Carl Caggiano, Jr.? An investment counselor and a Mafia Don's son. Look for another connection.

I dialed Heck's number, hoping he and Missy were back in the office by now, and hadn't stopped off somewhere for lunch after leaving Erica at her apartment. I got lucky, and Missy answered.

"Hi, Missy."

"Jack? Is everything all right?"

"Everything is fine. I'm in my office—"

"Damn you, why don't you go somewhere and get drunk, or something?" she demanded.

"I don't have time, dear," I said patiently.

"Did Walker Blue help?"

"You knew about that?"

"I, uh, yes, I heard Heck talking to him—"

"All right, all right, never mind. Yes, he did help. He started me thinking on another track, and that's why I'm calling you."

"How can I help?" she asked.

"I need someone to do some heavy research, someone with the patience for that sort of thing. Someone with an orderly mind, intelligence—"

"Someone susceptible to your particular brand of bull?" she asked, interrupting me.

"Right."

"Sounds like me, all right."

"Then you'll help?"

"As long as I don't have to do anything illegal, immoral, or fattening."

"I have to clear it with Erica Steinway—"

"Why her?"

"You don't like her, do you?"

"I don't know," she answered honestly. "Do you?"

"I...do, yes. Look, here's what I'd like you to do, providing I can clear it with her. I want you to go to Aaron Steinway's accountants' office and find out for me what other businesses he was involved in."

"What am I looking for, specifically?" she asked, and I knew she was making notes.

"Connections between Steinway and the Caggiano family. Connections, or potential connections, anything that looks...odd."

"All right, Jack," she said. "I think I know what you want."

"What?"

"Dirt."

"You're too smart," I said. "Gorgeous women are not supposed to be that smart."

"If I do find dirt, Jack, and it's on Steinway, how do you think Erica Steinway is going to feel about it?" she asked, ignoring my compliment.

"That's what I've got to find out before I give you the go ahead, Missy," I said. "That's what I'll find out tonight, at dinner."

"Jack," she said, sounding as if she were going to bring something up that she found distasteful, "have you read or gotten rid of that letter yet?"

I hesitated and then said, "No, I, uh, haven't had time."

"Don't you think you'd better do one or the other, so you can get on with your life? I mean, if you like Erica—"

"Missy, I can't deal with this now," I cut her off. "I've got too much else on my mind."

"You're going to have to deal with it sooner or later," she said. "It's been too long since you received that letter. This isn't...healthy."

"I will deal with it," I said, "I promise...and I love you for your concern. I'll call you tomorrow."

223

"If you want me to go ahead, call me at home tonight. Don't worry about the time. And Jack..."

"Yes?"

There was silence, and then, "Never mind. I'll talk to you later."

"Thanks, Missy."

We hung up and I made a mental note to mention to Heck that I needed Missy to do some research for me. I knew he wouldn't mind, but I had to clear it with him anyway.

Missy was right about one thing. I had to deal with Julie's letter one way or another, and deal with Julie's memory, but as far as I was concerned, I had other things to deal with first besides my personal life.

Although finding my brother's killer was pretty damned personal.

Chapter Fifty-four

I was sitting at the bar at Bogie's, listening to Billy Palmer apologize unnecessarily about not being able to attend Benny's funeral, when Erica walked in.

"There's your lady," Billy said, spotting her first.

"Okay," I said, sliding off my stool. "Don't let me hear any more apologies, Billy. You've done more than enough for me already."

He smiled and said, "All right."

Billy greeted Erica as if she had been a regular customer since they'd opened, and led us both to the same table we'd had last time.

"He's a nice man," Erica said after we were seated.

"And a good friend."

"How are you?"

"I'm fine," I assured her.

"You have nice friends," she told me, "and they all worry about you."

"Really?" I asked, remembering that she had driven back to the city with both Heck and Missy.

The waitress came over and we ordered drinks, a beer for me and white-wine spritzer for her.

"Missy gave me quite a talking-to on the way back from—on the way back to the city this morning."

I looked at the ceiling and said, "I'm sorry. Missy can get pretty protective at times."

"Don't apologize," she said. "She was just concerned about you."

"What did she want from you?"

"Well, in effect, what she wanted to know was what my intentions were," she answered, looking amused.

I covered my face with my right hand and peered at her from between my fingers.

"No," I said.

"She said you had been through a rough time a few months ago, and she didn't think you were quite ready to handle any pressure." She stared across the table at me and asked, "Have I been pressuring you, Miles?" She was half serious.

I took her hand and said, "Erica, I've been under a lot of pressure of late, but none of it has been coming from you."

"Whoever the girl was who hurt you, she's got an enemy for life in Missy," she said, "and I don't believe that she likes me all that much either."

"Well, Missy is—"

"—in love with you," she finished.

I shook my head and said, "No, you're wrong. She was in love with my best friend and he was murdered a few months back." I explained briefly the relationship between Eddie and Missy, and then my relationship with both of them. I told her how Missy had quit when I decided to keep Eddie's office open, and how we saw each other from time to time, but as friends.

"You can go on believing that if you want to, but—"

"Erica, can we go on to something else?"

"Okay," she agreed readily, "but ignoring the problem won't make it go away."

"I'm finding that out," I said. More times than one I had opened the top drawer of my desk, hoping that—somehow—the letter from Julie would be gone, and I wouldn't have that decision to make anymore.

"As I told you before, I need your help," I said.

"Doing what?"

"I want to look into all of your father's businesses, all his holdings, and I'll need written authorization from you for his accountants to open his books up to me."

"Why?" she asked. "Will that help find his murderer?"

"I'm hoping that it will turn up another link between your father and Carl Caggiano. I need a common denominator between all of these murders, other than the pulp magazines."

"Now you don't think they had anything to do with his death?"

"I'm just looking for another angle," I said.

"If you think it's important," she said, after a moment.

"I think it might be," I said, "but there's also something else."

"What?"

"If I find dirt on Caggiano, there's a chance some of it might get on your father. I want you to be aware of that before you give me your decision."

She played with her wineglass while she considered what I'd said, then looked at me and asked, "This is important to you as well, isn't it? I mean, towards finding your brother's killer as well as my father's?"

"Yes, it is," I answered, "but I want you to decide what's important to you."

She shrugged and said, "You mean, like my father's reputation?"

"Whatever, Erica. Just be sure of what you want."

The waitress came and Erica had some time to deliberate while we ordered dinner.

"I didn't know my father very well, Miles," she said after the waitress took our orders and left. "When you come right down to it, I really don't know how important it is to me to find out who killed my father—other than because he was my father."

"What are you saying?"

"I'm saying that I want you to do whatever you have to do to find out who killed your brother, and tried to kill you. If you have to get a little dirt on my father's name, then that's the way it will have to be."

"Just be sure of what you're saying, Erica," I advised her.

"I'm sure, Miles."

"Okay, then. After dinner we'll go into the office and write something up that Missy can show the accountants—"

"Missy?" she asked, frowning curiously.

"Yes, she's agreed to do the research I need. She's much better at that sort of thing than I could ever be. She knows what to look for, and has the patience to look for it."

"She sounds quite remarkable."

"She is," I said. "She'll do a thorough job."

"I'm sure."

"There's one other thing I'll need, Erica."

"What is that?"

"The key to your father's house. While Missy is checking out his accounts, I'd like to look around the house."

As she handed me the key, dinner arrived and we suspended our "business" conversation to eat, discussing other matters over the meal. We poked and prodded at each other, trying to find out more, and I sensed a reluctance on both parts to open up. Perhaps, given more time and different circumstances...

After dinner I paid the check and we went to the bar for an after-dinner drink with Billy and Karen Palmer. Erica and Karen got into a conversation while I pulled Billy off to one side.

"I have to go into the office to type something up. Could you keep Erica entertained?"

He looked past me at Erica and his wife, who were now deeply involved in some sort of discussion and said, "I think she's already pretty entertained. In fact, if you're not back soon Karen may talk her ear off."

I looked at both women and said, "She seems to be holding her own."

"Why don't you take her into the office with you?"

"I, uh, think it would be better this way," I answered evasively.

"It couldn't be that you're afraid to be alone with her, could it?" he asked with a grin. "Maybe you don't trust yourself?"

"I just want to get the thing done, Billy, that's all," I snapped.

"Okay," he said, backing off, "we'll keep an eye on her for you."

I put my hand on his shoulder and said, "Thanks,"

trying to ease the bite my voice had held a moment ago.

As I walked through the kitchen to the office, I admitted to myself that Billy might have been right. Maybe I was afraid to be alone with her in the office. Or maybe "afraid" wasn't the word. Maybe at this time, with my personal life and feelings as uncertain as they were, a better and more accurate word would have been... "unwilling."

I typed a short note saying that, as her father's heir, she had no objection to the "holder of this note" examining all of her father's business holdings. I dated it, left a space for her to sign, and went back to the restaurant.

Leaning on the bar she signed her name to the document, and I folded it and put it away in my pocket.

"I'll give it to Missy tomorrow," I said. "Come on, I'll take you home."

"Home?" she said, looking surprised. "All right."

We said good night to Billy and Karen and went out to find a cab on Eighth Avenue. After flagging one down, I gave the driver her address and leaned back in the backseat, leaving enough room between us for another person.

"Are you expecting someone else?" she asked.

"No, why—" I began, then stopped when I realized what she meant. The space between us was purely unintentional and I hadn't really been conscious of it until she spoke up.

"I'm sorry, Erica," I said. We both moved a bit to cut down on the space, but there was still some room between us.

"Don't apologize," she said. "I had been wondering why you hadn't come on to me yet, and the talk I had with Missy this morning explained it a bit. I guess it takes a while to get over being hurt, doesn't it?"

"Yes, I guess it does."

"It's an experience I haven't had," she informed me, "but I think I can understand it."

"Erica..."

"Don't," she said. "Don't apologize, and don't try to explain. It isn't necessary. Just let me tell you something. I had intended all along to come back, find out

229

how my father died, settle his estate, and then go back to Europe."

"And now?"

"Now I find that I may have a reason to stay here," she said as the cab pulled in front of her building. "No need to ask you if you'd like to come up."

"Erica—"

She leaned towards me, turned my face towards her with two fingers against my cheek, and kissed me softly on the mouth.

"No pressure," she said, "remember?" She stroked my cheek, then got out of the cab and walked into the lobby of her building.

"Hey, Mac," the cabbie said.

"Yeah, what?"

"Ain't you going up?"

"What's it to you?"

"Nothing," he said. "Just that if I had a date with a lady that foxy, I sure wouldn't let her go up to her apartment by herself."

The driver was a young guy in his early twenties, and his license identified him as Max Harris.

"Look, Max, you get paid to drive, not to tell me what a jerk I am. Take me back to where you got me."

" 'Scuse me," he said. "You're the boss."

I folded my arms and sat back. We had only gotten a few blocks away when I said, "Besides, I already know what a jerk I am."

He shrugged his shoulders and said again, "You're the boss."

Chapter Fifty-five

Before turning in I called Missy and arranged to meet her at Heck's office the next morning. At the same time, I'd clear it with Heck for her to take some time off to do me the favor.

After that meeting I stopped at my bank to deposit Carl Jr.'s check, then rented a car and drove out to Aaron Steinway's home in New Hyde Park, where the whole business first started.

I let myself in the front door and walked to his collection room. All of his other books and magazines were still there, getting dusty now from neglect. It would have been nice if the pulp magazine collection could have suddenly shown up back where it belonged, but that wasn't the case. The shelves where it had rested were still very much empty, and I left that room and walked to his library, where we had cemented our association.

I began with his desk, checking through all of the drawers. I found check stubs, carbons of certain agreements, balance sheets, folders bearing names of people and companies. If I had known exactly what I was looking for it would have been a lot easier, but since I didn't

I was forced to look at almost every piece or slip of paper that I found in his drawers.

I went through the canceled checks first. They were all from Steinway's personal account, and most of them were for bills. There were, however, three checks made out to three different people, none of whom I was familiar with, but I also found three checks for a thousand dollars each made out to cash. The three made out to cash I pocketed, and then I started going through the papers.

I found indications that Steinway was involved in one way or another with at least three businesses other than the one in which he was partners with Walter Brackett.

He was partners in a flea market that was located in Staten Island; he had some involvement—I couldn't tell how much, or on what level—with a publishing firm; and he owned a couple of race horses.

I picked up the phone and dialed Hank Po's number, hoping I'd find him in. When I didn't, I dug in my wallet for the phone number at Debbie's, and found him there. I gave him the names I had of the two horses, and asked him to check into the ownership of the animals for me. I gave him the number where I was, just in case he was able to get the information that quickly.

The carbons and Xeroxes of balance sheets were from the flea market, which, to my unpracticed eye, seemed to be doing fairly well. I wondered if any of his other businesses would be left to Erica, as well as his personal fortune.

I used my arm to sweep the top of the desk off, pushing the papers and checks into the top drawer, and what didn't fit I put in the other drawers. I didn't feel I had the time to be neat.

There were a couple of file cabinets in the room, and I went through those next. Each drawer was stuffed with file folders that appeared to have something to do with his investment and counseling business. I found a folder for Michael Walsh, but there didn't appear to be anything of interest to me in it. Steinway had simply made some investments for him, some of which apparently had panned out, and some of which hadn't.

The folders didn't appear to be in any particular order that I could see—and they certainly weren't in al-

232

phabetical order. The Walsh folder was in a top drawer. A few minutes later, in the bottom one, I found another folder that surprised me.

It was labeled: CAGGIANO.

And it was empty.

I took the folder out and opened it wide, just on the off chance that there might have been a small slip of paper inside, but it was completely empty. I looked at the label again, but there was no indication whether the folder had been made up for Caggiano senior or junior.

Somebody must have gotten there before I did and emptied the folder out, but why empty it and leave it behind? Why not just take the whole thing?

I put the folder back and closed the drawer. Supposedly the drawer contained folders on all of Steinway's clients. Why would a Mafia Don—or his son—go to an investment counselor? Surely the Mafia was not short on ways to launder money. Something wasn't right here.

I took the folder out again, and then chose two or three at random and compared the labels. They looked as if they had been typed on the same machine. They were stick-on labels, which would be typed, then removed and stuck on the folder. They peeled off easily, so that folders would be available for reuse. Taking advantage of that, I peeled off the label in question, and then two others as samples, found an index card, and affixed all three labels to the card. I then put the card in my pocket with the three canceled checks.

I looked around to see what else there was I could look through, but aside from taking all of the books off the shelves and shaking out the pages, I had pretty much finished with that room.

I stepped out in the hallway outside the door and stood with my hands on my hips. Some canceled checks, and file-folder labels. Not much of a haul. I decided to look through the rest of the house, just on the off chance that there might be another desk or file cabinet somewhere, but the time I put into that proved to be wasted. There were no other such items of furniture in the house, and I finally left with my small haul.

I got into my rented car and examined the items I had removed from the house once again. The three checks were virtually identical in handwriting and amount. The only thing that differed were the dates, which were each about a week apart, starting two weeks before Steinway left town. The third check could have been one of the last things Steinway had done before being killed. In fact, if the date on it was correct—the handwriting was awful—then it was dated the exact day that he died.

Which was very odd indeed.

I put the items back into my pocket, started the car, and headed back to town. The case was beginning to take on a new slant. I was looking forward to whatever information both Missy and Hank Po had been able to dig up for me. Depending on what that turned out to be, it was starting to look as if there were some sleight of hand going on behind the scenes.

Chapter Fifty-six

During the drive back to the city, things started falling into place for me, which was the way Eddie had always told me it would happen. "When it's right," he would say, "the pieces will all of a sudden just fit"; and that's what they were doing.

Some of them, that is. For the rest, I'd have to talk to Missy, Hank, and, finally, Hocus.

I dropped the car off at the rental agency, then walked to the Seventeenth Precinct. I waited to be announced by the front desk and then went up to the squad room. It was late, but Hocus was at his desk, as usual.

"Well," Hocus said, standing up from his desk, "how did you get along with Mr. Walker Blue?"

"As a favor to Heck Delgado, he did me a favor," I explained. "He gave me the benefit of his great experience."

"Well, there's no denying he's good at his job," Hocus admitted grudgingly.

"No, he showed me that," I said. "He gave me a new way to go, which is why I'm here."

"Don't tell me, let me guess," he said. "You're here to tell me where to go."

"Don't tempt me," I said.

We both sat down and I took the index card with the labels from my pocket and handed it to him.

"What's this for?"

"I'd like to borrow your lab."

"Oh sure," he said, dropping the card onto the desk top. "Take what you need."

"I'm serious," I said. "I want to know if those labels were typed on the same machine and by the same hand."

He looked at me, then picked up the card and examined the labels.

"They look to me like they're from the same machine."

"Me, too, but what I really wanted to know is if the same person typed them all."

"Where'd you get these?" For the first time he read all of the labels, and when he read the last one he said, "Caggiano?" in surprise and then asked again, "Where *did* you get these?"

"From Steinway's house," I answered. "He's got a file cabinet full of folders on all of his clients."

"His clients? Caggiano? Junior or senior?"

"Just what it says there."

"What was in the folder?" he asked eagerly.

"Nothing."

"What do you mean, nothing?"

"I mean it was just an empty folder. That's what started me thinking."

"About what?"

"Why would somebody empty the folder, then leave it behind, with the name tag on it?"

"I don't know. Maybe they just didn't think."

"Or maybe they thought very carefully."

He frowned at me when I paused and said, "Come on, come on, don't make me ask."

"What if someone put the empty folder there just to make us think there was a connection between Steinway and Caggiano," I suggested.

"In which case that particular label would most likely have been typed out by someone else and not Steinway." He flicked the card with his finger and said, "Okay, I'll send it to the lab with a rush on it."

"Great," I said, standing up. "Thanks."

"What will you be doing in the meantime?"

"Looking for other connections between all of our cases. Yours, mine, and New—" and then I stopped short because something occurred to me.

"What now?"

"New Jersey," I said, finishing my original statement. "When I had that run in with Caggiano's men at the house in Parlin, later on I saw their car pulling away from the station house."

"What the hell did they do, go and swear out a complaint against you?"

"I don't know," I said. "But it was odd then, and it strikes me now as even odder."

"Are you sure it was the same car?"

"I'm sure."

"I don't like what you're implying," Hocus said coldly. He hated even the sniff of a bad cop—even if it was a New Jersey cop.

"I'm not implying anything, Hocus," I argued. "I'm just telling you what I saw. Draw your own conclusions."

He worked hard to keep his mouth shut for a few moments, then said, "I'll call you as soon as I have something back from the lab."

"I'll let you know if I come up with anything else."

"You'd better," he said, making noises like a tough cop. He was upset, and I decided to back off, so I just said good-bye and left. I noticed that his partner, Wright, had witnessed the exchange, and was vigorously rubbing his stomach as I left, as if what I had said had upset his ulcer.

Come to think of it, my stomach didn't feel all that well either.

Chapter Fifty-seven

I went to Erica's apartment house and she cleared it with the doorman to let me come up.

"Here's your key," I said when she opened the door.

"Come in," she said, taking it. "Can I get you something to drink?"

"Coffee," I said. I noticed that the door to her father's den, where I had found his body, was closed. She saw me looking in that direction and explained.

"It's the only way I could stay here."

"I'm surprised you can stay at all."

"I'm not that squeamish, Miles," she informed me. "Sit down and tell me what you found."

"While you get the coffee, I'd like to use your phone."

"Of course. I'll be right back."

I dialed Hank Po's home number, and when he didn't answer dialed Debbie's, but he wasn't there either. She said that she hadn't seen him since he spoke to me earlier. I gave her Erica's number and told her I'd be there for a short time, otherwise he could call my office or Bogie's.

I called Heck's office next, but Missy wasn't back from the accountants' office yet.

"I'm sorry to be taking her away for so long, Heck," I said.

"Don't worry about it, Jack," he answered. "She's the best secretary I ever had and she's got this place running so smoothly that I can afford to do without her for a day—but only one day."

"Is she going to stay on permanently?"

"I'm going to ask her, but the decision is hers."

"Great. I knew you two would get along. Could you tell her to call me as soon as she gets in?" I gave him Erica's number just in case she came back in the next few minutes.

"I assume this is of some importance," he said.

"I think I'm getting close to the answers I want, Heck," I said, "but a lot depends on what Missy finds for me."

"Well, good luck."

As I was hanging up, Erica came in with a tray bearing a pot and two cups.

"What did you find at my father's house?" she asked with great interest.

"Some odds and ends that just may or may not mean something," I answered.

"Like what?"

I told her about the checks, the labels, and the empty file folder.

"Did your father ever have a secretary?"

"Not at home, I don't think."

"Wait a minute," I said, taking out my wallet.

"The coffee's on the house," she said, watching me curiously.

I fished in my wallet until I found Walter Brackett's phone number, then dialed him at his office. While listening to it ring I said, "Your father's partner should know if he ever had a secretary at home."

It rang a few more times before a secretary picked up, and I asked for Brackett.

When Brackett came on I posed my question to him, and he said, "Aaron has never allowed a secretary into his house that I know of. In fact, he allowed very few women in his house at all."

"All right. Thank you, Mr. Brackett."

"What are you investigating now, Mr. Jacoby?"

239

"I'm working on the same case, Mr. Brackett."

"That infernal collection?"

"The same. Thank you, again."

I hung up and said to Erica, "No secretary."

"I guess that's important."

"It could be."

"I've had calls from several lawyers," she said.

"About your father's businesses?"

"Yes. They are holding separate documents for the distribution of my father's separate business interests."

"Then I guess you have a few meetings to go to."

"Yes, I do, but—"

"But what?"

"I think I'd like to have someone with me, to advise me."

I didn't know if she meant me or not, but I had a better idea anyway.

"That'd be Heck Delgado," I told her. "You couldn't have a better man in your corner."

"Would he do it?"

"Of course. Your father was his client, and in going with you he's still looking out for your father's interests. On top of that, I'll ask him to do it."

"I'd be very grateful to both of you," she said. "I know I'm going to need some guidance over the next few days."

"And you'll get it," I promised her.

"That takes a load off my mind." Her voice sounded relieved.

"Okay," I said, standing up. "Now it's time for me to keep working towards taking a load off mine."

She stood up and put out both her hands, which I took. She held mine tightly and said, "Be careful, Miles. We have some things to discuss when we both get settled."

I squeezed her hands back and said, "We'll talk."

Out in the hall I took a deep breath and let it out slowly. I put Erica out of my mind, because there was no room for her there now, and decided to go to my office where I could sit in total silence and concentrate.

Ha!

Chapter Fifty-eight

I was preoccupied as I entered my office and didn't realize anything was out of wack until the door slammed
behind me. It didn't usually do that unless someone
helped it. I turned around and saw that there were two
someones in the room with me, and they were both Carl
Caggiano's men.

"Inside," one of them said.

We walked from the outer office to my office, where
Carl, Jr. was seated behind my desk. DeLauro was also
in the room with him, and now that made five of us.
Nice and cozy.

Carl looked up from my desk where he was reading
something and said, "I'm here for a progress report."

"No report," I said.

"Did you cash my check?"

I nodded.

"Then I get a progress report."

I shrugged and said, "No progress."

"That's not what I'm paying you to hear."

"You're paying me to find that collection," I said,
"and I haven't found it yet. That's called 'no progress.'
Do you want a 'no progress' report?"

He looked back down at whatever he had been reading, then back at me, and asked, "Have you found your brother's killer?"

"Not yet."

"You sound confident that you will."

"I'll find him."

"I hope you're that confident about finding that collection."

"Don't you think you'll be able to take Mrs. Brackett away from her husband without it?" I asked, leaning on my desk. In doing so I saw what he was reading and froze.

"You're an odd man, Mr. Jacoby," he said when he saw my reaction. "Take your mail, for instance. Here you've got a letter postmarked about two weeks ago, and you keep it in your top drawer, unopened."

"Put it back," I said coldly.

"I don't usually read other people's mail," he said, picking the two-page letter up off the desk. I recognized Julie's neat handwriting and made a grab for the letter. As he pulled it away, two sets of hands grabbed me from behind and pinned my arms.

"I find this very curious," Caggiano went on. "This letter is very interesting. All of this drivel about loving you and needing you...from your brother's wife?" He put the letter down, refolded it, and put it back in the envelope. "You know," he went on, "if the police ever saw this letter, it might start them thinking."

"About what?"

"About who had a very good motive to kill your brother," he said.

I felt my face flush and the two men holding me must have sensed something, because their hold on me tightened about 50 percent.

"You better hope these two jerks are strong enough to hold me," I told Caggiano, "because I'm about to tear your head off."

DeLauro took a step or two towards circling my desk, but Carl, Jr. stopped him.

"I could take this letter and see that the police get it, Mr. Jacoby," he said, then opened my top drawer and dropped the envelope back in it, "but I won't." When I didn't ask him why, on cue, he said, "Do you want to know why?"

"I want you out of my office."

He stood up and DeLauro backed up to let his boss by.

"I'll tell you why," Carl, Jr. said, coming around the desk. "I want you to believe that I didn't kill your brother. By sending that letter to the cops, I could make sure that they concentrate on you and never think of me. Think about it."

I didn't have to; it made sense.

He flicked his hand and both of my arms were suddenly free.

"I hope to hear from you very soon, Mr. Jacoby."

DeLauro led the way out, and Carl, Jr. followed, with his two strongarms behind him.

"Hey," I called.

They all turned and Carl, Jr. said, "Yes?"

"Did you know Steinway?"

"I'd seen the man, but never actually met him."

"Brackett?"

"We had some...business dealings."

"Were they investing your money for you?"

He smiled and said, "I don't need anyone to invest my money, Jacoby."

"That's what I thought," I said. "You can go now."

DeLauro took a step towards me, but Carl, Jr. put his hand on the man's chest and looked amused, then signaled them all that they were leaving, and they filed out.

I moved around behind my desk and almost unwillingly sat behind it. I pushed the chair back away from the desk until my back was to the wall and stared at the top drawer. The letter was open, which made it a whole new ball game now. All I had to do was take it out and read it. Carl, Jr. had given me a few words from it, but who knew if he was telling the truth.

There was only one way to find out. I pulled my chair back up to the desk and started to open the drawer, but the phone rang just then, and I answered it instead.

"Yeah?"

"Jack, that you?" Hank Po's voice asked.

I relaxed a little and said, "Yeah, it's me, Hank. What have you got?"

"Your man owns three horses," he said. "Up until a

couple of months ago all he had was two cheap claimers, but then he bought a class horse from another owner, and he's been doing all right with him. He's a two-year-old, won a couple of baby stakes before Steinway bought him, and he's made over three hundred grand since. Might be one of the winter book favorites for the derby."

"For somebody else, maybe. No co-owners on any of his horses?"

"Nope."

"Okay, Hank, thanks."

"You want to know who he bought the horse from?"

My brain must have been scrambled, or I would have asked that question myself.

"Of course," I said, feeling foolish. Caggiano had shaken me up with that damned letter. "Who did he buy it from?"

"If I tell you that the horse's name is Cagey Carl, would that give you a clue?"

"You mean—"

"Right. Steinway bought the horse from Carl Caggiano...junior!"

Chapter Fifty-nine

"How was the sale handled?" I asked.

"Hah," he said, "you've redeemed yourself with that question. There was an intermediary."

"Then they never met each other?"

"Not during the sale."

"Who was the intermediary?"

"Walter Brackett."

"Okay," I said. "Okay, that might explain how Laura Brackett happened to meet Caggiano. He was in her husband's office, working on the sale, and she dropped in. Maybe he heard them arguing about the collection, and he took a liking to Laura Brackett."

"I've seen her picture," Hank said, "and who could blame him?"

"Right. This lends credence to a theory of mine," I said, and then told him about the empty file folder marked "Caggiano" that I'd found in Steinway's drawer.

"So, as far as you know," he summed up, "the closest these two men have ever come is during the sale of the horse."

"Right. They were on the same floor of the same building, but somehow never got into the same office."

"Then that means that someone definitely planted

245

that folder in the house, hoping to implicate Caggiano."

"Or just keep the attention away from himself."

"The same person who stole the collection?"

"Probably the same person who physically stole the collection," I said, "but somebody paid him."

"And you think *that* somebody is behind the murders?"

"Maybe Steinway discovered that it was him who had the books stolen and he killed him. Maybe he killed Jimmy the Dime because he knew who he was, and he tried to kill me because I was on his trail."

"And what about the other guy who was killed in Jersey?" Hank asked. "What did you call him, Mr. Pulps?"

"Leon Battle, yes. That one's a little harder. Maybe he was involved in the theft after the fact."

"You mean fencing the collection?"

"Or hiding it for a while. Somebody once mentioned that to me, about a library being the best place to hide a book."

"Makes sense."

"I've got some more checking to do, though. This helped a lot, Hank. Thanks. Send me a bill."

"Don't worry, I will. Take care."

"Right."

I hung up the phone and a half a second later it rang. I picked it up and it was Missy.

"Hi," she said. "I got that information for you."

"About Steinway's other businesses?"

"Yes. What do you want first?"

"I want to know if he's ever been in business with the Caggiano family."

"No."

"That was fast. Don't you have to check your notes?"

"I anticipated the question, Jack."

"You're incredible, but maybe you should give me company names, partners' names, and I can check with Hocus—"

"I've already checked on whether or not any of the names are Caggiano family fronts, and the answer is no. Jack, I haven't been able to find any business connections between the Caggianos and Aaron Steinway

246

and, believe me, I looked. That's why it's taken me so long to get back."

"You're a wonder, Missy."

"I know. It's a gift."

"I owe you more than a dinner, honey," I said. "Thanks."

"Just be careful, so you're around for me to collect," she said, and I promised that I would.

I broke the connection and immediately dialed Hocus's number at his office.

"What are you, psychic?" he asked.

"Did you get anything back from the lab?"

"I just got it," he said. "Both labels were typed by the same hand, except for the one marked 'Caggiano.' The impression of the g's, or something, were heavier than on the others."

"That about wraps it up, Hocus."

"Wraps what up?"

"Caggiano had nothing to do with the theft of the books, or the murders."

"Well, that's fine," he said. "Can you come down from cloud nine long enough to answer a question for me?"

"Sorry," I said, reining in my excitement. "What's the question?"

"If they had nothing to do with it," he said, "who did?"

That had the effect of a bucket of cold water being thrown on me.

"I still don't know," I said glumly.

"Well, when you find that out, you can call me and we'll get all excited together. All right?"

"Yeah, sure."

He must have heard the depression in my tone, because he said, "Well, look on the bright side. You're not dealing with any of the Caggianos, so it won't matter if your life insurance lapses."

"I don't have any—" I started to say, but then I stopped short and started to get excited again. "Insurance," I said.

"What?"

"I've got to go," I said. "I've got to see a man about insurance."

"You don't need—" he was saying when I hung up on him.

I called Missy back and asked her, "Do you still have your notes?"

"Of course—" she said, but I didn't give her a chance to finish.

"How deeply did you probe into Steinway's businesses?"

"Deep enough," she said, sounding puzzled. "What do you need, Jack?"

"Insurance," I said. "All businesses have to be insured, right?"

"Well, of course, but—"

"I want to know who insured his businesses, Missy. Have you got that?"

"Do you want all of the companies' names?"

"They're not insured by the same company?"

"No, there are several—"

Undaunted, I said, "What about the man, the insurance man? The one through whom Steinway did his business. Did he use the same man every time?"

I gave her a moment to scan her notes, and then she said, "Yes, as a matter of fact he did. How did you—"

"What's the man's name?" I asked, enjoying the rush of excitement I felt.

And then, as I knew she would, she said, "Michael Walsh."

Chapter Sixty

Look elsewhere, Walker Blue had said, look for other connections, and in doing so I had cleared Caggiano, but another name had popped up.

Just because Michael Walsh was more than just a client of Aaron Steinway's did not make him guilty of anything, but it brought him to the fore, so to speak, and it made me think of him again, and want to speak to him again.

When I got to his office his secretary told me that Mr. Walsh was not in.

"Can you tell me where he's gone?" I asked. "It's of the utmost urgency that I speak to him as soon as possible."

"I'm sorry, but Mr. Walsh is not even in the city," she said. "He's gone to a meeting in New Jersey."

"New Jersey?" I said. "Does Mr. Walsh have many clients outside of New York?"

"He is a very busy and successful man," she said, as if that was an answer. She was a fiftyish, spinsterish-looking woman with a bun, and I had the feeling that she was fonder of her boss than a secretary should be.

"I have another question, miss, after which I'll let you get back to work." She listened expectantly, looking anxious to do just that. "Has Mr. Walsh taken any steps to settle the insurance claim on the Battle account?"

"Battle?" she repeated, looking at me with disapproval.

"Yes, Leon Battle. He had a large collection of books insured, and he recently...died."

"I don't think I should be discussing—"

"Oh," I said, taking out my wallet and showing her my I.D. "I'm sure it's all right. Mr. Walsh has retained me to try and track down some of Mr. Battle's relatives. That's what I have to speak to him about."

"Well," she said, wavering and then slipping over the edge, "as a matter of fact, that's where Mr. Walsh has gone."

"To the Battle house in New Jersey?"

"Yes, but—"

"Thank you, ma'am. Thank you very much."

I rushed from the office, found the nearest car rental agency, made one phone call, and then started for Parlin, New Jersey, where I hoped to finally find all of my answers.

Chapter Sixty-one

When I reached the house in New Jersey there was a
Plymouth parked in front. There were at least a hundred
yards between this house and the next closest one, and
I parked about halfway between them, not wanting to
announce my arrival. Further, instead of approaching
the house from the front, I cut through the woods, which
also cut down on the distance I had to walk.

The way Walsh's name was turning up now was too
much of a coincidence to suit me. I approached the house
with care, totally unsure about what kind of a reception
I was going to find.

The back door—thanks to Leon Battle's meticulous
care—was no problem. I tried forcing the lock, and the
rotted doorjamb actually splintered.

Once inside I shut the door behind me and kept it
that way with an eye-hook lock, then stood very still
and listened. I was in a hallway, and moved along it
until I came to the kitchen. From there I did hear some
noises, and a man's voice, coming from behind the basement door, which was closed. I opened it a crack and listened.

"...got to be here someplace," someone was saying.
There was anger and bewilderment in his voice, and I

could hear him shuffling books about. "Damn, where the hell did he put it?"

Michael Walsh was apparently having trouble finding something, and I decided to try and give him a hand. After all, we were probably both looking for the same thing.

I opened the door and walked down the steps, not bothering to try and minimize the echoing effect my feet had on the wooden steps. Before I reached the bottom I could see Michael Walsh, standing amidst the clutter of books that were still strewn about the floor. He turned abruptly and when he saw me his eyes widened.

"Jacoby."

"Mr. Walsh," I said, coming down the rest of the way. "What are you looking for?"

"What—" he said, off balance for a moment, but he recovered quickly and said, "I might ask you the same question."

"Fair enough," I said. "I came here looking for you."

"Oh? Why is that?"

"Maybe because I need insurance."

He studied my face doubtfully and answered, "I'm sorry, but I deal only with large companies, Jacoby. I could recommend someone, however—"

"You insured this collection, didn't you?" I asked.

He looked down at the books on the floor, then said, "Yes, I did, but that was an exception. As a collector, I could appreciate—"

"Did you insure Steinway's collection as well?"

"Yes, as a matter of fact, I did."

"Another exception?"

"Yes," he said, then showing annoyance he added, "Why are you asking me all these questions?"

I ignored his question and asked another of my own.

"Why didn't you tell me that before?"

"You never asked," he said, giving me the stock answer.

"You handled the insurance for all of Steinway's businesses, didn't you?"

He hesitated, then said, "You're asking me, but you already seem to know the answer."

"I do. I did some research, Walsh, all of which has led me to you."

252

"Which means?"

"You insured Steinway, you insured Battle," I said. "Steinway bought a horse from Carl Caggiano, Jr. Did you also insure the horse for him?"

"I...had some dealings with Mr. Caggiano, yes."

"And that's what gave you the idea."

"What idea is that?"

I took a few steps towards him, moving books aside with my feet, and said, "The idea of planting a folder labeled 'Caggiano' in Steinway's file cabinet. You were trying to implicate Caggiano, or at least focus attention on him, and away from yourself."

"What are you talking about?" he demanded, taking a couple of steps himself to maintain the distance between us.

"I think you did it all, Walsh," I said, pointing my finger at him. "I think you had someone steal the collection, and had them bring it here; only now you don't even know where it is. What happened? Did Battle try to go into business for himself?"

"You're wrong."

"And I said you did it all," I added. "That includes killing Steinway, Denton...and my brother."

"I didn't—" he started, then stopped himself short and looked away.

"Come on, Walsh. It's all over now. The fact that you're here..."

"I have every right to be here," he insisted. "I insured all of this. I'm merely taking inventory."

"You have a photographic memory?" I asked, indicating the fact that he had no pad or pen. "No, you're here looking for Steinway's collection, but I could have told you it wasn't here. I had an expert come in and search for it among all of these books. Battle obviously moved it, Walsh, and he's dead. You killed him—or had him killed—and he was probably the only one who knew what he did with it."

"I didn't—" he started to say again, but once again he stopped himself. He looked like man struggling with something, and I decided to play on that.

"Walsh, I think you started out trying to get that collection, one way or another. I don't think you meant to kill Steinway."

He began to move books around with his feet, looking much like a little boy shuffling his feet.

"Walsh," I said gently.

"I only meant to scare him," he said softly.

"What?"

"I said I only meant to scare him," he said louder, much too loud this time. He looked at me and said, "He was always rubbing it in my face, the fact that his collection was so complete. I offered to buy it again and again, but he always upped the price on me, just to be mean. Every time I was able to come up with the price he asked, he'd up it again. So—"

"So you decided to steal it?" I prompted.

"Yes."

"After you had Jimmy Denton front for you with another offer."

"That's right."

"How did you meet Denton?"

"I came across him when I was dealing with Carl Caggiano, and I remembered him."

"Did you realize that you'd never be able to show it once you stole it?" I asked. "That just having it in your house would be dangerous?"

"I did realize that eventually, but I just wanted to get back at him, so I had the books brought to Leon's house—here—"

"Didn't he know they were stolen?"

He grinned tightly and said, "Leon was not averse to dealing in stolen items."

"Are you telling me he was a fence?"

"He was," he said. "Where do you think he got the money to build up his collection and keep his Mr. Pulps catalogue going?"

"Makes sense," I said. "Walsh, why don't you tell me what happened with Steinway?"

He walked to the corner of the room, righted the chair Battle had kept behind his desk, and sat down. I moved closer to him, but kept a respectable distance.

"After I realized what a problem the stolen collection was going to be, I decided to make him pay through the nose to get it back."

"He must have loved that."

"He got angrier than I've ever seen him," Walsh said. "First, because then he knew I was the one who had had it stolen, and second because I had the audacity to try to make him pay for his own property."

"Did he get violent?"

"He took a gun out of his desk," he said. "We struggled for it and it went off, striking him."

"You hit me when I came out of the elevator."

He nodded. "I panicked. I was trying to get out when I saw that the elevator was coming up. When you came out I hit you with the gun, and then ran."

"So it was an accident," I said. "You should have gone to the police."

"I would have had to admit that I hired someone to steal the collection, and then tried to extort money from Steinway in order to give it back."

"That would have been better than the charges you face now," I said. "There are four murders to be paid for now."

"But I didn't kill the rest of them," he insisted. "I didn't kill your brother, Jacoby, I swear!"

"Then who did, Walsh?" I asked. "Who did?"

His eyes widened at that moment and I heard a noise behind me and turned too late. Both of them had come down the stairs quietly and now stood on the basement floor with their guns trained on me.

"Answer his question, Walsh," Detective Seidman said. "Go ahead."

"The man is waiting for an answer," Abel chimed in. "Tell him who killed his brother, and the others."

I looked back at Walsh, who looked miserable and frightened, and said simply, "They did."

Chapter Sixty-two

"Before we discuss this matter any further," Seidman said, "are you carrying a piece?"

"You killed my brother?" I demanded in disbelief.

Abel cocked the hammer back on his gun and said, "Our questions come first, Jacoby." Smiling benignly, he added, "You understand."

"Not yet I don't," I answered, "but I'm looking forward to. Yes, I am carrying a gun."

"Good," Seidman said, smiling. "Shoulder holster or belt?"

"Belt."

"Put your hands straight out from your body," he instructed me, and when I did so Abel handed Seidman his gun, approached me, removed my gun from my holster, then patted me down, searching for any additional weapons. Satisfied, he tucked my gun into his belt and backed up next to his partner, who handed him back his gun without taking his eyes off me. They were very good together, practiced and precise.

That didn't make me feel any better about possibly getting out of there alive.

"Is it my turn to ask questions yet?"

"Excuse me a second," Seidman said with exaggerated politeness. He looked over at Walsh and asked, "How much did you tell him?"

Walsh, seeming to shrink with every passing moment, shrugged his shoulders and said, "Everything."

"Everything?" Abel asked.

"Not quite everything," I said. "I've still got plenty of questions."

"How far *did* he get in his story?" Seidman asked.

"He told me he killed Steinway by accident, during a struggle."

"Yeah, he told us the same thing," Seidman said, "but who knows?"

"I told the truth," Walsh argued feebly.

"Sure you did," Abel said. He looked at me and asked, "Did he tell you it was him who tried to run you down?"

"I only wanted to scare you," Walsh assured me.

"How did you know I'd be there?"

"I called your home and your brother told me," he explained. "Mr. Jacoby, these two got involved because they knew Battle. They worked with him—"

"With him, or for him?"

"Work for Leon?" Seidman asked, laughing. "Leon was good at doing what he was told, but when it came to using his brains, he needed guidance."

"Which you were only too happy to give him, right?"

"Of course," he answered. "We're servants of the people, right?"

"When I panicked that night I came out here," Walsh said. "Battle called them. They took the gun from me, Mr. Jacoby, and said they'd take care of it for me."

"I think I understand," I told Walsh. Once they had the gun, which was evidence against him, they could force him to go along with whatever they had in mind.

All at once I had an idea of who had been in control of this whole business, following Steinway's death. If there's anything worse than a couple of crooked cops, it's a couple of opportunistic, crooked cops.

"You're a smart P.I., aren't you?" Seidman asked.

"Always ready to get a little smarter, though," I said.

"Well, we can see that you're just busting to ask some questions," Abel said, "so since Mr. Walsh has already told you much of it, ask away."

"I assume you fellas have always had a close association with Leon Battle's fencing operation."

"We've kept a close eye on it, yes," Seidman answered.

"And when you heard about the collection, and how potentially valuable it was, you had your own idea about what to do with it."

"We offered our help," Abel said, and Seidman nodded.

"Which of course meant killing Jimmy the Dime, Battle, and my brother."

"Nobody wanted to kill your brother," Seidman said, and for the first time it looked as if they didn't agree on something. The sidelong glance that Abel tossed his partner said that he wished he hadn't said that.

"I didn't think so," I said. "The bomb in my apartment was meant for me. I guess you just wanted to make a clean sweep of things." I looked pointedly at Walsh and added, "Or were you going to do that here, today?"

Walsh didn't even pick up on what I was saying, which gave some idea of how far out of it he was at that point.

"Who planted the bomb? I know it was a pro."

"We don't have any trouble coming up with people to do things like that," Seidman assured me.

"I wouldn't think so. You just blackmail them into it, right?"

"We use our positions to our best advantage," Abel informed me.

"I can see that. Who's the fuckup who killed Battle?"

"That was unfortunate," Abel admitted. "He and Denton got into an argument, apparently over the split—".

"And you solved it?"

"Denton killed Battle," Seidman explained. "We got here just as he stabbed him. I plugged him to keep him from doing it again, but once was enough. They both died, and we covered them up."

"And waited for someone to find them," I added. "It's unfortunate that Battle was killed, all right, considering he was the one who knew where the collection was."

"That's okay," Seidman said. "That's why we arranged to meet Walsh here today. So he can tell us where it is and we can get business out of the way once and for all."

I had the distinct feeling that Battle was smart enough to try and hold an ace in the hole on these two, and it had kept him alive long enough for Denton to kill him.

"Okay, Walsh," he went on, turning his attention away from me, "how about it? Where's the collection?"

I caught Walsh's eye and pinned him with a hard stare, hoping to send him a message. As long as they thought he knew where it was, they had to keep him alive. If he told them that he didn't, they didn't need him anymore. Alive, he was more of a danger to them than anything else. I hoped he'd see that and lie.

"Seidman," Walsh said, shaking his head and spreading his arms out in a helpless gesture, "I don't—"

"Don't tell them, Walsh," I interrupted him. "Once they know where it is they don't need you anymore."

"Shut up," Abel snapped at me. They were the first impolite words I had heard either one of them speak.

"Walsh, we've waited long enough for you to get your ass out here," Seidman told Walsh tightly. "Now where the hell are those fucking books?"

Abel kept his gun trained on me while Seidman switched his over to Walsh. Walsh, seeing this, opened his mouth, but no sound came out.

"He's too scared to talk," I shouted at them. "He needs a drink to get him going." They exchanged glances and I said, "You can't shoot a man because you scared him speechless."

They both looked at Walsh, who seemed on the edge of apoplexy. His mouth was flapping open and closed so fast he looked like he was in a chewing-gum contest.

"He's right," Seidman finally said. "Let's go upstairs where we can all sit down, have a drink, and discuss it." Suddenly, he was polite again, but he didn't fool me. He wanted to calm Walsh down enough to get him to talk, and then they'd kill us both.

Then again, seeing as how they didn't need me for anything, they might even kill me before the drink.

Seidman walked over to Walsh and said, "Take it

easy now, Walsh. We're just going to go upstairs and have a drink. Come on."

He walked Walsh over next to me, and then we all started for the stairs. When we reached them I stepped aside and said to Seidman, "After you."

"Don't be cute, Jacoby," he said. "You first."

What I did next may not have been very nice, but Walsh had a free pass with these guys, at least for a while. The walk I was taking up the stairs could have very well been my last. That's why I didn't particularly feel guilty when I stiff-armed Walsh, who was right behind me, and sent him tumbling into the two armed detectives.

As I sprinted up the steps a shot rang out, but I figured that was a result of the collision. One of them must have squeezed one off in surprise. At the top of the stairs I tried to close and lock the door, but it had no lock. I pulled a chair over from the kitchen and propped it under the doorknob, like they do on TV, but the chair itself was so flimsy it wouldn't hold them for very long. Maybe just long enough to get me to my car.

I took off down the hall the way I'd come in and yanked on the back door. When it didn't budge I yanked harder and pulled the eye-hook lock right out of the wall. Real smart of me to remember.

I was just out of the house when I heard wood splinter as the kitchen chair came apart and they burst through the door. I ran straight back into the woods, wanting as many trees between me and the back door as possible before they reached it.

"Jacoby!" one of them shouted, but I kept running. There were two shots, and then they must have given up and taken out after me.

It took me a few seconds before I realized I was running the wrong way. I had approached the house through the woods from the side, which meant I was now running away from my car, not towards it, and on top of that I had no idea what I *was* running towards.

Undecided about which way to go, I tripped on a large root and went *down*. I was on all fours when I heard someone call my name again, but I couldn't tell which detective it was.

"Jacoby, damnit!" the voice shouted then, sounding really annoyed.

I scrambled to my feet but found that I couldn't put all that much weight on my left ankle, the one I'd caught in the root.

"Oh, great," I hissed at myself, and suddenly the pain started, working its way up my leg.

I heard someone pounding through the woods behind me and looked around for a place to hide and something to use as a weapon. I spotted a tree that was twice as wide as I was and dragged myself over behind it. On the ground were several lengths of tree branches, and I picked up two or three before I found one with the heft that suited me. Maybe I could take one of their heads off before the other one killed me.

I stood with my back against the tree, holding the tree branch like Reggie holds his bat, and favoring my left leg.

I tried to quiet my breathing so I'd hear when they were approaching me. After a few seconds I heard someone's feet tramping down on leaves and bark and tightened my hold on my club.

The man called out, "Jacoby!" just as he came into view and as I started to swing at him I recognized him and tried to stop myself.

"Jesus!" he shouted, ducking under my swing. With all my weight on one foot, swinging and missing him threw me off balance and I went tumbling to the ground again, losing my club as I tried to break my fall.

"Didn't you hear me calling you?" Hocus demanded, looking down at me.

"That was you?"

"Who the hell did you think it was?" he demanded. His face was red, either from anger or exertion. "I been chasing you since you came running out of that house like your ass was on fire."

"*You've* been chasing me?"

"We grabbed those other two as soon as they came out of the house behind you," he explained. "Their lieutenant is reading them the riot act right now. You called me, damnit, why didn't you wait for me to get here?"

"I heard shots. I thought they were shooting at me."

"They were lining up on you, so I let two go to attract their attention," he said. "Do you want to get up now?" He extended his hand to me and I stared at it, still breathing hard and trying to realize that it was all over and I was still alive.

"My ankle," I said, pointing. "I twisted it."

"Well, I'm not carrying you," he said. "Who the hell told you to run from me—oh, shit," he said. I grabbed his hand and he pulled me upright. "Lean on me and let's get back to the house so we can wrap this thing up."

As we hobbled back he said, "You know, Jacoby, sometimes you're a real pain in the balls."

Happy to be alive, I grinned and said, "Yeah, ain't it great?"

Epilogue

A week later I was sitting in my office, wiggling the toes of my right foot. This was the first day since I had hurt it that my ankle hadn't been wrapped, and it felt pretty good. It was the first real encouraging thing that had happened during the week we'd wrapped up the murders.

Walsh had killed Steinway. Whether or not it had happened like he said was for a jury to decide.

According to Seidman and Abel, Denton had stabbed Battle, who had then shot Denton, but both Walsh and I could testify to the story the way they told it to us in the basement that day. On top of that, we could testify that they admitted hiring—or blackmailing—some poor torch to put a bomb in my apartment in an attempt to kill me, and had killed my brother instead. And on top of all that, all kinds of indiscretions on the part of the two detectives were coming to light, and they wouldn't be *seeing* the light for a long time to come.

On the personal front, Tracy was gone. She had called a few days earlier to say she got a "legit" offer to act in a picture in California. It was temporary, and she was going to accept, unless I could give her a reason not to—which I couldn't, so she went.

I was still living out of the back office at Bogie's, not having found anyone else willing to put me up for an occasional stint behind the bar. I didn't have any ready cash, because I had returned Cagey Carl's five grand to him. I had not found the collection, and had returned my fee in the interest of goodwill, good business—and good health.

The letter from Julie was still in my desk, and I was beginning to think I would leave it there forever. A psychiatrist might say I was trying to punish myself for what had happened to Benny, but I didn't have the money to pay one and find out.

And then there was Erica. She had gone back to Europe, and her trip—like Tracy's—was supposedly temporary. It was obvious that there was an attraction between us, but—as she said—I was obviously unwilling or unable to take a step forward, so her solution was to put a little time and distance between us and see what transpired.

So I wiggled my toes because it was the only thing that felt good and was a good way to start off the day. Maybe it would even get better.

Then the door opened, and it got worse.

Laura Brackett walked in, all smiles and elegance, and behind her came Cagey Carl himself, Carl Caggiano, Jr.

"Hello, Miles," she said.

"Mrs. Brackett."

I looked at Caggiano, who simply said, "Jacoby," and I just as simply nodded.

"What can I do for you, Mrs. Brackett?" I asked, because I doubted that coming to see me had been Caggiano's idea.

"May I sit?"

"Please do," I said. She sat in the visitor's chair and crossed her legs. Conscious of Carl, Jr.'s eye I tried not to stare, but I am only human, after all.

"We would like to hire you," she said when she was comfortable.

"We?"

"Yes, the both of us," she answered. She took Carl, Jr.'s hand and said, "Carl and I."

"I see. Uh, to do what?"

264

"Why, to find the collection of books, of course. I understand everything has been solved—the killings, I mean—but that the books still have not been recovered."

"That's true."

"Then we would like you to find them."

I looked at Caggiano's face, which was not wearing a happy expression, and asked, "Is that true?"

"Whatever Laura wants," he said, and she squeezed his hand and smiled lovingly up at him.

"He's a dear," she told me. "He wants to give them to me as a wedding present."

"Wedding present?"

"Yes. As soon as my divorce from Walter becomes final, we're going to be married."

"Congratulations," I said, "but, uh, I'm sorry I can't help you."

"Can't?" he asked. "Or won't?"

"Can't, won't, it's the same difference," I said. "I went through too much, Mrs. Brackett," I said, directing my remarks to her, "looking for that collection, and it cost me my brother. I think I've had quite enough of it."

"But it's still out there," she said. "The job's not done. How can you let it go unfinished—"

"Mrs. Brackett, I'm sorry," I interrupted her, "but I am not one of your pulp magazine private eyes. If you'll excuse my directness, I really don't give a damn where that collection is, or if it ever shows up again. Please understand."

I looked from her to Caggiano's scowling face, and then back to her and said, "Please."

She regarded me for a moment and as Carl, Jr. started to move forward she said, "No, dear," to him and stopped him on a dime. It was amazing to me to see the control she had over him. "I do understand, Mr. Jacoby," she informed me, standing. "I'm sorry to have taken up your time."

"I'm sorry I couldn't help you."

"Let's go, dear," she told Cagey Carl, and he looked at me as if saying, Tell anyone about this ring through my nose and I'll be back.

I'd be the last one to make a remark, Carl old boy, I said to myself. Touching the drawer where Julie's letter lay, I added, We're all under some woman's influence, one way or another.

FREE!!
BOOKS BY MAIL
CATALOGUE

BOOKS BY MAIL will share with you our current bestselling books as well as hard to find specialty titles in areas that will match your interests. You will be updated on what's new in books at no cost to you. Just fill in the coupon below and discover the convenience of having books delivered to your home.

PLEASE ADD $1.00 TO COVER THE COST OF POSTAGE & HANDLING.

BOOKS BY MAIL

320 Steelcase Road E.,
Markham, Ontario L3R 2M1

IN THE U.S. -
210 5th Ave., 7th Floor
New York, N.Y., 10010

Please send Books By Mail catalogue to:

Name _____
(please print)

Address _____

City _____

Prov./State _____ P.C./Zip _____

(BBM1)